LOVING AND LOSING

MARION REYNOLDS

POOLBEG

Published 2020
by Poolbeg Press Ltd.
123 Grange Hill, Baldoyle,
Dublin 13, Ireland
Email: poolbeg@poolbeg.com

A catalogue record for this book is available from the British Library.

ISBN 978178199-387-3

www.poolbeg.com

ABOUT THE AUTHOR

Marion Reynolds is from Dublin. She read English at Trinity College, Dublin, and was awarded an M.A. in Communications by DCU. During her career, she worked as a teacher and lecturer in both Ireland and the UK. She was a regular contributor of articles, interviews and book reviews to newspapers such as the *Irish Examiner* and the *Evening Echo*, but now concentrates on creative writing. She also teaches creative writing, and mentors writers of memoir and historical fiction.

She lives in Greystones, County Wicklow, with her husband. They have two grown-up children.

Her ideas for the *Devereux Family Trilogy* arose out of research into her own family. She is currently writing the third part of the series which began with *A Soldier's Wife*.

ACKNOWLEDGEMENTS

Thanks to everyone at Poolbeg, especially Paula Campbell and Gaye Shortland, my wonderful, supportive editor.

Fiona Reynolds, my daughter, has been my IT advisor and webpage designer. Liz Mellon read the first draft and gave me insightful feedback.

C3 80

To Patrick, my husband and partner in everything I do. Your encouragement and love continue to inspire me.

Also to my daughter, Fiona, who gives me love and support.

CHAPTER 1

New Year's Eve 1931

Ellen looked around her crowded kitchen where family and friends stood chatting in small groups. Occasionally, there was a burst of laughter. The debris of their meal was still on the table. Turf and logs glowed and spat in the fireplace and paper chains hung across the ceiling in scallops. Holly and ivy, withering from the heat, crowned every picture while red candles danced with their reflections in the mirror. Christmas cards stood crookedly on the overmantle, displaced by smudged glasses.

She loved times like this when all her loved ones came together, safe and well. The years since 1922, when the Irish Free State was established, had been a difficult time for many people, she reflected. She was lucky. James had come home safely from the war, unlike many of his friends. He had found it difficult to get work, but they had managed on his small army pension and whatever temporary work came his way. The nineteen thirties looked set to be difficult but their children had good jobs at a time when many people were unemployed. Harry was an army officer and Joseph was a civil servant. Mary was studying to be a teacher and Kathleen – well, Kathleen was an actress.

James was standing between his two sons, looking as handsome as ever with his curled moustache and his thick hair, now more white than blonde. Harry, their oldest son, dark-haired and brown-eyed like Ellen's father, towered above the others. He held his little daughter in his arms while his wife, Julia, leaned against him, her pregnancy swelling her slender frame.

"They still look like love birds, don't they?" Violet, her friend and Julia's mother, nodded at the two young people.

"Yes, they do. It's hard to believe that they have three children already. They'll soon fill that house of theirs. It's great to see them so happy."

"I wish my twin girls were settled too," said Violet. "Joseph isn't as keen to marry as his brother was. I hope he makes up his mind soon. I know Esther and Ellie are both mad about him, but they can't wait for ever. It's time for them to settle down."

Ellen didn't answer her outspoken friend. Joseph would marry when the time was right. He had a good job in the Civil Service when so many young men were idle because of the depression. He had a lot of interests that kept him busy in the evenings. She looked across the room at her second son. He was talking to the two identical young women with tumbling auburn hair and making them laugh.

Joseph felt her eyes on him and smiled across at her. He was so different to his older brother – smaller, quieter but just as good-looking with his silky brown hair and dark-blue eyes.

There was a flurry beside her as Kathleen pulled on a coat over her fashionable dress.

"Mother, we have to leave now. George has been invited to a party at the Gate Theatre and he wants me to go with him."

She turned and waved at a young man who was lounging on the sofa, a cigarette held aloft and a look of boredom on his face.

"George, come here and say goodbye to my mother."

The young man came towards her and offered a limp hand. Ellen forced a smile to her face.

"Sorry you have to go. Will you make sure that Kathleen gets home safely tonight?"

"Oh Mother, don't fuss. I'm staying with Grace tonight, it's all arranged. You'll be at the party too, won't you, Grace? Everyone who is anyone in Dublin theatre will be there." Her eyes glistened with excitement.

Had she some of that black stuff on her eyelashes, Ellen wondered.

"I'll call in for a few minutes but I won't stay long," said Grace. "Don't be too late, Kathleen." Grace was Ellen's friend and an actress with the Abbey.

"See you all tomorrow. Say 'bye for me to Dad and everyone."

With a toss of her blonde hair and a wave she was out the door, followed by George as he lifted his hat and coat from a chair in one swift movement like a detective in a murder film leaving the crime scene.

Ellen looked at Violet. "You don't know how lucky you are having such sensible daughters. Kathleen hasn't an ounce of sense in that blonde head of hers. I don't know where we got her. We couldn't get her to stay on in school. Since she joined the Abbey Theatre Company I spend half my life worrying about her. I'm glad you are there, Grace, to keep an eye on her. Now she's talking about trying to get a role in the next production at the Gate Theatre. If George is anything to go by, they are quite a racy crowd."

"Oh, I think Kathleen is well able to take care of herself, but she is very different to Mary. Where is Mary, by the way?"

"Upstairs, with the two boys. They were being a bit too boisterous so she took them up to play card games and give Julia a rest."

"She's so good, always thinking about other people. How is she getting on at the teacher training college?"

"Great, she really loves it. She reminds me of her mother Annie, God rest her soul. When I encouraged Annie to study to become a nurse and offered to look after Mary, she put all her energy into it even though she missed her child. Mary is the same. When she wants anything, she puts all her energy into it. She studies hard and is really cut out to be a teacher. She has the patience of Job with children."

"Well, my patience has run out with these two. They wouldn't let me win even one game." Mary had just come down the stairs in time to hear Ellen's worrds.

The two little boys ran over to their grandmother.

Ellen scooped the smaller child into her arms. "Pádraig, have you got a kiss for me? What about you, Michael?"

"Maeve has a kiss for you too." Harry came and lifted up his daughter so that she could join in the kissing. "We'd better go now, Mother. The weather is getting worse and Julia is tired."

"All right, son. I'll help the boys with their coats. Be careful going home. The footpaths will be slippery."

Joseph joined them. "I'll walk them home. I can carry one of the boys. Don't wait up for me, Mother. I'll stay and have a chat with Harry. He's so busy these days that we seldom get to talk."

The three older women fussed around Julia and the

children, making sure they were well wrapped up.

Violet kissed her daughter. "Be careful going home, Julia. Hold on to Harry so you don't slip."

James had been outside, getting turf and logs for the fire. He built up the fire as the children clamoured for just one more game with Grandad. After he had done his magic trick of finding some sweets in their ears, they were ready to go.

"Goodbye, Mam," said Julia. "Goodbye, Mother Devereux. Goodbye, Grace." She embraced them one by one. "Happy New Year to you all!"

With a flurry of goodbyes and a few retreats to find gloves or hats, they were out the door into the gathering storm.

As soon as the door was opened, the heat seemed to be sucked out of the room, the candles guttered and went out and some cards fell from the overmantel into the fire where they quickly turned to ash.

Mary and the twins stood at the front door to wave them off. When they came back inside their hair was glistening with snow.

Mary closed the door and leaned against it. "I don't think there will be any dancing in the street at midnight this year. It's freezing out there."

Ellen shivered and felt a sense of foreboding. "I just hope they get home safely and that Joseph has the sense to stay in Harry's."

"If they still lived in the cottage in Black Street they'd be home in two minutes," said Violet.

"They would, but the new house is lovely, and it even has a garden for the children. Harry was very lucky that Mrs Major left him enough money to buy it. Of course, she was delighted when I asked her to be his godmother. She was always very fond of him and kept in touch even when we came home from India. My God, that snow is getting heavier. I hope they will be all right."

James put his arm around his wife. "Don't do so much worrying. They will all be fine. Now, let's all sit at the fire and have a drink. Violet, will you have a port? How about you, Grace?"

Violet settled back comfortably. "I think I will for the night that's in it. Hard to believe that it's almost 1932, isn't it?"

Grace nodded. "Yes, it is. Ten years since the British left Ireland. I remember Harry raising the Tricolour at the barracks. He looked so handsome in his uniform and we were so proud that he was chosen from all the cadets."

Ellen smiled at the memory.

James motioned to her with the bottle of port.

"No, James, I'll just have a cup of tea. Girls, will you put the kettle on, please? And help yourselves to a mineral."

"I suppose that all the preparations for the Eucharistic Congress will start in the New Year. I saw them installing a public telephone kiosk down near Kingsbridge Station. I hear that they are putting them all over the city. And Count John McCormack is to sing at the Mass." Violet sipped her port. "Isn't it a great honour for Ireland that the Congress is to be held here?"

Grace looked thoughtful. "I suppose it is, but it will cost a fortune and we would be better spending the money on building houses for the unfortunates living in tenements. After all, Dublin has the reputation of having some of the worst slums in Europe."

James gathered the smudged glasses from the overmantel,

relit the candles and joined the others around the fire with a glass of whiskey in his hand. "Harry was telling me that there could be trouble when the election takes place in February. Cumann na nGaedhael has been in power for the last ten years but there is talk that they might lose the next election to Fianna Fáil. They won't like handing over power to their old enemies in the Civil War."

"I wish Harry wasn't so involved in politics. He should just concentrate on his career in the army and forget the politics." Ellen's face darkened with memories of the Civil War.

James was quick to reassure his wife. "Don't worry, love. As long as he is in the army, he can't be too actively involved. He just likes going to meetings and discussing politics."

"I hope you're right. Well, here's to a happy 1932!" She accepted the teacup from Ellie and raised it. There was a chorus of "Happy New Year!" and they all settled down to a game of cards.

CHAPTER 2

Kathleen and George ran down Aberdeen Street to the bus stop at the Park Gate where they could get a bus to the city. They were out of breath and laughing when they clambered on to the bus and made their way upstairs.

"My hair is ruined – I don't know what I'm going to do with it." Kathleen ran her fingers through her hair and fluffed it out around her face. She then took a compact out of her bag, opened it and patted her nose with the small powder puff inside it. "Will Micheál and Hilton be at the party?"

George took a cigarette from a gold case, tapped it on the case, lit it and drew on it deeply, watching her as she applied red lipstick to her pouted lips. "Of course they will. The party is to celebrate the first year of the Gate Theatre in the Rotunda building. They are so delighted to have their own place at last, having spent two years in the Peacock Theatre in the bowels of the earth below the Abbey Theatre."

Kathleen gave herself a last satisfied look in the compact mirror, snapped it shut, replaced it in her handbag and turned to look at George. "Will I do?"

"You'll be the prettiest girl at the party."

"But have I any chance of getting into the Gate Company? The Abbey is so boring with Mr Blythe laying down the law and all their domestic dramas. I want to appear in Ibsen and Shakespeare and –"

"Just be nice to everyone at the party, especially me."

"Of course I will. And, George, introduce me to everyone as Kay Devereux. It sounds so much more glamorous than Kathleen. Kathleen is all right for the Abbey but …"

"Kay? Why Kay?"

"After the Hollywood actress Kay Francis. Do you think I look like her?"

"I don't remember what she looks like. But a shorter name is better in the theatre, so Kay it is."

The bus was moving down O'Connell Street past Nelson's Pillar. They climbed down the stairs and stood on the platform until it stopped at the end of O'Connell Street. They could see groups of people in evening dress heading for the imposing granite frontage of the Gate Theatre. Seeing the glamour on display made Kathleen look down at her own dress and fluff her hair out once more. She pushed back her shoulders and made herself as tall as she could.

At least I'm young – some of these people must be at least forty, she consoled herself.

She clung on to George's arm and tripped along beside him to the theatre entrance, her face lit up with excitement. Inside, she could see a dark-haired man in a wine-velvet smoking jacket greeting people as they arrived.

"Oh my God, there is MacLiammór at the top of the stairs! Isn't he handsome! Is that Hilton Edwards beside him?"

The crowd moved slowly up the steep staircase and suddenly they were at the top and Micheál MacLiammór was shaking hands with George.

"George, my good man, how lovely to see you. And who is this lovely lady?"

His velvet voice was caressing. He took her hand and kissed it, appraising her as he did so, his dark-brown eyes intense.

She could see that he was wearing make-up. Still, he was an actor.

"This is Kath– I mean Kay Devereux. She is with the Abbey at the moment but she would love to join the Gate."

"Would she indeed? Such a pity to waste such sweetness on the desert air of the Abbey! Talk to Hilton later about that. As you can see, he is engaged at the moment."

He drifted away, head up, cigarette held aloft, as though he was exiting the scene, stage left.

Hilton Edwards was surrounded by a group of young actors, who were hanging on his every word. He was taller and heavier than Micheál, with a long nose and a rather lugubrious face. From time to time there were guffaws of self-conscious laughter from the group as he entertained them with some story, his resonant voice and English accent carrying through the foyer.

"Come on," said George. "Let's get a drink at the bar. There are some people I would like you to meet."

George was soon in animated conversation with a group of young actors and actresses. He paused to introduce her and remembered to call her Kay but, as soon as the young people ascertained that she was not anybody famous, they ignored her. All the talk was of the next production at the Gate and who was likely to get a part in it. She stayed on the periphery of the group, sipping her wine, noting the women's clothes, their accents and their extravagant mannerisms.

She felt annoyed with George. He could have taken the opportunity to introduce her to Hilton Edwards. She felt that if she got talking to the director there was a chance he would offer her a place in the company. She moved slowly back to the foyer, hoping that George would see her and follow. He didn't. She stood on the edge of the group surrounding Hilton, feeling very conspicuous since the others were all male. Eventually there was a pause in the conversation while people moved to the bar to replenish their drinks.

She moved closer to Hilton.

"Mr Edwards, my name is Kay Devereux. I'm with the Abbey Theatre at present but I would very much like to be in the Gate Company. I've been with the Abbey for four years and have played a variety of small parts. I think I am more suited to the types of plays that you produce at the Gate."

She was conscious that she was gabbling and using a posh accent that wasn't her own.

Hilton looked at her intently for a few moments before answering. "How do you do, Miss Devereux. I am afraid that we have a number of young ladies, very similar to you, already in the company. Contact me again in a year's time and I will consider the situation. In the meantime, get all the experience you can. There are some excellent playwrights writing for the Abbey at the moment. Lennox Robinson and Paul Vincent Carroll are two that come to mind. Have you a part in the current production of *Things That Are Caesar's*?"

"Yes, I have a small part in it, but I also understudy the female lead."

"Excellent. That is exactly the type of experience I was speaking about. Get as much experience as possible and then come and see me again. Now, my friends are waiting for me. I'll see you again, Miss Devereux."

Kathleen was thrilled to have spoken to the great Hilton Edwards but devastated to learn that she would have to wait a year for a chance to join the Gate. She couldn't bear to think of spending another year at the Abbey. Anyway, she had heard rumours that only fluent Irish speakers were to be employed by the Abbey in the future. The only subject she had been good at in school was English. She would have to think of another way to get into the Gate.

George eventually came looking for her and brought her back to join the group. This time they were more friendly and she found herself chatting to a group of young women. They were all in the Gate Company. She told them that she had spoken to Hilton about joining them.

"He said come back in a year?" Olivia, a flame-haired actress in a green dress, was scathing. "Pay no attention to him. The thing to do is make sure that he sees you as often as possible. Hang around after the show or get a job in the bar. That's how I got in here."

"Yes, they are always looking for people to work in the bar," another girl said. "They have a notice up at the moment, have you seen it?"

Kathleen shook her head.

"Come, I'll show you where it is. You just have to see the manager of the bar and convince him that you can do the job. The pay is not bad, and you often get tips, especially from famous people that come here."

Working in a bar? Her parents wouldn't hear of it. But

she was almost twenty-two – she should be able to decide for herself.

She turned to the girl. "Show me where the ad is and point out the manager to me."

She was soon waiting to see the manager who turned out to be an affable man of about sixty.

"I'm delighted that you turned up tonight. One of our regular girls has decided to seek her fortune in London so in a week's time I'll be short-staffed. Have you any bar experience?"

"A little," Kathleen lied.

"All right. When can you start?"

Kathleen thought quickly. *Things That Are Caesar's* was just finishing a run and the Abbey Company would begin rehearsals for a new play the following week. She hadn't been given a part yet.

"I'll begin in a week's time."

Her parents would go mad, but she was an adult and should be able to make up her own mind.

CHAPTER 3

The snow was falling more heavily now than when Joseph and his family left the house, but powdery and dry so that it was not too slippery. There was a magical quality about the streets, houses tucked under an eiderdown of soft snow, gaslights gleaming overhead, the smell of wood and turf in the air and normal sounds muffled and hushed. Harry carried Maeve and Julia linked him. Joseph carried Pádraig and Michael walked beside him. The boys were captivated by the snow.

"It's just like where Heidi lives!" Michael said, remembering one of his favourite books.

They all had to keep their heads down against the falling snow and didn't talk again until they reached the house.

Harry lowered his daughter to the ground and put his key in the door. Julia still clung to him.

"Are you all right, love? I'll soon have the fire going and you can relax. Joseph and I will get the children to bed."

"I just have a bit of a pain in my back and I feel very tired. I'll be fine once I lie down."

The fire, which Harry had banked up before he went

out, sprang to life when he riddled it and put some coal on.

"Sit down here, love, and get warm. Will I make you a hot drink?"

"I think I'll go straight to bed. I just need to lie down."

"I'll put a hot-water jar in the bed for you. Will I help you up the stairs?"

"No, I'll be able to manage."

Julia was already in bed when Harry came up with the hot jar. She looked pale and drawn.

"Don't look so worried," she said. "I just need to sleep. Say goodnight to the children for me. Thanks, love."

Harry leaned down to kiss her. "I love you, my darling. Sleep well."

When he came downstairs, Joseph had already made hot milk for the children.

"Right, it's time for bed," Harry said as soon as they had drunk their milk. "Boys, you go up and get into your pyjamas. I'll be up in a minute when I've changed Maeve. Don't disturb Mammy."

Half an hour later, Harry and Joseph were sitting either side of the fire, each nursing a glass of porter.

Joseph leaned towards his brother. "It's great to have a chance to have a chat. Remember when we used to share a room? We used to chat for ages every night before we went to sleep."

"I think I did most of the chatting. I used to tell you about my great ambitions and my plans for the future."

"How are all your plans coming along? You seem to be doing very well in the army."

Harry sighed. "I really enjoyed it at the beginning. It was exciting. A new Free State, a new army and a new beginning. Everything seemed possible. I got a commission and I married Julia. My godmother died and left me enough money to buy a house. I have a great life and I am very happy but, to be honest, I am a bit bored with the army. Life is very routine – there is none of the excitement of the early days. Most of the work I do at my rank is repetitive and mundane. I don't think there is any chance of further promotion unless someone dies."

"What will you do? Will you stay in the army? There are not many jobs around."

"Don't tell anyone about this for the moment, Joseph. You know that I've been very active in Cumann na nGaehael recently? I've been canvassing for Paddy Geoghegan, the sitting TD. In fact, I'm his election agent. The General Election in February is going to be a tough fight. Cumann na nGaedhael has lost the confidence of some of the electorate. Anyway, it has given me a taste for politics. I'm putting myself forward for the Council elections and maybe for the next general election."

"Surely you'd have to resign your commission in the army to stand as a candidate? Then, if you lost the election, you'd have no job!"

"Well, there is some risk involved."

"What does Julia think about all this?"

"Julia knows how bored I am at present. She's not very enthusiastic about me standing because she knows how much time politics takes up. But I know she'll support me whatever I do."

"Have you told Mother and Father?"

"Not yet. I know they would prefer that I had a steady job. They have too many memories of Father being unemployed when he came back from the war. Anyway, I haven't made a decision yet. And I would have to go through a selection process first. Well, that's enough about me. As usual, I am doing all the talking. What are you up to? I thought you would be married to one of the twins by now!"

Joseph looked down. "That's the trouble. I can't choose one and hurt the other. We've been friends all our lives. Anyway, I want to see a bit of life before I settle down. I want to travel. I want to write."

"But you've had a good few things published already."

"Yes, some poems and articles and a short story. But I have an idea for a novel and it's hard to find the time and the space to write it. I'd love to go to Paris or Berlin and just concentrate on writing."

"Isn't that a bit of a romantic notion?"

"No more romantic than you wanting to be a TD."

Harry could see that he had upset Joseph. He tried to change the subject. "What do you think of Kathleen's new boyfriend – what was his name? George."

"Not much. But I don't think she's serious about him. She just likes showing off her theatrical friends."

"Well, we'd better get off to bed soon. The children wake up very early. You don't mind bunking in with Michael?"

"Not at all. Your children are lovely, Harry. They are a credit to you and Julia. You are very lucky."

"I know. Now, let's have a drop of whiskey to celebrate the New Year. I hope it is a successful and happy one for you, Joseph."

"And for you, Harry. Here's to your success."

Joseph lay in bed, listening to the quiet breathing of the child beside him and thinking about Harry's reference to the twins. The hints from his parents, Violet and even

Harry were becoming more frequent. The truth was he didn't want to get married at all. He didn't want to be tied down with responsibilities like Harry was. He didn't want to put an end to his dream of travelling and becoming a writer. He had tried to convey that to the twins, but they were convinced that he simply couldn't choose between them.

He could hear Harry and Julia talking quietly in the next room. Then the sounds became more urgent and agitated. The door opened and Harry was standing beside him.

"*Shhhh* . . . I don't want to wake the children. I'm going to have to go and get Dr Byrne. Julia is in a lot of pain."

"Is it the baby?"

"It's too early for the baby. Something must be wrong."

"Can I do anything?"

"Just be here in case the children wake. Don't go in to Julia unless she calls you. I'll go on my bike – it will be faster." Then he was gone.

Joseph managed to extricate himself from the bedclothes without waking Michael. He went downstairs and made himself a cup of tea to distract himself from the stifled groans from upstairs. Then he could stand it no longer.

He went up the stairs, two at a time and opened the door. The sharp, metallic smell of blood hit his nostrils. Julia was writhing in a tangled heap of bedclothes. There was a large towel, darkened with blood, on the floor. She was so consumed by her pain that she didn't notice him. He stood there, horrified. Then he heard the crunch of wheels on snow.

He rushed down to open the door.

"She's bleeding badly!" he told the doctor.

The doctor was up the stairs in a flash, followed by Harry. They closed the bedroom door. He could hear muffled questions from the doctor and hesitant, sobbed-out answers from Julia.

It seemed an age before Harry came downstairs, white-faced and shaken.

"I have to go out again to call an ambulance. She needs to be in hospital." He ran out the door.

Joseph grabbed Harry's coat and ran after him. "Here, Harry, your coat! You'll get pneumonia."

Harry grabbed the coat but didn't pause to put it on.

Joseph turned back to the still-open door. Michael was framed in the doorway.

"Why is Daddy running out? I heard noises and I looked for you. Why is Mammy crying? Where's Daddy gone?"

Joseph lifted the little boy up. "Mammy is all right. The doctor is looking after her. She wasn't feeling very well. Daddy will be back in a few minutes. Come on, let's get back inside. Would you like some hot milk and a biscuit?"

He was settling Michael in the kitchen when he heard the sound of the ambulance. The door opened and Harry rushed in, followed by two ambulance men. The doctor hurried downstairs and conferred quietly with the men.

As they hurried up the stairs, he turned to Harry.

"Harry, can you pack a few things for Julia? She'll tell you what she needs. She's likely to be in hospital for a few days. She's calmer now but still in a lot of pain." He put a hand on Harry's shoulder. "Don't worry – hospital is the best place for her. She will be well looked after."

The men had some difficulty negotiating down the narrow staircase with the stretcher but soon Julia was safely in the ambulance.

Michael's eyes were wide with terror. "What's wrong with Mammy? Where is she going, Daddy?"

"She's going to hospital so the doctors there can make her better." Harry picked him up, kissed him and handed him to Joseph. "I don't know how long I'll be, Joseph. Can you look after the children for the moment? And let Julia's mother know later if I'm not home? Let our parents know too."

"Of course."

As soon as the ambulance pulled away, Michael began to cry loudly and Joseph tried to comfort him.

The ambulance made its way slowly through the snow-covered streets. Harry sat beside Julia, holding her hand. She was barely conscious. He kept talking to her as the doctor had advised. Occasionally, he glanced out the window of the ambulance to check their progress. Sometimes he saw groups of revellers emerging from houses or standing on street corners, chatting and laughing, their breath hanging on the icy air. Mostly the streets were deserted, pristine and gleaming with virgin snow.

The huge granite building of the Rotunda maternity hospital looked grim and imposing. Harry followed the ambulance men carrying Julia's stretcher and Dr Byrne into the building, along the deserted corridors and to the door of an operating theatre where gowned figures took charge. He barely had time to say goodbye to a frightened Julia before the doors closed, excluding him.

"They'll come and tell us when there is any news. She will be a while in there so I think we should go and get you a cup of tea." The kindly doctor led the way to the cafeteria.

There was a rattle of cups over low conversations. There were a few people sitting at tables, relatives or friends Harry supposed, from their anxious faces and frequent glances at the large clock on the wall. He realised that he was shaking when he tried to pick up the cup which the doctor had placed before him.

"Harry, I have to get back to my practice and I have a few house calls to make first. I'll look in on Julia later. You stay here until they can tell you what's happening. I'm fairly sure that she is losing the baby. She's also lost a lot of blood and will need a transfusion. They'll keep her here for a week or so until she recovers. "

Tears were running down Harry's face. "If anything happens to her …"

"Nothing will happen to her. She's a strong young woman. Say a few prayers for her while you're waiting." He put a hand on Harry's arm. "Now, I have to go. Will you be all right?"

"Yes, I will. I'll have to go home to see to the children – Joseph said he would stay with them until I return. Thanks, doctor."

He couldn't sit still once the doctor went. He walked up and down corridors and found his way back to where they had taken Julia. He felt sick and disorientated so he sat down on a seat in the corridor. He tried to say a few prayers but the white face of Julia kept flashing across his mind.

After what seemed like hours, the door opened and a doctor emerged. He sat down beside Harry.

"I'm Dr Devine. You're Mrs Devereux's husband? I am glad to tell you that she is out of danger, but I am afraid she lost the baby."

The tears came again with relief. Harry had to wait a few minutes before he could speak. "Will she be all right? How long will she have to stay in hospital?"

"We'll be able to tell you more in a few days. We'll do some tests as soon as she is strong enough. You can see her now for a few minutes. Then she needs to sleep."

He led Harry into an adjoining ward where patients were being served breakfast.

Julia lay in a curtained-off cubicle. She looked up at Harry drowsily.

"Harry, our baby! I lost the baby." She began to cry, wrenching sobs that shook her small frame.

Awkwardly, fearful that he might displace the tubes attached to her, Harry tried to put his arms around her.

"As long as you get better, that's all that matters to me." He kissed her gently.

She was already drifting off to sleep when he was ushered out of the room.

Outside the hospital, he felt completely disorientated. He walked up O'Connell Street toward the quays, wondering why there were so few people on the streets. What time was it? He hadn't put his watch on. He could see Clery's clock. It was nine o'clock. Why were there no people going to work? Why were there so few buses? Then it hit him. It was New Year's Day!

He hopped on a bus in O'Connell Street and put his hand in his pocket. No money. The conductor listened to his story.

"Don't worry, son. If an inspector gets on just tell him you're coming from the Rotunda. Was it a boy or a girl?"

Harry felt his eyes filling up again. "She lost the baby."

"Ah, God love ye. I'm sorry for your trouble."

Julia's mother opened the door before he could use his key. "We were watching out for you. How is she?"

"She is out of danger, thank God, but oh, Violet, we lost the baby."

Violet put her arms around him. "Thank God that he spared Julia. I'm sorry about the baby. I know how much you were both looking forward to it. Now come and have some breakfast."

The two little boys sat as close to him as they could while he ate breakfast.

"When is Mammy coming home?" Pádraig wanted to know.

"Is she very sick?" Michael understood more than his brother.

"She's very tired so she has to stay in hospital for a few days. She told me to give you both a big hug. Where's Maeve?"

"Still asleep." Violet sat down beside him, a cup of tea cradled in her hands. "Joseph has gone for a lie-down. He stayed up all night until he could get one of the neighbours to stay with the children so he could come and tell me and Ellen. Ellen will come here later and we'll all go back to the hospital."

Harry suddenly felt exhausted. "I think I'll have a sleep for a few hours. They said we could visit Julia about four o'clock. You two be good boys now for Granny Vaughan."

Later that day, Harry, Violet and Ellen made their way to the hospital. In the ward, visitors surrounded every bed and there was a happy hubbub of voices. A baby cried and was soothed. The nurse drew the curtains around Julia's bed to give them some privacy.

Julia was asleep, her red hair fanned out on the pillow around her, highlighting her pallor.

Harry kissed her gently on the forehead.

Julia stirred, opened her eyes and smiled at them. "What time is it? Where are Maeve and the boys?"

"It's about four o'clock. The children are at home with Joseph. How are you feeling, sweetheart?"

"Very tired and weak." The tears started again when she remembered the lost baby.

Violet stroked her daughter's hand as Ellen patted her arm.

"We'll soon have you home again. The children send their love. They are being very good although they have Joseph worn out from playing games."

They chatted for half an hour and then it was time to go.

Harry felt his shoulders relaxing as they walked to the bus. "She looks a lot better than she did last night. I was so afraid that she was going to –"

"Don't even think about that, love." Ellen linked her arm through that of her son. "Everything will be all right."

CHAPTER 4

The children were ecstatic when Julia at last came home from hospital but were also very demanding. Maeve wanted to be in Julia's arms all the time and the boys asked questions constantly. Harry could see how exhausting it was for his wife, so he arranged to take some compassionate leave. With his mother's help, he also found a neighbour, Lily Dempsey, who was willing to help with the children for very reasonable pay. She was very reliable and had grown-up children of her own.

At the weekend Mary came around in the afternoon to sit with Julia and Maeve while Harry took the boys for a walk to his mother's.

The two women chatted easily. They were good friends but Julia was always amused at Mary's seriousness. Mary's main topic of conversation was her studies and her end-of-year exams.

"Mary, I'm delighted that your studies are going so well but do you have any time for a social life? Any boyfriend?" Julia was teasing but also keen for a good gossip.

Mary blushed and then smiled. "There is someone but don't tell anyone, not even Harry. You might know him –

the family live in Black Street. His name is Liam O'Broin."

"Oh yes, I know his sister. She's a teacher. In fact, I think his parents are teachers too."

"That's how I got to know him. I was chatting to him at the bus stop and I told him that I was looking for someone to help me with Irish and he volunteered. That was in early December and we have been seeing each other a bit since then. He had got his first teaching job in September and he's been very busy so it's not really serious."

"It sounds as though you really like him."

"Yes, I do. We went to a few *ceilidhs* at the college together but neither of us have much time at the moment."

"Well, you will have to bring him here some evening. Harry will want to vet the man who is interested in his favourite sister."

"Oh, please, don't tell Harry or anyone else."

"Don't worry, I'm only teasing you. Your secret is safe with me."

The noisy entrance of Harry and the boys put an end to the conversation.

That evening Dr Byrne paid them a visit. He was pleased to see Julia up and dressed. They engaged in small talk for a few minutes but then his face became serious.

"Julia, I am delighted to see you looking so much better. You still need to take it easy and avoid any bending and stretching or physical work. I know it is not easy with the children, but you need to be careful for a while. The tests they did in the hospital were, on the whole, satisfactory, but there is still a weakness there. A pregnancy in the future would likely result in a miscarriage and probably, a haemorrhage. It could be very dangerous."

Julia looked stricken. "Dangerous? What do you mean? Do you mean I shouldn't have any more children?"

"That is up to you. I am simply warning you of the danger. Now, I am afraid I have to go. I have evening surgery. Harry, will you see me out?"

Harry was rigid in the chair, staring first at the doctor and then at his wife.

The doctor put a hand on his shoulder. "Harry, walk to my car with me."

Dragging himself out of the chair, Harry walked stiffly behind the doctor.

When they reached the car, Dr Byrne put his medical bag inside then turned to face Harry, his face sombre. "I wanted to have a word with you on your own, Harry. You heard what I said to Julia about the dangers of another pregnancy. It's up to you to be careful."

"Careful? What do you mean, careful?"

"You know what I mean. You will have to control yourself. I'm sorry to have to tell you this." He patted Harry's arm then got into his car and drove away.

Harry stood for a few minutes on the footpath, trying to compose himself before he went inside to Julia.

She was sitting on the couch, her head bowed, crying silently. He couldn't bear to see her like that.

"Come here, love, and let me hold you. Let me dry your tears. Everything will be all right, I promise you."

"How can it be?" She turned a tearstained face up to Harry. "You heard what he said. No more children. How will we manage that? Oh Harry, I love you so much."

"I love you too. You are my life and my love." He held her close to him and kissed away her tears.

She held her mouth up to be kissed. He felt a longing

27

for her, for the way it used to be. If he ever made love to her again, he could be putting her life at risk. Was he never again to be able to express his love for her?

She clung to him as he carried her up the stairs and into the bedroom. Then the image of her on the bloodstained sheets flashed across his mind. He loosened her arms from around his neck, sat her on the bed and helped her into her nightgown.

"You go to sleep now, love. We'll talk about it in the morning."

He could hear her crying again as he went downstairs. He didn't know whether his own tears were tears of sadness or anger. The Church's teaching was that it was a sin to deliberately prevent conception. He had never really had to think about it before. Julia had breastfed each baby and that had given her nearly two years' protection from pregnancy each time. She had seemed happy with that. She loved children and her previous pregnancies had been straightforward.

The doctor hadn't been much help. Who else could he talk to? His father or mother? No, he couldn't do that. Joseph was his usual confidant but he was inexperienced in these matters. He thought of his friend, Brian Boyle. He and Brian had gone to school together and then joined the army as cadets. Harry had been surprised when Brian left during their second year to study for the priesthood. They had kept in touch and he had asked Brian to be godfather to Maeve. Yes, he would talk to Brian.

A few evenings later, Violet came to spend the evening with her daughter. Harry said he had a political meeting and made his way to Rathmines, where Brian was a curate. The priest's house was an imposing redbrick, right beside the church. The housekeeper let him in.

Brian met him in the hall, surprised to see him. "Harry! I'm delighted to see you. Come in, come in!" He led the way into a small parlour full of dark furniture, the walls heavy with portraits of saints.

"We'll have some tea and scones, please, Rita," he said to the elderly woman who had opened the door.

Brian wanted to know all about the children, especially his godchild Maeve. Harry told him some amusing stories about their antics. Then Brian asked about Julia, which gave Harry an opening to raise the topic which was monopolising his thoughts.

"I'm afraid she's not very well. She had a late miscarriage a few weeks ago. She haemorrhaged very badly. The doctor told us that she should not have any more babies, that it would be dangerous for her."

Brian sat back and digested this news. "I'm very sorry that Julia had such a terrible experience. How is she now?"

"Physically, she's getting stronger but she cries all day. I hate leaving her alone. I committed myself to campaigning for Cumann na nGaedhael and there's only a few weeks to the election so I'm very busy. Her mother and mine spend a lot of time with her and help with the children but they have their own families to look after. I managed to find a local woman, Lily Dempsey, who is able to come in every day and help with the children and do some cleaning. Mary, my younger sister, is also very good. She is back at college now, but she comes at the weekends."

"I'll call in one evening and say a few prayers with her. I'd like to see the children too. Maeve must be getting big now. I didn't know you were so involved in politics. You must tell me all about it."

Harry could feel the opportunity to have a serious talk with Brian slipping away from him. He leaned forward.

"Brian, I want your advice about something. The doctor told us that another pregnancy would be very dangerous for Julia. He didn't tell us what to do. His only advice was that I should be careful. I don't know how."

Brian sat back and studied the ceiling. Eventually he looked at Harry.

"You know what you have to do. The Church's teaching is that it is a sin to prevent conception. I can't advise you otherwise. I know it's very hard but if you love your wife you will control yourself for her sake."

"Control myself? You have no idea what you're asking. I have loved Julia since we were very young. We are very happy together." He searched for the right words. "Our physical relationship is wonderful. If that is no longer possible for us, it will put a terrible strain on our marriage."

"I know it will be difficult. You are not the first and you won't be the last with this problem. God will give you the strength you need. You must pray for strength. Having separate bedrooms would help."

Harry looked at his friend in disbelief. "Is that all the advice you can give me?"

"I am afraid so, Harry. I will pray for you and Julia."

Harry got to his feet, knocking over the china cup and saucer, and left the house.

The next thing Harry remembered was standing at his own front door, the key in his hand. He had no recollection of walking home. He went in quietly, checked on the children, and opened the bedroom door. Julia was asleep, lying on her side, her hand under her cheek, her beautiful hair like a halo around her. He was reminded of the Titian print that Joseph had in his room. He undressed and slipped in beside her. She snuggled back against him when he put his arm around her. He held her close and eventually fell into an exhausted sleep.

CHAPTER 5

At the beginning of the New Year Joseph felt very unsettled. He was passed over for promotion at work in favour of an older colleague. Not that he really wanted the promotion, but all the same it brought home the lack of any real prospects of advancement for him.

One evening on his way home from work he began to think seriously about his future. He had confided in Harry about his ambition to be a writer. Harry had dismissed it as a romantic notion. Yet, when he had a short story published in *An Claidheamh Soluis* the previous year, Harry had been impressed, probably because one of the original editors of the magazine had been Pádraig Pearse, an idol of Harry's. His father and mother were amazed that someone paid him for his stories and the twins were disappointed that they were not more romantic. They loved the romantic, nationalist novels of Annie P. Smithson. As for writing as a career, they all thought that writing was simply an eccentric pastime that he enjoyed. No one he knew was a professional writer. Even James Joyce could not make a living as a writer – he had to teach English to support his family. *A Portrait of the Artist as a*

Young Man was one of Joseph's favourite books. Maybe he too, like Joyce, would have to go into exile to become a good writer.

He had told Harry that he had an idea for a novel. It had come to him when he had read *A Portrait of the Artist as a Young Man* for the third time. He researched Joyce and discovered that his first novel was described as a Bildungsroman, one which traced the personal development of the protagonist from childhood to adulthood. That was precisely what he wanted to write about. He was becoming aware that, as he developed intellectually and morally, he was increasingly conscious of the restrictions that his culture and religion imposed. He wanted to write his own Bildungsroman. He already had a title for it: *Chrysalis*. He often felt that he was hearing and experiencing the world through a cocoon, as though he were not yet part of it. He wanted to emerge as a butterfly, soaring above the inequalities and cruelties of life. Joyce had written about his early memories, his parents and family life, his experience of school and religious education and the effect his voracious reading had on his developing and complex imagination. Harry knew he couldn't be as cruel as Joyce in his judgements of people, but he hoped to be as insightful. He too was an avid reader. He had recently read John Steinbeck's *Of Mice and Men*, *Tobacco Road* by Erskine Childers and *Down and Out in Paris and London* by George Orwell. The terrible poverty depicted in those books led him to read books about socialism, especially the writings of Karl Marx.

His job left little time to write during the day so he would have to write at night. But where? His parents' house was always full of comings and goings and there was nowhere to get away from it. Then he thought of the library. He could go there in the evening and he wouldn't be disturbed. He was a regular visitor to Phibsborough Library which had opened recently. It was calm and quiet, an ideal place to write. He could go there in the evenings after work. He could bring a sandwich from home, eat it before he left the office and then have two, maybe three, uninterrupted hours to write. He would begin the very next day.

But the very next day, it turned out, was the twins' birthday. He had forgotten all about it until they reminded him that morning as they walked together to the bus.

"Joseph, don't forget we are all going to the pictures tonight," Ellie reminded him.

"What? Tonight?"

They usually went on a Saturday night.

"It's our birthday, or had you forgotten? You promised to take us." Esther looked aggrieved. He was always forgetting arrangements lately. "We're going to the cinema on Mary Street. *Red-Headed Woman* is on."

"Jean Harlow is in it," said Ellie. "She's gorgeous. And Charles Boyer! I love his French accent."

A romantic comedy, no doubt – a genre he hated. "All right, girls. I'll call for you at seven." His first night of writing would have to wait.

To his surprise, he enjoyed the film – maybe because he knew it would be his last for a while. On the way home, he made the girls laugh by talking to them in Charles Boyer's French accent.

"You're in great form tonight, Joseph," Ellie said.

"Yes, for a while there we thought you had found another girl," Essie added.

"Well, I had a lot on my mind. But I have come to a decision."

He stopped and turned to face them. The two girls were looking at him hopefully.

The words tumbled out. "You know I told you that I want to write a novel? I have an idea for one but I couldn't seem to get started. I thought I had no time and no suitable place for writing, but I was wrong. I have decided to go to the library to write every evening after work, maybe even Saturday morning as well, until I finish my novel."

The two girls stared at him in silence.

Then Essie said, "Every evening and every Saturday morning? When will we see you? You'll have no time for anything else."

"You'll miss your tea every evening," said Ellie. "What will your mother say?"

"I haven't told her yet, but I think she'll understand. I hoped you two would understand as well. It's very important to me that I at least *try* to write my novel."

"Oh, of course we understand," said Essie, frowning.

But he wasn't at all sure they did.

Ellen did seem to understand when he told her that evening. She agreed to make a sandwich for him each day to have in the evening. He always came home from work for his dinner in the middle of the day so she was happy that he got at least one good meal daily. He suspected that she was glad he was settling down to something – he had been very unsettled for a long time.

The next evening he felt elated as he walked into the library, his thick notebook and pens in an old briefcase of Harry's. To his surprise, he wrote thousands of words the first evening. They seemed to flow as though a dam had burst.

His earliest memories were of living in luxury in India where his father had served with the British army. He had talked to his mother about her perceptions of India and found that they coincided to a great extent with his own. He had loved the two servants who had looked after the family, Vinod and his niece Prithi. Even as a child he had wondered where their own family was. His mother had told him that servants sometimes didn't see their families for years if they lived at a distance from their home villages, and that they were frequently mistreated. He had witnessed a boy of his own age kicking and hitting a servant who was taking him to school. The teacher saw what was happening but did nothing. Ellen described seeing "the natives", as they were called, working in the fields and the hard lives that they endured.

When they came home to Ireland, he realised that they had left their life of privilege behind and were now part of the ordinary people. His mother had to work like Prithi used to and his father had to accept heavy manual work so that he could provide for his family. Sometimes, he couldn't find any work. It was difficult to convey, writing through the prism of a child's eyes, how these experiences began to hone his political views.

He didn't pause until he heard the librarian announcing closing time. That night he hardly slept – his mind was racing ahead with the plot.

The next evening he read through the previous night's work. It needed some revision. This time he wrote more slowly and thoughtfully. He moved on to his family's experience of The Lockout in 1913, when workers in

Dublin had been locked out of work by their employers for almost a year because they tried to join trade unions. His family had been protected by the fact that James had a small pension from the British Army but the pension also alienated them from many of their neighbours who were starving. One neighbour, Mrs Doyle, often used to send one of her seven children to knock on their door to ask for any food scraps for the dog. Ellen knew that the food would go to the children and always put aside for them as much as she could spare.

Dublin at that time had some of the worst slums in the British Empire because many landlords were absentees and collected their rents from the safe distance of London. Landlords who were from the emerging middleclass of Catholics were not much better. Tenement houses usually had one family, often as many as ten or twelve people, to a room, and one shared toilet and one tap for drinking water for the whole house. He had once accompanied his mother on a visit to a woman she had known in India. The tenement the family had been living in had collapsed. She and her son had serious injuries and were sent to hospital. Her husband and her mother were both killed. When she was able to leave hospital, his parents had helped her and her son to get a room in a slightly better house and gave her a few pieces of furniture from their own meagre possessions. The landlord was never prosecuted even though many people had been killed as a result of his negligence.

The Church never spoke out against these injustices. On the contrary, it seemed to him that they were always on the wrong side. They seemed obsessed with the morality of sexual relations but said nothing about the

37

terrible evils visited by the rich land and property owners on the poor.

For the first few weeks it was difficult to spend every evening writing. He felt tired and he missed his friends and the easy company of the twins. However, as the novel progressed it became his world and the characters became his friends.

He found himself observing people at work rather than joining in the office banter. He wondered how they could be happy in jobs that were safe and pensionable and guaranteed for life, when the jobs were so boring. They seemed to endure the week and live for Saturday night when they could go to a dance with their girlfriends or have a few pints with the lads. As soon as they got married and had children, the men looked much older and weighed down by responsibility. The main topic of conversation at tea break was football and they never discussed books. If they discussed politics, they simply repeated party lines fed to them by politicians. If Joseph expressed even mild socialist opinions, they looked at him aghast. They called him the Professor because he always had a book with him and needed glasses to read.

Even at home he became more introspective, leading to his sisters observing that it must be his love life that was distracting him. He usually saw the twins on Sundays when they all walked to Mass together and then went for a walk in the park. The two girls still had a lively social life and chatted to each other about people and places that he didn't know.

He became increasingly aware that he needed more from life.

CHAPTER 6

One evening, not long after after she joined the Gate bar staff, Kathleen was washing glasses when she heard an unfamiliar voice.

"I don't remember seeing you here before?"

The accent was American. Kathleen turned slowly, head tilted to show her best profile. A very tall, well-built young man with blonde hair and tanned skin was standing at the bar, smiling at her.

"Nor I you," she said.

"I'm Sven Olsen. I'm with the Gate Company. I just had some time off before the next production."

"I'm Kay Devereux. I used to be with the Abbey Company but I'm hoping to get into the Gate. That's why I'm working behind the bar here."

"What a lovely name! A lovely name for a lovely lady! And you were with the famous Abbey? What productions have you been in? Maybe I saw you – although I'm sure I would remember if I did."

"Oh, you wouldn't remember. I've only had small parts so far and the costumes are designed to make us look like drab country girls."

"I can't imagine you looking drab! I've been lucky. I've only been here a few months but I've got some great parts." He drained his glass. "I think I'll have another drink."

"Kathleen, what on earth are you doing here?"

It was Grace, her mother's friend and a member of the Abbey Company.

Oh, now the cat's out of the bag, Kathleen thought.

"I'm working behind the bar. I'm leaving the Abbey. I'll get into the Gate Company when I've worked here for a few months."

Grace looked horrified. "Have you told them at the Abbey? Have you told your parents?"

To Kathleeen's dismay, Sven moved discreetly to the end of the bar.

"Not yet," she said. "I'll tell the Abbey on Wednesday, my day off. My parents don't need to know for a few weeks. I'm still coming and going at the same time so they haven't noticed anything."

"How can you do that to your parents?" Grace said, dismayed. "You should have told them before you left the Abbey. And how do you know that you'll get a part here just by working behind the bar?"

"I've been assured that most of the girls who work behind the bar end up getting parts. I spoke to Mr Edwards about it."

Grace looked sceptical.

"If I'd told my mother and father, they would have stopped me," Kathleen went on. "Working as an actress was bad enough but working in a bar would be the last straw. You know how old-fashioned they are."

Grace was now looking angry. "You have to tell your parents immediately or I will. And you owe it to the

Abbey to resign as soon as possible. They took you in on my recommendation, remember?"

Kathleen was trying to keep an eye on the young American who was still at the end of the bar.

"It's beginning to get busy now, Grace. Are you staying for the performance?"

"No, I just dropped in to see a friend of mine who is the costume designer for this production. Kathleen, please tell your parents immediately or they will hear it from someone else. I'll see you soon."

A group of people approached the bar and began ordering drinks, almost drowning Grace's parting words.

The American, Sven, waved goodbye and disappeared backstage.

After the performance, the bar was very busy with animated patrons discussing the show.

Then last orders were announced and Kathleen had just finished clearing the bar and washing glasses when Sven appeared again.

"Would you like to have a drink with me?"

"Yes, I would but last orders have been called."

"Not for the actors. There is a little sitting room where we can sit for a while and have a chat. I would like to know more about you. Let's take a bottle of wine and two glasses with us."

He put a note on the bar and she gave him his change. He pocketed it, took the bottle and glasses and led the way. She fluffed her hair out and wondered what she looked like after a night of hard work. No time to check her make-up. He guided her to the room where they found a couple in discreet, low conversation. They went to the opposite corner where there was a squashy red-velvet couch. Kathleen sank into it gratefully. Her feet were aching. She shouldn't have worn such high heels to work in the bar.

Sven went back to the bar and reappeared with a plate of what looked like some small pieces of bread with something spread on them.

"Here, have a canapé. Somebody left them in the kitchen."

Kathleen took one of the limp pieces of bread and tasted it. It was horrible, with a dry bitter aftertaste. "It's lovely but I'm not hungry. I had a meal with my family before I came out."

"I'm starving. They don't pay enough in this theatre to keep me in food. Still, it's good experience. Folks will be very impressed when I get back home to the States."

"Where are you from?"

"Well, I'm from Nebraska, but I'm going back to Hollywood, California. That's where all the big breaks are. I want to get into the movie business."

Kathleen couldn't believe it. She was talking to someone who was going to be in the movies! She gulped down her wine and coughed as it hit the back of her throat. "That's what I want to do too," she managed to say then. "I want to be in the movies."

Her head was beginning to swim. She hadn't actually eaten much all day. She wanted to look as thin as possible, like Kay Francis. She sank back into the couch. Sven sat beside her and put his arm around her. His head was very close to hers and he was looking deep into her eyes. They kissed, gently at first, then more passionately. Some more people came into the bar and they sat back on the couch.

Sven introduced her to other members of the company

and soon there was a rising hum of conversation and laughter.

Kathleen suddenly jumped up. "Oh my God, my bus! I'm going to miss the last bus!"

She ran back to the bar and, darting behind, grabbed her coat and bag.

Sven was close behind her. "I'll come with you in case you miss it."

They ran up O'Connell Street and were just in time to see the bus pulling out.

"*Oh, no!* I'll have to walk home."

"I'll walk with you. I spent my last few pounds on the wine, so I have no money for a taxi. Is it far to your home?"

"No, it's just off the North Circular Road. You don't have to come with me. I've walked home on my own before."

"I want to come with you. I'd like to get to know you and we can have a good chat on the way."

He offered his arm and Kathleen took it, grateful for some support for her aching feet. They walked slowly, chatting and laughing about their experiences. He told her that he was from a large family in Nebraska and had gone to New York to try to get into acting. He worked as a waiter and tried to get into the Group Theatre which was directed by Lee Strasberg, a disciple of the famous Stanislavski method of acting. Hundreds of aspiring actors auditioned every year and only a few were chosen. Kathleen had never heard of either Lee Strasberg or Stanislavski but they sounded exotic.

"I failed the audition twice in two years, so I decided to get some good experience before I tried again. I had heard of the Gate Theatre in Dublin and decided to try my luck there. MacLiammór liked my style and I exaggerated my experience a bit and so I got in. I've been given some great parts and experience which I wouldn't have got in New York. But now, as I told you, I want to get into the movies – that's the coming thing and it all happens in Hollywood. But that's enough about me. Tell me about yourself. How did you become interested in acting?"

"Oh, there's not much to tell about me. When I left school, I got a job in an office answering phones and I hated it. My mother's friend Grace, the woman who came into the bar tonight to talk to me, is an actress in the Abbey and she managed to get me in. At first I was just making tea and helping with costumes but then I began to get small parts. But I don't like the plays that they do. They are dull and boring and set in rural Ireland. I want to act in Shakespeare and Ibsen and Chekov. I want to travel and, like I said, get into the movies." She looked shyly at Sven. "Do you think I have a chance?"

"Of course you do. You have great looks and, although I haven't seen you acting yet, I am sure you're very good. But I heard great things about the Abbey when I was in New York, so I'm surprised you didn't like it."

"Oh, it's not that I didn't like it. I was happy enough there for a while but, like you, it was time to move on. The Gate will give me wider experience. I'll need that if I want to go to Hollywood. Oh, just up the hill there, that's my street. We can say goodnight now and thanks for coming with me. Will you be able to find your way back? I never asked you where you live."

"I share one room on the quays with another actor. It's basic but all I can afford. I know Dublin quite well now so I can find my way home. It's been great talking to you. I hope you will come out with me soon."

He leaned down, kissed her quickly and she responded.

She watched him as he walked off down Infirmary Road, heading for Parkgate Street and the quays.

Her mother was waiting for her when she opened the door.

"Thank God you're home safely. I was worried about you. Did you miss the last bus? Did you have to walk home?"

She decided to leave telling the news about leaving the Abbey and working in the bar at the Gate until the morning. It was high time she told them but right now she didn't have the energy for the inevitable row that would follow.

Sven came to the bar after the Saturday matinée performance. Kathleen was just tidying up and preparing for the evening show. She pretended not to see him at first and then acted offhand, just like Kay Francis in her latest film.

"Oh Sven, it's you. I wondered who was lurking in the shadows. How are you?"

He smiled his toothy smile and took her hand. "Kay, I wanted to see you again. Will you come and have a cup of coffee with me?"

"I have an hour free before the evening performance. Just let me get my coat. I won't be a minute."

She was conscious that some of the actors were taking a break in the bar and were watching her and Sven. As an American and a handsome one, Sven was a source of gossip. She didn't care – let them gossip about her if they wanted.

She took his arm as they left the building and headed for Bewley's on Westmoreland Street.

"I like it here because I can get a fairly decent coffee. Would you like one? No? Tea? How about a sticky bun?"

Over their tea and coffee and while he attacked a sticky bun, they made small talk about the play for which he was rehearsing.

Then he leaned close to her. "Kay, I have been thinking about you since we met. I'd like to see you again. It's difficult with us working every night but we are both free on Sundays. Will you meet me tomorrow, Sunday?"

Kathleen thought quickly. Her mother would be suspicious if she wasn't there for Sunday dinner.

"I could meet you about three o'clock. I don't want my mother to know though so we'll have to meet where nobody will see us."

"How about meeting in the park at St Stephen's Green? You could get a bus into the city."

"That's a good idea. If it's a fine day my family will go for a walk in the Phoenix Park. They wouldn't think of going to Stephen's Green."

Kathleen tried to contain her excitement as she ate her dinner. Harry and Julia and his family were also there, so in the general fuss that surrounded Julia whose first outing this was since she came home from hospital, Kathleen was able to leave in good time. She had told her mother that she would be meeting some of her friends from the Abbey.

She could see Sven as soon as she got to the top of Grafton Street. He was standing at the memorial gate at the entrance to St Stephen's Green, smoking a cigarette, wearing a cream raincoat and a black fedora hat. He looked like a character in a gangster movie. He was so tall that he could see over the groups of people out for a Sunday stroll. As she got closer, his eyes locked into hers.

She felt a shiver of anticipation as he took her arm and led her under the arch and round to the duck pond. They found an empty park bench and sat down. Children, muffled up in hats, scarves and gloves were feeding the ducks.

He put his arm around her shoulders. "Are you cold?"

She smiled up at him. "No, not at all. I'm delighted to see you."

Actually, she was cold. There was a biting wind whipping up waves on the pond and sending the hats of unwary people skittering along the path. She should have worn her warm coat instead of the flimsy coat which flattered her but didn't keep her warm. She pulled her hat down firmly and tucked her scarf more tightly around her neck.

"If we walk along the pathway through the trees it will be more sheltered. I thought Nebraska was cold but this is a different kind of cold."

They walked briskly and soon left the Sunday strollers behind. They came to a clearing which curved back into the trees. He guided them in and when he was satisfied that they could not be seen from the pathway, he drew her to him and kissed her. Her face was numb with the cold, but his mouth was warm and demanding. She responded and felt a warmth going through her body. He had his hand on her breast, fondling it through the thin material of her coat.

She pulled away. "Someone might see." She could hear people chatting in the distance.

He moved back reluctantly. "OK. I think I have just about enough money for two coffees in Bewley's. At least it will be warm in there."

Bewley's Café on Grafton Street was buzzing with people. They found a table and when the waitress came Kathleen asked for a coffee too. It was bitter but when she added two spoons of sugar she found that she quite liked the taste. They chatted easily for about two hours, repeating their coffee order once, and after that ignoring both the waitress, who asked did they want anything else a few times, and the queue of people still waiting for a table. Sven was good company and very amusing. From the frequent glances in his direction, she realised people at adjoining tables were listening to his stories.

At six she said that it was time for her to go. She didn't want to arouse the suspicions of her parents. He wanted her to stay longer but she promised to meet him at the same place the following Sunday and perhaps to stay a little longer. He walked her to her bus stop and waited until the bus pulled out. She stood on the platform until his figure became smaller and eventually disappeared. She felt like Helen Hayes in *A Farewell to Arms*.

The following Sunday was still bitterly cold. Harry's family stayed at home. After she had helped to clear up after the meal, Kathleen went upstairs to get ready to meet Sven. She was seeing him later than usual that day. He was having lunch with friends – the couple he stayed with when he first arrived in Dublin. By the time she was ready to leave she was running late.

As she hurried down the stairs there was a soft knock on the door and she saw Mary rushing to answer.

Mary then reappeared with a young man. He was tall and thin with sandy hair and a nervous smile on his face. Mary looked shy and happy.

"Mam, Dad, this is Liam O'Broin. His family live in Black Street. He has been helping me with my Irish for the exams. He's a qualified teacher."

"Liam, you are very welcome," said Ellen. "I know your parents and I remember you when you were a little boy. Sit down here and have a cup of tea."

James held out his hand. "How are you, Liam? This is Kathleen, our other daughter."

Kathleen smiled and shook hands. She could see her parents were delighted with Liam. Of course they were – he was a teacher. They wouldn't be so pleased with Sven.

"I'm just leaving to meet some friends, Mary. Delighted to meet you, Liam." They were all too involved in conversation to notice when she gathered her things and slipped out the front door.

Sven was waiting anxiously at the bus stop. "I thought you weren't coming."

"Well, I'm here now. Are we going to the Green or Bewley's?"

"Neither. Those friends of mine want to meet you. They live quite close to here in South King Street. You'll like them."

Elizabeth and Daniel proved to be a very likeable couple. Elizabeth was English, a costume designer as well as an actress. Daniel was an actor. They were both older than Sven. Their flat was small, upstairs over a shop, but they had made it very warm and welcoming, with throws over the chairs and worn but colourful rugs on the floor. The walls were adorned with pictures of each of them in various productions. Elizabeth was wearing what looked like a Japanese robe with her black hair tied up in a knot on the top of her head. Daniel was wearing a corduroy suit which looked as though it was too big for him but he wore it with aplomb.

Kathleen sank into a sofa and had to move to accommodate the springs which stuck up in places.

Elizabeth brought over two glasses of wine and sat down beside her. "Now, tell me all about yourself. Sven has been talking about you a lot. I hear you are with the Abbey?"

The two women were soon in deep conversation about the theatre and Elizabeth's experience on the London stage. They disappeared into the bedroom when Elizabeth offered to show Kathleen some costumes she had designed. The two men remained in the kitchen, drinking porter and exchanging theatrical gossip.

Later, they came together and Elizabeth made pancakes – crepes, she called them. They were delicious, sprinkled with sugar and lemon juice and then rolled up. They were also very filling.

Kathleen knew that this was the kind of life she wanted. Bohemian, her mother would have called it.

Sven walked her to the bus when it was time to go home. It was dark enough for them to kiss in a doorway before she boarded. Again, she stood on the platform and watched his receding figure for as long as it was visible. This time she wasn't acting. She would miss him during the long week that followed.

CHAPTER 7

Mary had met Liam in early December when they were both walking to the bus in the morning, she on the way to college and he to his new job in a primary school. At the end of the term he asked her to come to a dance in the college with him. She had danced all night with Liam and other boys she knew but, when the last dance was announced, Liam took her arm.

He retrieved their coats and hurried them out so that they were alone on the walk home. After a while, he stopped in the street and turned to her.

"Mary, will you be my girlfriend? I love being with you and enjoy your company. I know you're only eighteen, but I would be happy to ask your parents if I could see you regularly."

Mary was delighted. "Liam, I'd love to be your girlfriend. I'll introduce you to my parents after Christmas if that's all right with you. The whole family will be there for Christmas and it could be a bit overwhelming. I would rather you met my parents on their own first."

Liam took a small wrapped box out of his pocket. "I hope you like this. I didn't know what to get you." He looked bashful and shy.

It was a slim silver bracelet.

"Oh, it's beautiful! Thank you, Liam. I will wear it always."

She put it back in the box. As soon as Liam met her parents, she would start wearing it. Shyly, she kissed him on the cheek. He smiled and took her hand and they walked home chatting easily.

At her door, he kissed her quickly on the lips.

"Goodnight, Mary. I'll see you very soon."

She knew she was flushed when she met her mother in the kitchen.

"You look happy. Was it a good evening? Was there anyone at the dance that I would know?"

"It was a great evening. I danced all night and I have sore feet because of the new shoes. There were a good few people from around here who are students at the college. You would probably know them or their parents."

"Would you like a cup of cocoa? I'm just making one for myself."

"No, thanks, Mam. I'll just get a drink of water. Goodnight and God bless."

She wasn't ready to tell her mother about Liam yet. She ran up the stairs and was soon in bed, thinking about Liam and his goodnight kiss. She placed the bracelet under her pillow.

Eventually, Mary invited Liam to call on a Sunday afternoon when she thought everyone except her parents would be out. As it happened, Kathleen didn't leave as early as usual that Sunday so she was still there. Mary had wanted to avoid her meeting Liam for the moment. Liam wasn't very good-looking and Kathleen would joke about that later.

Her parents liked him immediately and it turned out that they knew his parents quite well. They were delighted to give their permission for him to take her out and were impressed that he was old-fashioned enough to ask.

When Liam was leaving, he asked her to go to the pictures with him on the following Saturday. They had agreed that one date a week was enough for the moment since they both were so busy, she with her studies, and he as a new teacher needing to prepare his work every night.

After he left, she showed her silver bracelet to her parents and put it on her wrist. She was smiling and humming to herself as she prepared for bed that night.

CHAPTER 8

With only two weeks to go to the election, Harry was very busy in the constituency office organising the canvass. One evening he was approached by the chairman of the local branch.

"I have bad news, Harry. Paddy is very ill. He has been diagnosed with lung cancer. In fact, he is dying. We hope he will live, at least until after the election."

"Oh, I'm sorry to hear that. I knew Paddy wasn't too well, but I didn't realise that he was dying."

"He will be badly missed. What concerns us now is that if we lose this election we are going to have to hand over the reins of government to the very people that we fought in the Civil War. Every seat we win will count. It's vital that we win this seat and hold on to it. I am afraid that Cosgrave is not getting through to the electorate like De Valera and the Fianna Fáil are. People blame us for the economic problems in the country when actually they are partly caused by the financial crash in America and the protectionist policies of other European countries. Cosgrave is still promoting the idea of free trade while De Valera is preaching protectionism, an end to paying land annuities and the removal of the oath of allegiance to the king. Added to that, De Valera is a much more charismatic leader than Cosgrave, who is a good man but one who refuses to promote himself."

"Yes, I got some idea of those issues when I was canvassing. De Valera is certainly very popular. But I didn't fully realise that we are likely to lose the election."

"Well, we are. Anyway, the reason I came to see you is this. When Paddy dies, there will be a by-election. We need a new candidate, a strong candidate to replace him. The committee has decided to ask you to go forward."

Harry was still absorbing the news of Paddy, his friend and mentor. He began to realise the implications for himself.

"Me? A candidate? But I have no experience."

"We have very little time and you have made a strong impression on the local members of the party. Paddy thinks a lot of you and he gives you his blessing. You'll have to represent him for the next few weeks. That will give you a high profile. Of course, there will be a selection meeting when the by-election is called but there's no one else in the constituency that has as good a chance as you to win this seat."

The chairman began to outline the hectic schedule for the coming weeks. The first thing he wanted Harry to do was to resign his commission. Half listening to the urgent tones, Harry thought of Julia. She would support him of course but she needed his support too. He knew what the last weeks of a campaign were like: he would hardly see his home. He would be knocking on doors, speaking at church gates, talking to newspapers and rallying Paddy's supporters. He would have no time to spend with Julia. But that might be no bad thing. A break from the intensity of the past few weeks would do them both good. Their families would give her plenty of support.

He walked home rehearsing how he would break the news to her. She was still up, still dressed, her hair brushed and shining, drinking a cup of cocoa.

"Hello, love," she said. "We haven't had much time together over the last few weeks so I thought we could have a chat." She moved over on the sofa. "Come and sit down. Would you like a cup of cocoa?"

He took a seat in the chair opposite her, settled himself and took a deep breath. "No, thanks. I had a cup with Jim, you know, the chairman. He wanted to talk to me about something. I'm sorry to say that poor Paddy is very ill. He has lung cancer. They don't expect him to last long after the election."

Julia was shocked. "Oh, the poor man! And his poor wife!"

"Yes, he will be a great loss. When he dies, there will be a by-election," Harry continued, choosing his words carefully. "We can't afford to lose a seat so they need someone to stand in his place, someone who knows the constituency and has a good chance of winning the seat."

Julia was staring at him, dawning awareness in her eyes. "So they asked you?"

"Yes, they did. I was very sorry to hear of Paddy's illness but honoured to be asked to take his place."

"Did you accept?"

"Yes, of course I did. It's a great opportunity and I never thought it would come so quickly. I will have to resign my commission, but you know that I was getting tired of army life. They say that my chances of winning the seat are excellent."

"And what about me and the children? We'll hardly see you. It was bad enough when you were just an election worker. I know what political life is like for the TDs."

Harry leaned forward and took both her hands. "Yes, you are right. It will be hectic until I'm elected but, after that, things will calm down and life will return to normal."

"Will it?" Julia freed her hands and rose, her shoulders slumped, her head down. "Anyway, you have made your decision. I think I'll go to bed now."

The fire was almost out. He raked it, added some wood and turf and it slowly smouldered back to life. He sat for a long time, thinking about the events of the evening. He would put all his energy into supporting Paddy in this election and making himself the best candidate for the by-election. It wouldn't leave much time for worrying about his marriage.

Afterwards, Harry would remember the few weeks before the election as a blur of speechmaking, handshaking and constant walking. It was both exhilarating and exhausting. He left home every day before Julia was up and returned late in the evening when she was in bed. Usually she was asleep but, on the evenings when she was awake, he avoided going to their room and squeezed in beside Michael or Pádraig.

On the day of the election, she accompanied him to the local voting station in the primary school. He was proud of how elegant she looked in her green tweed suit with its fitted jacket and calf-length skirt. She had made it herself, with the help of her sisters, from a paper pattern. A fashionable fedora hat sat at a rakish angle on her shoulder-length hair. She chatted and talked to people with ease. He excused himself and made his way to her side.

"Julia, I'll have to stay here until the polling station closes. I'll get someone to see you home as soon as you want. If, *when*, we win the seat, there will be a party tonight. I hope you will come."

Her green eyes looked steadily into his. "I don't think so. You will be busy talking to people. I'd prefer to stay at home with the children. I'm going now. I can walk home by myself."

He watched her walk the length of the hall to the door. The room seemed to darken when she left. He suddenly felt lonely.

"Harry, there's someone here I want you to meet." The chairman was steering him towards a group.

He loosened his shoulders, smiled and strode forwards. There would be time to talk to Julia, to find a solution to their problem, when this was all over.

The result of the election was expected that evening about eight o'clock. There was prolonged cheering when Paddy won the seat by a narrow margin. However, although the counts from all the constituencies were not in, it was obvious that *Cumann na nGaedhael* would not win enough seats to form a government. For the first time, since the beginning of the State in 1922, Fianna Fáil would form the government with the support of the Labour Party. The celebrations of Paddy's supporters were tempered by this knowledge. They still went ahead with the planned party, but it was subdued.

Ellen and Violet arrived with Mary to join in the celebrations. There was someone else with them and for a brief moment Harry hoped that it was Julia. It was Grace, his mother's friend and the adopted aunt of Harry and his brother and sisters. There was a flurry of greetings and then Harry felt he had to circulate. By the time he got back to where he had left the group, they were gone. Only Grace remained, chatting to a group of party workers and obviously entertaining them with stories of her life as an actress in the Abbey Theatre. Harry joined the group and listened for a few minutes.

Then Grace made her excuses and took his arm. They moved away from the group.

"How is Julia? I thought she would be here. I haven't seen her since I visited her when she was in hospital. And how are you? You look well. Ellen tells me that you have an exciting time ahead of you. How is Paddy holding up?"

"Paddy is as well as can be expected. I saw him earlier, when we were certain that he had won the seat. I went to his house as soon as we knew the result. His wife, Alice, was there and she said that he was well enough to talk to me for a few minutes but I had only congratulated him when he took a terrible fit of coughing and I had to leave. The poor man looks dreadful. I'm afraid he won't last much longer." He lowered his voice. "I can't really talk about my own future at the moment."

"Of course, I understand. Listen, will you walk home with me? I know it is out of your way but I'm a bit nervous. Fianna Fáil supporters are out on the street celebrating and there could be some trouble."

"Of course I will. Let's go. The party has fizzled out anyway. People are very disappointed with the overall results. At least Paddy won his seat. That means a lot to him."

The night air was damp and cold. Harry breathed it in deeply, trying to clear his head. Grace linked him and chatted to him for a few minutes about the election results. Then she stopped and turned around to face him.

"What's wrong, Harry? You don't seem yourself. Are you worried about Paddy?"

"Yes, of course I am. I have known Paddy since I met him with Michael Collins in the weeks before Independence. He is a good man and he worked very hard for his constituents. We are all devastated by his illness. But it's not just that. I have been asked to stand as a candidate in the by-election in the event of his death. Keep that to yourself for the moment."

Grace resumed walking, digesting this piece of news. "That's a great honour, Harry. How does Julia feel about it?"

"She would prefer me to stay in the army. She knows what life is like for the family of a politician. And there's another thing. We have been having some difficulties. I don't know, maybe I could talk to you about it. I need to talk to someone."

His muted tone conveyed that he wanted to talk about something personal.

Grace linked his arm again and began to walk faster. "Let's wait until we are sitting down in my house before we discuss whatever it is that is troubling you."

When they reached her house, the fire was black in the grate but the rich colours in the room and the soft velvet throws on the furniture made the room seem warm. Grace made a hot whiskey for Harry and a hot port for herself before sitting down opposite him.

"Now, Harry, what is it you wanted to talk to me about?"

He shifted uncomfortably in his seat and put his drink down. "I don't know how to say this. You know Julia has been very ill. She lost a lot of blood when she miscarried.

She is much better now but we have a problem which we are finding it hard to discuss. The doctor told us that it would be very dangerous for her to have another baby. He didn't tell us what to do about it, other than that it was my responsibility. I went to see my friend, you know, Brian, the priest who was Maeve's godfather? He was no help either. He told me what the Church's teaching is. He even suggested that separate bedrooms would help."

He clenched his fists at that memory and looked at the floor, trying to find the right words.

Grace looked at him, understanding in her eyes. "I know what you are trying to say. Julia should not have another baby, but you don't know how to prevent that without going against the teaching of the Church."

Relief flooded Harry's face at hearing his dilemma put so clearly. "Yes, that's it. I couldn't put Julia's life in danger. I love her so much. But I can't imagine a life where we can't have normal relations either. I know she feels the same, but I can't discuss it with her. For the first time, we can't talk to each other." He put his head in his hands.

She could hear him choking back the tears. "Harry, do you want me to speak frankly?"

He nodded without looking at her.

"We both know that any kind of birth control other than abstention is forbidden by law in this country," she said. "That is not to say that people do not practise it. Because of what your mother calls 'my bohemian life' I know more about the subject than many women. You probably know most of this already, but I will do my best to clarify things for you."

"Thanks, Grace. I'm sorry, I'm just a bit awkward talking about this. But do go on."

"Have you heard of 'coitus interruptus'? Yes? It's the most commonly used form of contraception. Your Latin is good enough to tell you what that entails. It is commonly and humorously called 'getting off at Dolphin's Barn' – you know, getting off before you reach the inner city. Its success is completely dependent on the man's ability to withdraw in time. Accidents happen, so it's not reliable."

Harry smiled. "I never heard it described like that."

"Well, it is more descriptive than the Latin term. Then, you've probably have heard of French letters?"

Harry nodded. "I've heard of people importing them."

"They're not legally available in the Free State but people import them illegally or get them from friends in England. They are reasonably reliable but again, accidents happen. Then, there is the rhythm method which involves counting days and avoiding the fertile days in a woman's cycle – needless to say, that too is unreliable. I am afraid that if you are looking for a completely safe method of contraception, there isn't one."

Harry looked at her, his expression bleak. "I suppose, somewhere at the back of my mind, I knew that. Thanks for putting it so clearly, Grace. I just can't bring myself to discuss these methods with Julia. Something that was so private and beautiful and profound begins to sound sordid when you have to discuss it like this."

The misery on Harry's face made Grace go over to him. She put her arms around his shoulders. "Go home to Julia and talk to her about it. You will have to talk about it sometime. Not talking is making it worse for both of you."

Harry walked home slowly, ignoring the rain which was turning to fog. He went over the events of the day as he walked, trying to avoid thoughts of his conversation with Grace. There would be a lot of work to do in preparing for the by-election. The other parties had got wind of Paddy's illness and, no doubt, were preparing their own candidates. It would be a hard-fought battle but he would give it all his energy. There wouldn't be any time to talk to Julia until afterwards. It was just as well. The whole problem was too raw at the moment. The few times he tried to talk to her about it had ended with Julia in tears and him leaving the house, walking aimlessly for hours, not wanting to go home.

He didn't want to go home now either, although he was soaked. He could feel rainwater trickling down the back of his neck. He took a detour and found himself near Kingsbridge Railway station. The sounds of shunting and whistles were muffled by the fog which had descended like an eiderdown, obscuring familiar sights. He could hardly see a foot ahead of him. The enveloping fog smothered the gas lamps, allowing only a glimmer of light to peer through. Parkgate Street was deserted except for a few travellers making their way to Kingsbridge for the last train. The faint lights of Ryan's pub shone out like a beacon. He pushed in the door and was hit by the warmth and the cloying smell of porter. Along the bar three men gazed philosophically at their reflections in the mirror and took slow sups from their pints.

"Is it yourself, Harry? We don't often see you in here. What'll you have?" Willie Ryan looked closely at him, taking in his soaked hat and overcoat.

"A large whiskey, please, Willie."

He lowered the whiskey without tasting it, then made his way to the Gents', avoiding the curious eyes of the few clients. His coat and hat were sodden. He took them off and stared at himself in the mirror. Almost every night lately when he left the constituency office, instead of heading for home he had walked aimlessly down Parkgate Street to the quays or along the North Circular Road. He didn't return home until he thought Julia would be asleep. Sometimes she was, other times she would be weeping softly into her pillow. Those were the nights that he slept uncomfortably on the sofa or beside one of the boys.

Willie was now talking to one of the men at the bar. Harry ordered another large whiskey and downed it quickly, feeling the warmth spread through him. The door opened, admitting a blast of cold, damp air.

A young woman came in, her face almost obscured by the sodden brim of her hat.

"Terrible evenin', isn't it, love?"

She stood close to him. He moved away and sat at a table. She followed and sat down.

"Any chance ye'd buy me a nip, love? I'm frozen to death and half drownded."

Willie was staring at him.

"What would you like?" Harry asked.

She was thin and slight, her brown hair escaping in wet strands from under the ruined hat. Streaked dabs of rouge on her cheeks highlighted her pallor.

"Ah, you're terrible good. I'd love a drop of gin."

"A gin, please, Willie, and another large whiskey."

Willie arrived with the drinks which he slapped down on the table without looking at Harry. "Drink that now and be on your way, Biddy. I told you before that you are not welcome here." He returned to polishing glasses behind the bar.

The woman seemed to shrink into herself as she lowered her head and pulled the drink towards her. She took a sip and then gulped it down, grimacing at the bitterness.

"Never seen you in here before, love. I'da noticed a good-looking young fella like you. D' ye live around here?"

She smiled at him, revealing a missing side tooth. She was young, only about eighteen or twenty, he reckoned.

"No, I don't live around here. Well, I have to be off now. Don't want to miss my train."

He put on his sodden hat, wincing at the cold clamp of it.

He was outside the door, fumbling with the buttons of his coat when he realised she was beside him, her arm linking his.

"My place is just around the corner. Why don't yeh come in with me for a few minutes to get warmed up? Yeh can still catch yer train."

He could smell the gin and something else, an earthy muskiness both repellent and attractive. He didn't want to go home and he didn't want to go back in to Willie's disapproving stare. He allowed her to pull him in the direction of the station, putting his head down against the slap of cold air. Familiar buildings retreated into the fog and became swirling sketches. An open door seemed to suck them in. He struggled to control his movements in the hall, avoiding a broken-down pram and trying not to inhale the urine-soaked air. She pulled him up the broken staircase, into a small room which reeked of dampness and mould. She lit a candle and pulled off her coat and hat.

"C'mere, chicken, and let me get that wet coat off yeh. Yeh'll get your death."

He had seen how thin and pale she was when she took

off her coat. She was wearing a flimsy shift-like garment that revealed the curves of her small breasts. She leaned up to take off his hat and then kissed him. He felt himself responding. She peeled off his coat and put her arms around him.

In the next room he heard something moving. The small sounds became a cry, a baby's cry. The woman moved away towards the door.

"Oh, sorry, darlin'! She'll go back to sleep in a minute. I'll just settle her."

The cry had sobered him up. By the time she came back into the room he had his coat and hat on again. He pressed some money into her hand.

"That's all the money I have on me. I'm sorry. I have to go."

Her thin shoulders slumped. "That's all right, love. I didn't think yeh were the type anyway."

The smell of the squalid room was still in his nostrils as he walked home, the shame of what he had almost done like a weight on his shoulders. He had almost betrayed Julia in a most horrible way. How could he have been tempted by that poor woman? What was he going to do?

CHAPTER 9

Mary and Liam had settled into a happy routine. Saturday evenings they usually went to the pictures or a dance. Sometimes on Sunday afternoons they went for a walk in the Phoenix Park and back to her parents for tea. Other times, he helped her with her college studies. They liked reading the same books and discussed them on their walks. She felt she could tell him anything.

One Sunday, as they strolled in the park, she confided in him about her family. She had decided to do it as they walked as it would be easier if she didn't have to meet his eyes.

"Liam, there's something I need to tell you. I hope it won't make a difference."

"A difference? What do you mean?" He sounded alarmed.

"I'm not the natural daughter of Ellen and James. My mother, Annie, was Ellen's youngest sister. Their family lived on Lord Lucan's desmesne in Castlebar, County Mayo. Annie fell in love with Lord Lucan's chauffeur, Albert Dunne. She didn't know that he already had a wife and children in Dublin. When she told him that she has going to have his baby, he ran away to Dublin and joined the Dublin Fusiliers. She never heard from him again. He was killed fighting in France three years later."

"Oh, the poor woman!" he said, and she was relieved to hear the sympathy in his voice. "I'm so sorry to hear that. But what happened to her? How did you end up living with the Devereux family?"

"My grandmother was afraid the neighbours would get to know about Annie and Albert so she and Jane, her eldest daughter, brought her to Dublin. Ellen wasn't bothered about the neighbours and what they thought so she took Annie into her own house. James was away fighting in France at the time. I grew up calling Annie "Mama Annie" and Ellen "Mama Ellen". When James came home he became my father. I look on Harry, Joseph and Kathleen as my brothers and sister and I know they feel the same about me."

"That's an amazing story."

"So that's how I became Mary Devereux. I was christened Mary Ainsworth – that's my mother's maiden name." She looked at him for the first time since she began to speak. "Look, please don't tell anyone else this story. People are very judgemental. Around here people think that Annie had a husband who died in the war and that Ellen took me in when Annie went off to study to be a nurse."

"Do you ever see Annie now?

"She died of a heart attack when I was ten."

"Oh, Mary! I'm so sorry."

"I really miss her because we were very close, and she always encouraged me in my ambition to be a teacher."

"Thanks for confiding in me, Mary. That's a sad story but you are lucky to be part of such a loving family and remember that you have me now to love you and encourage you as well."

CHAPTER 10

Meeting with Sven on Sunday afternoons had become an important part of Kathleen's week. Her mother accepted that she was meeting a group of friends and asked no questions. Sometimes she met Sven in Bewley's, especially when the weather was very cold, sometimes in St Stephen's Green, sometimes in Elizabeth and Daniel's flat. The older couple were always pleased to see them and Kathleen became very fond of Elizabeth. She was in awe of her experience on the stages of Dublin and London and learned many tips about fashion and make-up from her. When she got a small part in the play that Sven was in, Elizabeth helped her rehearse.

On a cold, blustery Sunday in March, she and Sven met at the bus stop as usual. There were very few people about. Kathleen had to hang on to her hat as they made their way along the street.

"We can't stay out in this weather. Will we go to Bewley's?"

"No, we're going to Elizabeth and Daniel's." Sven took her arm.

They walked quickly, heads down against the wind

which was making talking difficult. She was surprised when they arrived at the flat and, instead of knocking, Sven took out a key and opened the door.

"Daniel and Elizabeth are away in London. She was called for an audition for a West End play and got the part. He had nothing on, so he went with her. He's hoping to get a small part in the same play. They asked me to look after the flat so I'm staying here for the moment. It's a lot better than the bedsit I share with Tom."

Kathleen didn't know what to say. She was glad to have a warm place to meet but felt anxious about being alone with Sven. She knew how demanding he could be during their few private moments in the park. He was watching her, trying to gauge her reaction.

"It's great to get in out of the wind. How long will they be away?"

"That depends on the run that the play gets. Daniel might come back to Dublin if he doesn't get a part."

He hung up their coats and went outside to get some wood and turf to make a fire. Soon they were sitting on either side of a spluttering clump of damp turf.

Kathleen got the bellows and soon pumped the fire into life. "Now, that's much better. Would you like a coffee?"

She found some of Sven's favourite coffee and some sugar. No milk, of course – Sven didn't take milk. She brought the cups over to the fire, handed one to him and sat down.

"This is like playing house, isn't it?" she said.

"I suppose it is," he said with a smile.

When they had finished their coffee, Sven put a record on the gramophone and wound it up. "Come on, let's dance."

"When the Blue of the Night Meets the Gold of the

Day" was one of her favourites. He held her close and looked into her eyes as they danced. She could feel his heart beating. He leaned down to kiss her. The tune was just finishing.

She pulled away. "Put on something faster. Do they have any Louis Armstrong?"

Soon they were bouncing along to "I Got Rhythm". They were breathless by the end of the song.

"Let's have a breather. I haven't much food in the house. Would you like some bread and cheese and another coffee? There might be a few biscuits too."

She put more turf on the fire and relaxed. It was going to be all right. When it was time for her to leave, Sven put his arms around her. He kissed her, gently at first and then more passionately. She responded but then the thought of missing her bus and her mother finding out about Sven made her pull away.

"I really have to go, Sven. It's been lovely being here alone with you but, if my mother finds out I've been seeing you, she won't let me out anymore. I'll see you next week."

The following week Kathleen spent most of her time dreaming of Sven and picturing the future they would have together. They would get married and go to live in Hollywood. They would both get parts in big movies. She would change her name to Kay De Vere. They would be a Hollywood golden couple. Her parents would be upset about her leaving Ireland but once she and Sven got married, they would be happy. They would get married in Dublin and the papers would be full of stories of the Dublin girl who became a star in Hollywood. She would ask Elizabeth and Mary to be her bridesmaids. Elizabeth would design her dress. They would go on their honeymoon to New York.

The following Sunday she confided her plans to Sven. Well, not all of them – just the ones about getting married and going to Hollywood.

He listened indulgently. "I haven't any money, you know. I can just about look after myself."

"Oh, we don't need any money. My parents will pay for the wedding and I can borrow the money for my fare from my brother Harry. When we get to Hollywood, I'll be able to work. There are a lot of Irish actresses in Hollywood. Look at Maureen O'Sullivan. She's doing very well. When do you think we should go?"

"We don't want to rush into things. This play will run to the end of May. Then I'll decide what to do. Now, let's just relax and listen to some music. We had a full house last night and I am really tired."

There was finality in his tone, so she didn't tell him any more of her plans. There would be time enough for that. She snuggled up close to him on the lumpy sofa. The fire and the music were making her drowsy.

She woke up feeling chilly, to find the fire had gone out. Sven was beside her with his hand on her breast. The buttons of her blouse were open. He was kissing her, his lips demanding and his tongue pushing into her mouth. She found herself responding, the warmth flooding down through her body. He was pushing her skirt up. What was she doing?

"*No, Sven. I can't!* I don't want you to do that. I have to go now. Please let me up."

He watched as she rearranged her clothes. He was angry – she could tell by the coldness in his eyes.

"Will you walk me to the bus?"

"I told you that I'm very tired. It's not very far."

She went to kiss him goodbye but he didn't respond. By the time she had put on her coat and hat, he had pulled a throw over him and his eyes were closed.

The tears rolled down her face as she ran for the bus.

Kathleen almost missed her cue for her few lines during Monday's performance. The director had a word with her afterwards. He said that if she couldn't keep her mind on the performance, he would give her part to another girl. She had worked so hard to get that small part. Now she didn't care if she lost it. But the reprimand gave her an excuse to cry. The other members of the cast were very sympathetic and she wallowed in the kind words and cups of tea which they offered.

She couldn't decide whether to see Sven the following week. She knew what he wanted, and he was determined to get it. But if they were going to get married, it didn't really matter, did it? If she gave in to him, it would show him that she really loved him.

On Sunday morning, she was still undecided.

"I suppose you are off into the city to meet your friends," her mother said. "We are going around to Harry's for tea so you'll probably be home before us. Don't wait up."

That decided her. She could have a few hours extra with Sven! She hurried to get ready, while choosing her clothes carefully. She took out the new, silky, flesh-coloured slip which Grace had given her for Christmas. It was time to start wearing it. She surveyed herself critically in the mirror before putting on her dress. She looked like a star. Only her eyes betrayed the nervousness that she was feeling.

He wasn't waiting at the bus stop. Her eyes searched the Sunday crowds on O'Connell Street but there was no sign of him. He probably thought that she wouldn't come. She ran the distance to Elizabeth and Daniel's flat and banged the knocker loudly on the door. No answer. She tried to blink back the tears so as not to ruin her make-up and knocked again.

The door opened slowly. Then he was standing in the doorway, looking sad and forlorn.

"I didn't think you would come. I'm sorry about what happened last time. You looked so beautiful when you were asleep. I just couldn't help myself. I do love you, you know."

It was the first time that he'd said he loved her. She threw herself into his arms.

"I love you too. I was just afraid. I've never … you know."

"Don't worry. I will take care of you."

He led her into the room where the fire was glowing, removed her coat and hat and tenderly sat her on the sofa. He sat down beside her and put his arm around her shoulders. She snuggled into him. He kissed her gently and tenderly. She soon found herself responding, lying back on the sofa and allowing him to caress the length of her body.

He spoke very quietly, punctuating sentences with kisses which started at her throat and travelled downwards. "I won't force you to do anything you don't want to do. I'll be very careful. Remember I love you."

Afterwards, she felt warm and euphoric nestled in his arms. She wanted to talk, to discuss their wedding plans, but he fell asleep. She watched him sleeping and felt such tenderness towards him that she cried. She wanted to stay all night with him, but her parents would be worried at first and then angry when they found out where she had been. She consoled herself that once she told them that she and Sven were to be married they would be happy and she could spend as much time as she wanted with him. As soon as they had made their plans, she could tell her family.

"A penny for them." Sven was awake and smiling at her.

"Oh, I was just thinking about when we are married."

"Come on, let's get our coats – you don't want to be late home."

CHAPTER 11

On the final day of Mary's exams in May, Liam was waiting for her outside the college. Students were thronging the footpath and there was a general air of euphoria.

Liam caught her in his arms and swung her around and around.

"I'm sure you did very well! I'll be free in a few weeks and then we'll have the whole summer to ourselves."

"All I have to do now is find a job before September – assuming I've passed!"

"Of course you have! You're a fine student, you know that."

"But I'm very nervous when it came to exams."

"I'm sure you've done brilliantly." Liam had been working on helping her to overcome her nerves.

"Fingers crossed. Anyway, now I want to celebrate by going to the Palm Grove and having a Knickerbocker Glory."

Liam laughed. Mary loved ice cream and was a connoisseur of the best ice-cream parlours in Dublin.

As they walked off, he felt proud of her. She was into a lovely, confident young woman.

The sun shone for the next couple of weekends and

Mary and Liam had a wonderful time. They walked in the Phoenix Park, went to the Zoo, took the tram to Howth and had a fish-and-chips tea there and travelled on the train to Bray where they walked the promenade, had an ice cream and swam in the sea.

On that day in Bray, they were lying on their towels on the shingly sand, toasting themselves in the sun, when Liam sat up and leaned over Mary.

"Mary, will you marry me? I love you and want to spend my life with you."

Mary sat up and kissed him. "Of course I will – but not until I get a job! I need to get some teaching experience before I marry. You know it's very difficult for a married woman to get a teaching position. It's bad enough that married women are paid less than men and single women but it's even worse that it's so hard for them to get a job."

"You have it all figured out! Once you get a job, we could get engaged at Christmas and then get married a year later. I'll ask your parents the next time I see them."

"No, don't say anything to them until near Christmas. I want it to be a surprise for everyone. Anyway, it will save you having to think of a Christmas present for me. The ring will be enough!"

Liam laughed. He hated having to choose presents and, after his first gift to her of a silver bracelet, he usually took her with him to choose even the tiniest gift like a scarf or some scented soap.

Mary began to apply for teaching posts and the first interview she was called for was in Liam's own school. She couldn't believe it when she was offered the job, subject to her passing her exams. Of course, the parish priest

Father Mongey, who was manager of the school, and the principal Mr Murray had no idea that she knew Liam.

Her parents were jubilant and her mother danced around the kitchen with her. Her father hugged her and had tears in his eyes when he said, "You are the best daughter that a man could have."

She ran around to Liam's house with the letter. His parents were delighted for her. Liam managed to contain his excitement until they were outside, on their way to the Park.

"We'll be able to travel to school and home again together. We'll see each other at breaktimes. I can't believe it – it's perfect. Of course, we'll have to pretend that we don't know each other at the beginning. They don't approve of relationships between staff members. But once we're engaged that will all change."

"We're so lucky, Liam. Everything is working out so well. I say a prayer every night to thank God for sending you to me. I love you very much and I know we will be happy together."

She linked him and they strolled along, in step with each other, to the duck pond.

CHAPTER 12

The play had finished at the end of April and Sven's contract had run out at the same time. He was offered a part in the next production, but it wasn't a lead part. Kathleen was also offered a small part. The new production went into rehearsal in early May with the opening planned for July.

Kathleen was delighted that they were appearing together, but he was annoyed that he wasn't playing the lead. He was in a bad mood all the time and didn't even offer to walk her to the bus on some Sunday evenings. He was annoyed by the crowds in the city. He scoffed at the decorations and flowers which could be seen all over the city in preparation for the Eucharistic Congress which would attract hundreds of sightseers.

For the first time she found that she was suffering from nerves before every rehearsal, feeling sick and clammy before she went on. Then one morning she began to suspect that it wasn't nerves making her feel ill. She realised that her time of the month had come and gone and nothing had happened. For days every twinge or tingle in her abdomen sent her rushing to the nearest lavatory. She examined her body in the mirror for signs of any changes. Finally, she had to face the truth.

She was going to have a baby – Sven's baby. She didn't know how she was going to tell him. They would have to arrange the wedding quickly.

She decided to wait until Sunday when they would be alone together in the flat. On Sunday morning, her mother remarked on her wan appearance. She said that appearing in the play was very exhausting. Then she almost vomited at the smell of sausages and rashers. Her mother looked worried.

"Did you eat anything last night that could have made you sick? The weather is very warm and it's easy for things to go off."

"Yes, I ate some sandwiches at the theatre. They did taste a bit off."

Then she excused herself and went to put on her make-up, using extra rouge to make herself look healthy.

By the afternoon she felt much better. She managed to eat a little dinner to please her mother and was able to leave at her normal time.

Sven wasn't waiting at the bus stop – he had given up that practice a few weeks before. She made her way to the flat, rehearsing different ways of telling him about the baby. There was no easy way to tell him. She didn't think he would be happy to hear the news. When she arrived at the flat, she stood on the doorstep for a minute before knocking. When she finally knocked, the door flew open and Elizabeth was standing there.

"Elizabeth! When did you get back?"

"Kay! How lovely to see you! We got back last Tuesday. Come on in."

"No, no, I was just calling to see Sven."

"Oh, did he not tell you?"

"That he would be going back to his flat? No, he didn't."

Elizabeth stared at her. "But Sven left for New York this morning. From there he was going on to California and Hollywood. Some friends of his are doing a road trip along Highway 66 and they invited him to join them. He wasn't very happy with the small part he had been given so he decided to accept. He said he would tell you. Obviously, he didn't."

Then Kathleen was sobbing convulsively on the doorstep. Elizabeth put her arms around her and drew her into the kitchen.

"You poor girl, you've had a terrible shock. That bastard should have told you. Let me make you a cup of sweet tea and we'll talk. I can't believe that Sven didn't tell you he was leaving."

Kathleen sat on the sofa where she and Sven had spent so many happy Sunday evenings and drank the tea. What was she going to do now?

"Did he leave an address where I can write to him?"

"I'm sure he will write to you when he gets to Hollywood," Elizabeth said without conviction. "He borrowed some money from Daniel to make up the fare so he will have to write to us."

Kathleen was tempted to tell Elizabeth the real reason for her distress but Elizabeth would tell Daniel and he might tell someone else and her reputation would be ruined. No, she would have to find a solution to her problem on her own. She chatted to Elizabeth for a while longer, trying to appear confident that Sven would write to her.

When she left, she automatically headed for St Stephen's Green. It was a beautiful day and the park was full of families and young couples. Kathleen found a seat on the bench near the duck pond where she and Sven used to sit. She began to examine the options that were open to her. She doubted that Sven would return or even write to her – certainly not in time to prevent her disgrace becoming obvious.

She could continue with the pregnancy. She knew a girl who had done that. Maybe her parents would let her stay at home and accept the baby into the family. Her mother had accepted her own sister Annie into her home and adopted her daughter, Mary. But that was during the war and the Rising. Her father wasn't at home and her brothers were just children then. People did heroic things at times like that, but in normal times they were more interested in their reputation.

She could go to a mother and baby home, one of the dreaded Magdalene laundries. There was one in Goldenbridge. She had caught sight of the miserable women a few times when she passed by. She could take the boat to England where nobody knew her. Any of these options meant that her reputation would be ruined, and it would be very difficult to return to Dublin. There was one final option: she could somehow get rid of the baby. She could feel the bile rising in her throat at that thought. There were always rumours about girls who had done it themselves and died or girls who had gone to illegal abortionists and died. They always seemed to die. No, she couldn't go down that route.

She decided to walk home rather than take the bus. It might help to clear her head. She was beginning to feel queasy again. She got up and walked around the duck pond before heading for the bus.

When she got home, even her father noticed her pallor.

"Kathleen, are you all right? You look very pale and tired. That acting is taking too much out of you. You should look for another job."

Her mother was solicitous and made her hot milk with a drop of brandy in it. It would settle her stomach and make her sleep, she said. To her surprise, she did sleep.

CHAPTER 13

The next day Kathleen went to the theatre for rehearsals as usual but found she could not concentrate. She pleaded a sick stomach and was replaced by an understudy. Other members of the cast looked at her knowingly. They thought she was pining for Sven whose part was now being rehearsed by someone else.

She walked up O'Connell Street, not wanting to return home too early.

"Kathleen, how are you? I thought you'd be in the theatre at this time."

It was Liam, Mary's boyfriend.

"Oh, hello, Liam! What are you doing in town?"

"I came in after school to go to Eason's Bookshop. I was looking for some Ibsen plays. I read one when I was at college and I really liked his writing."

"Ibsen? Oh, I love Ibsen too. He writes great roles for women. Have you read *A Doll's House?*"

"Yes, I have – that was the first one I read and I have just got *Hedda Gabler*. I'm really looking forward to reading it."

"I'm going across to the Gresham to have a coffee.

Would you like to join me?"

Liam hesitated. "That would be nice. I've never been in the Gresham."

The hotel lounge was full of fashionably dressed people. They found a seat in the window overlooking the street. When they had given their order to the waitress there was an awkward silence. Then they both spoke together.

"I didn't know …"

"I thought that you …"

They both laughed.

Kathleen spoke first.

"I didn't think that you were interested in theatre. I thought that primary school teacher training was just about education."

"Well, it is, to an extent. But we also study literature in both English and Irish. I particularly like drama and poetry. I can't afford to go to the theatre very often, but I have seen a few plays in the Gate and the Abbey."

"Oh, I didn't know that. Did you see *Mourning Becomes Electra*? I was in that. Only a small role but it was a start."

"No, Mary doesn't like the theatre so I haven't seen anything since I started going out with her. She prefers the pictures."

"Oh, I love the pictures too. I would love to be in the movies."

Liam smiled. He wasn't so plain when he smiled.

"You'd be great in the movies. You look like a star already."

The waitress put a tray on their table with a pot of coffee, cups, milk and sugar and some scones with butter, cream and jam.

Suddenly, Kathleen was starving. "They do the best scones here and very good coffee," she said as she layered on the fresh cream and strawberry jam.

"I've never been here before. I always thought that it was very expensive."

"Only a little bit more expensive than an ordinary tea shop, and it's worth it for the atmosphere. You never know who you might meet here. Have you ever been backstage in a theatre?" A plan was beginning to form in her mind.

"No, never. I'd love to see what goes on behind the scenes."

"Well, now's your chance. When we finish our scones, I'll take you over to the Gate and show you around backstage. Rehearsals will be finished and the evening performance is not for a couple of hours."

"Oh, that would be great. I have plenty of time. Mary is meeting some college friends tonight. They're all celebrating getting new jobs."

The mention of Mary made her think for a minute. She loved her sister but Mary was young and she would meet someone else. She had a good job and she wasn't even engaged to Liam.

When they got to the theatre it was very quiet. The stage manager was in the foyer, a big plan of the stage laid out before him on a table.

"Oh, hello, Kay, I didn't expect to see you back here this evening."

"Hello, Jack. I'm just going to show a friend around backstage – is that all right?"

"Yes, of course. They've all gone out to get something to eat. Later, we're going to start constructing the set. You'll have the place to yourself until then."

She loved the eerie feeling of the theatre when there

was no one else there. The place was in semi-darkness with only the odd light throwing shadows around. She took Liam's hand.

"Be careful. Don't trip over anything. Come on. I'll show you backstage."

They looked out from one of the wings to the empty rows of seats.

"Can you see the audience when you're performing? It must be very unnerving."

"When I'm waiting in the wings for a cue, I sometimes study the audience. If the play is going well, you can tell immediately from their facial expressions. But the lights onstage make it difficult to see anything but the first few rows."

"I'd love to appear on the stage but I'm far too nervous. I would probably forget my lines."

"Have a go now. What plays do you know? We could rehearse a scene."

"I don't know any plays by heart, except maybe *Romeo and Juliet*. I did that at school."

"I know it too. I played Juliet in a school production. Come on, let's rehearse a scene from it. It will be fun and you can get a feel for what acting is all about. Do you know the scene where Juliet finds Romeo and thinks he is dead? It's my favourite scene."

"Yes, I think I do."

"Right. You are Romeo. Lie down on the ground here. Then I enter, stage left. I am distraught because I think that you're dead."

Liam lay down in the centre of the stage, arranging himself in an awkward heap. He raised his head. "I can't remember my lines."

"You have none in this scene. Just look like you are

dead. I'll take a minute to get into character." She disappeared into the wings.

Liam was just thinking of getting up from his embarrassing place on the floor when a distraught Juliet emerged onto the stage.

"*What's here? A cup closed in my true love's hand?*
Poison, I see, hath been his timeless end.
O churl, drunk all, and left no friendly drop
To help me after? I will kiss thy lips."

At that, Kathleen gave him a lingering kiss.

"*Haply some poison yet doth hang on them,*
To make me die with a restorative.
They lips are warm.
Yea, noise? Then I'll be brief. O happy dagger,
This is thy sheath. There rust and let me die!"

Making a stabbing motion, Kathleen dropped gracefully on top of Liam, and remained for a minute, eyes closed. Then she sprang to her feet.

"Well, what do you think? Was I a convincing Juliet? I'd love to play that part."

Liam was still lying on the floor, stunned by Kathleen's kiss, which had been warm and passionate and rather longer than necessary, and the sensation of her body on top of him when she "died".

He got awkwardly to his feet. "You were amazing, but I didn't have to do much acting. Anyway, I'm hopeless at remembering lines. I think I'll leave the acting to you."

"Come on, then. I'll show you around the rest of the place. I think I can sneak us both a drink from the bar. I know where the keys are kept."

Liam followed her and watched as she poured two large whiskeys.

"We can go into the little snug to have our drinks in comfort." She led the way to the very couch where Sven had first kissed her.

They chatted amiably for a while and sipped their whiskies. Liam was very entertaining once he relaxed and had her laughing at his stories about school.

"Would you like another whiskey?" she asked.

"No, thanks, I'm not used to whiskey. A glass of porter is my usual tipple."

"Would you like another kiss?"

Before he could answer she was kissing him, her lips warm and sweet, demanding and tasting of whiskey. Her first kiss had aroused him and now he responded by kissing her hungrily, his arms around her, forcing her back onto the couch. He knew he shouldn't be doing this, but he couldn't stop. Her hands were caressing him, working their way down his body. He knew what was going to happen but he couldn't help himself. His fingers ran up the silky length of her stocking until they came to the warm flesh. She leaned back further to accommodate him.

When it was over, he was overwhelmed with guilt. He had never done anything more than kiss Mary. He also felt a sense of excitement as though a new world had opened up to him.

Kathleen rearranged her clothes and snuggled back in his arms.

"That was wonderful, Liam."

"It was wonderful for me too. I think I'm in love with you."

Kathleen smiled and kissed him, gently this time. He was so sweet. And so naïve!

"What are we going to do? I'll have to tell Mary. She'll be heartbroken."

"Don't tell anyone for the moment. We can see each other secretly until we decide what to do. Mary is young – she'll get over it."

He was surprised at her matter-of-fact tone.

"The others will be back soon so we'd better get moving," she said. "Will you walk me to the bus? You'd better get the next one so that no one will see us together."

The following Sunday, Liam met her at the bus stop as Sven used to. The weather was beautiful and the park was full of people but they found a secluded spot and sat on Liam's coat, kissing passionately. She knew that Liam wanted more.

"Next Sunday, let's go to the Phoenix Park. I know some very secluded places where we can be alone. It's quite a long walk up to the Fifteen Acres but very few people go there. Would you like to do that?"

Liam looked embarrassed. "If you think that's a good idea. I just want to be alone with you."

The following week, Liam pretended that he had a lot of admin work to finish. Mary was disappointed when he told her.

"Never mind," she said then. "You will be finished school soon and we can meet whenever we like."

He said nothing.

He was besotted with Kathleen. Most evenings that week he waited outside the Gate so that they could have a few minutes together before she had to go to do her make-up. On Sunday, he took the Number 10 bus to the Phoenix Park Gate as she had instructed and then followed her into the park. It was early in the afternoon and most people, being creatures of habit, were still enjoying their Sunday dinner. There were fewer and fewer people around as they walked further. They came to a copse of trees and Kathleen stopped.

"I think we have walked far enough. This will do. We're very near to the special altar where the final Mass of the Eucharistic Congress will take place, but they won't be working there on a Sunday. The Mass is next Sunday, I hear."

"Yes, Mary is going with her mother. She invited me to go along with them, but I don't think I'll go."

"I definitely won't go. I hate all that. My mother was trying to persuade me to go to the Women's Mass but luckily I could say that I would be busy in the theatre."

They came to a place among the trees to where there was a hollow.

"We can sit down here. We can't be seen from the track and we can hear if anyone approaches."

Liam wondered how she knew this exact spot. Maybe she had played here as a child. Kathleen began to unpack a bag which she had been carrying. She took out a bottle of red lemonade and a packet of biscuits.

"We used to have a picnic up here when we were children. Half a pound of broken biscuits and a bottle of water and we thought we were in heaven."

Liam pictured the young Kathleen playing in that spot. She might have been playing with Mary. He was overcome with guilt. Mary was so good. He loved her, but not the way he loved Kathleen.

Kathleen had taken a thin rug from her bag and was spreading it on the ground. "I hate insects. They always bite me. Now, sit down beside me and have a drink. You must be thirsty. It's only red lemonade but they didn't stock champagne."

They shared the biscuits and lemonade and Liam began to relax. He took off his jacket and lay back on the rug. Kathleen snuggled up to him.

"Isn't this lovely? Look at the way the sun is shining through the leaves. I used to imagine that this was a fairy forest and I was a fairy princess."

"You are a fairy princess. You have enchanted me."

"And you are the frog who became a prince when I kissed you."

"You better keep kissing me in case I change back into a frog!"

They spent the afternoon in each other's arms. Occasionally, they heard voices in the distance but no one intruded into their idyll. When the sun started going down, Kathleen sat up, rearranged her clothes and packed away the rug and the empty bottle.

"We better go now. It's a long walk back. It's been such a lovely day. I don't want it to end."

They parted before they reached the park gate. They were afraid of being seen by someone who knew them. Liam walked ahead to the bus stop and joined the waiting queue. Kathleen passed him and continued down Infirmary Road.

She was elated. Liam was in love with her.

CHAPTER 14

June was a very busy month for everyone in the family, indeed in the country, because of the preparations for the Eucharistic Congress. For weeks before, the city was abuzz with people connecting an elaborate public-address system for the Papal blessing which would take place on O'Connell Bridge, cleaning the streets and decorating them with flowers and papal bunting.

Days before the start of the Congress, which was to last for five days from the twenty-second to the twenty-sixth of June, huge ocean liners moored along Sir John Rogerson's Quay and in the port basin. They acted as floating hotels for the many Catholics of different nationalities who had come to Dublin to participate in the Congress. The Pope would be represented by the Papal Legate, Cardinal Lorenzo Lauri.

Mary went with her mother to view the ocean liners, some of which could accommodate over one thousand people. Liam was supposed to accompany them but, at the last minute, he announced he had too much work to do for the end of term. They also planned to go to the final Mass of the Congress which was to be held in the

Phoenix Park on the Sunday, but Liam couldn't go to that either. He said that he would never get his reports finished if he spent the whole day out. Mary was surprised because she had assumed that Liam was as anxious to go as she was. Almost everyone she knew was going. Harry and Julia were attending the Mass with their children and Joseph was walking there with a group of friends. Her father, however, had a chest infection which recurred from time to time. It was a result of his inhalation of gas in the trenches during WWI. He was staying at home to listen to the event on the wireless. She didn't know whether Kathleen was going or not – she hardly saw her at home and, anyway, she was not very religious.

She and her mother set off early to walk to the place in the Park where a special altar had been built. It was a magnificent edifice, designed by a prominent Irish architect. A vast crowd had gathered. The famous Irish tenor, John McCormac, sang "Panis Angelicus" at the offertory of the Mass and was joined by the Palestrina choir, of which Harry had once been the boy soprano soloist. There was a live broadcast from the Vatican by Pope Pius XI using a very extensive PA system which also broadcast the whole Mass throughout the city. After the Mass, four processions left the Park and walked to O'Connell Street where about half a million people gathered around O'Connell Bridge for the concluding blessing given by the Papal Legate.

Mary and Ellen were tired but elated as they walked home.

"Wasn't it a great day! I really feel as though I have been part of something wonderful." Ellen linked Mary as they walked with the crowds.

"Yes, it was wonderful. I never thought that I would hear a famous singer like John McCormack in the flesh. And the Palestrina Choir was as good! Do you remember when Harry sang with them? It's a pity that Liam couldn't come – he would have enjoyed it. He seems to have so much work to do at the moment."

"He should have come – it was a once-in-a-lifetime experience."

"Are you all right, Mam?" Mary noticed that Ellen seemed to be a little breathless. "It's been a long day and we have a long way to walk yet. Would you like to stop somewhere for a cup of tea and a rest?"

"No, love, I doubt that we would get in anywhere with these crowds. I heard it said that there must have been a million people at the Mass. I'm a bit tired but it was worth it. It's a pity that James couldn't come but he wouldn't have been able for it. I only hope he got good reception on the wireless."

CHAPTER 15

Mary hadn't been seeing much of Liam as he'd been so busy with end-of-year reports and all the administration that was necessary at that time of year. They still went to the pictures on a Saturday night, but he was usually busy on Sunday afternoons. She sensed a change in him but put it down to tiredness after the demanding school year.

One Saturday, he seemed even more preoccupied than usual as they walked home from the cinema. She stopped and turned to face him.

"Liam, is there anything wrong? You don't seem yourself these past few weeks. Are you feeling all right?"

He didn't meet her eyes. Sadness – and something else – masked his usually cheerful face.

"Mary, I'm sorry. I've been seeing someone else. I want to break it off with you. It's all my fault. You are a wonderful girl but since I met her everything has changed. I didn't mean to hurt you. Please forgive me."

Mary couldn't breathe. She felt as though her world had fallen apart. "How do you mean, you have met someone else? Who is it? When did it happen?"

Her mind was racing, trying to find answers. Could it

be someone at his school? But they were mostly middle-aged women teaching there. Where else could he have met someone in such a short space of time?

"*Who is she?*" she burst out. "*Where did you meet her? How could you do this to me?*"

She was crying and, instead of comforting her, he was looking at the ground. He kept repeating "I'm sorry" until she could have choked him. She started walking again, crying silently now. He put a hand on her arm.

"I'm sorry," he said again.

"*Stop saying that!* How could you do this to me? We had so many plans. We were going to get married. I'll be working in the same school as you. I'll see you every day! How am I going to do that now?"

They had reached Aberdeen Street. She took out her key and opened the front door.

"I don't want to see you ever again. You have broken my heart."

He put out a restraining hand, but she quickly slipped in and closed the door. The house was dark. Her parents were in bed. At least she wouldn't have to face them in this distraught state. By morning she would have found a way to explain her break-up with Liam. She fought to quieten her sobs as she climbed the stairs.

CHAPTER 16

Early in July, Kathleen told Liam that she was pregnant. He immediately said that he was happy to marry her. He was, indeed, happy. The only cloud was the thought of telling his parents about his marriage and the reason for it. And, of course, revealing the truth to Mary and her parents.

"We'd better go to Aughrim Street and see the priest as soon as possible to arrange for the wedding," Kathleen said. "Then I have to buy a wedding dress. Oh, and we will need a place to live. We can start looking for a flat immediately." Her mind was racing ahead, making plans. She was so relieved that her problem was solved that she felt euphoric.

That evening, they went to tell Kathleen's parents. Ellen and James were stunned by the news. They knew that Mary had been very upset recently and Liam had not been seen in the house for a couple of weeks but she had refused to talk about it. They surmised that she and Liam had had a row but thought that it was only a lover's tiff and would blow over.

They looked at each other in disbelief. Kathleen was talking about the wedding, which was to be in the next few weeks. So that was it. A shotgun wedding! It was common enough and, as long as the young man did the right thing by the girl, there was little gossip.

Harry was so busy with the upcoming election that he barely registered the fact that Kathleen was getting married to Mary's boyfriend. Julia was horrified and couldn't believe that Liam had abandoned Mary for flighty Kathleen.

Joseph saw the effect on Mary and tried to support her. He did his best to talk to her, but she was silent and pale and uncommunicative.

Kathleen let Liam tell his own parents and went to his house for a frosty tea a few days later. She knew that his parents didn't like her. They looked disapprovingly at her make-up and her fluffed-out hair. They did, however, ask about their financial situation and offered to loan them a deposit on the rental of a flat. His brother and sister were also teachers and almost as serious as their parents.

The worst experience was the arranging of the wedding with the priest. Father Dempsey had been in the parish a long time and knew both of their parents. He guessed immediately the reason for the wedding when they asked for it to be as soon as possible. He didn't look at them as he took notes for the banns to be read. Then he looked sternly from Liam to Kathleen.

Liam moved slightly away from her.

"You must go to confession before the wedding and remain chaste until you are man and wife. Ask God to forgive your weakness and to bless your union. The wedding will have to be at the seven o'clock Mass in the morning, at a side altar, so as not to give scandal."

Kathleen had to bite her tongue so as not to say

something rude to the priest. Liam kept his head bent all the time and seemed grateful. They felt they had been released when they got outside.

"What an old grouch! He treated us as though we were criminals," Kathleen said.

"We did commit mortal sins," Liam said.

Kathleen laughed. "Let's go up to the park and commit some more! Then we can go to confession before the wedding and be forgiven."

She kissed him and he responded, reluctantly at first, then hungrily.

The wedding was in the middle of August, on a Monday. Kathleen wore a pale-blue dress which matched the colour of her eyes. A playful, feathery hat sat on top of her blonde curls. Her pregnancy was beginning to show in the fullness of her breasts and the rounding of her stomach but the dress showed off her figure to great advantage. Liam felt he was the happiest man in the world. Ellen cried during the Mass, mostly for Mary but also because she knew that this marriage was doomed. She knew her daughter and realised that Liam was not the man to keep her happy. Mary had insisted on coming to the wedding even though Ellen had tried to discourage her. Now she sat beside her mother, dry-eyed and white-faced. Elizabeth was matron of honour and tried to support Kathleen as well as she could. She had been stunned by the speed with which Kathleen had found a new man after Sven abandoned her. She guessed the reason for the sudden marriage and also knew that the baby must be Sven's. She felt sorry for the young man who was marrying her friend. Kathleen would be a handful.

The wedding breakfast was an awkward affair. Liam's

parents were stony-faced and only talked to their own family. Their older son, Declan, who had been best man, did his best to lighten the atmosphere with his speech but his jokes fell flat. Only James, as father of the bride, got any reaction with his heartfelt speech about his beloved daughter. Kathleen and Ellen were both in tears at the end of it.

Once the breakfast was over, Liam and Kathleen said their goodbyes and went off on their honeymoon. They were to spend three nights in County Wexford in a cottage which had been lent to Liam by a friend. They were showered with good wishes and confetti as they left for the train. Most of the wedding party repaired back to Ellen and James' house to continue the festivities. Mary said she was tired and went to bed. Liam's family all excused themselves and went home.

The cottage in Wexford was not up to Kathleen's expectations. It was cold and damp and quite a long walk from the beach. The house was surrounded by fields which were full of cows. Kathleen hated cows. The village shop wasn't too far away but had very limited supplies. It looked like they would have to live on rashers and eggs for the three days. She bought a big bag of sweets to compensate and a small bottle of whiskey to ward off the damp. Liam was delighted with the cottage and especially the old Tilley lamp which they had to light at night. There was a range for cooking and a pile of turf to keep them going. Each night Liam cooked rashers and eggs and Kathleen toasted some bread at the range with a toasting fork. They had a hot whiskey before going to bed. They made love in the old iron bed and Liam thought that he had never been so happy. Each morning they were woken by the lowing of the cows and the low burbling of wood pigeons. Too soon, for him, it was time to go home.

There was less than two weeks left of the holidays before Liam had to start back at school. They spent that time making their small flat on the North Circular Road as comfortable as possible. Frances, a friend from the Gate, had told Kathleen about the flat which she and her husband were about to vacate. Liam's parents gave them some furniture, including a bed, and his sister gave them a present of blankets and sheets. Kathleen's parents gave them some pots and pans and crockery. None of the presents were to Kathleen's taste but she consoled herself that they would soon buy new things for themselves. She wanted their flat to look bohemian and artistic like Elizabeth's. Elizabeth gave them a purple velvet throw which Kathleen draped over the old brown sofa which came with the flat.

CHAPTER 17

Liam started back in school in early September. His colleagues were surprised that he had got married but congratulated him and presented him with a present of a tea set from the staff. The principal spoke to him about the stabilising influence of marriage and the fact that his salary would increase since he was now a married man with responsibilities. He and Mary avoided each other where possible. He was overcome with guilt every time he caught a glimpse of her pale, thin face. However, she was teaching the High Babies class and he taught Fifth Class so their paths didn't cross very often.

Kathleen was working in the wardrobe department at the theatre. She had spoken to Hilton Edwards when her pregnancy began to show. He said that she could help with costumes as long as she was able but that after the baby was born he wouldn't be able to offer her any work. They were a small company, he explained, and they couldn't afford to employ someone who might be absent from time to time. Kathleen was devastated and assured him that she would never let anything interfere with her acting career.

Hilton patted her arm and said, "We'll see."

She hated the way she looked. None of her clothes fitted her anymore. Julia loaned her some clothes but they were very different to her own taste. She felt dowdy and unattractive and she spent a lot of time alone at home, crying. Liam couldn't understand her moods. He was looking forward to the birth of their baby and was always suggesting names for him or her. He wanted to call the baby an Irish name, but she wanted to call the baby after a film star.

She managed to keep working until her seventh month but then the travel by bus to the theatre became too much. Morning sickness had abated after the third month but was soon replaced by claustrophobia which made travelling by bus difficult. It soon began to make work in the crowded costume department impossible.

Staying at home all day with her feet up on the couch at first seemed like a luxury but soon became boring. There was no one to talk to and nothing to do. Her mother visited every afternoon and tidied up the flat. She often brought something for their dinner. Kathleen was glad of the company but she wished that her mother wouldn't be so full of good advice. She seemed to know everything about having a baby. She even predicted that it would be a girl.

Liam wanted her to attend the Rotunda hospital during her pregnancy but she refused. She insisted that she wanted to have her baby at home, as many women did. The truth was, she was afraid that hospital check-ups and official records would reveal the fact that her pregnancy was more advanced than she was pretending it was. If she had the baby at home, she could simply pretend it was a bit premature. She could engage a midwife who would be discreet.

However, in mid-December she began to feel unwell. Her legs swelled and she felt nauseous most of the time. She went to Dr Byrne. He looked serious as he took her blood pressure. Then he told her that it was high and that she was suffering from something called pre-eclampsia. He would have to admit her to the hospital. They would have to monitor her until the baby was born. She phoned Liam at his school during lunchtime. He wanted to rush to the hospital but she told him there was no need. He could bring her bag, which she had left ready, that evening.

Liam and her mother arrived together that evening. He had called to the house to tell Ellen on his way home from work. She insisted on giving him his tea before they both set out. There was a crowd of visitors in the main area of the hospital, waiting to visit loved ones. Liam got directions and they found their way to Kathleen's bedside. She was sitting up, refreshing her make-up.

"Oh, my poor girl, what happened to you?" Ellen hugged her daughter.

"I'm all right, Mam. I was feeling a bit sick and my legs were swollen so they said I have to stay here until the baby is born. But they think the baby might come a bit early."

Liam looked anxious. "Is the baby all right?"

"Of course it's all right. It's me you should be worried about."

"I didn't mean I wasn't worried about you. Of course I worry about the two of you."

Ellen tried to calm them both. "You will be well taken care of here, anyway. Did they say anything else?"

"Only that my blood pressure is too high. They might have to induce the birth. I could die."

Liam looked stricken.

"Don't exaggerate, Kathleen. You'll be perfectly all right. They're just keeping you in here as a precaution."

Kathleen dissolved into tears. "I know that, Mam. I'm just scared."

Ellen put her arms around her daughter. "Of course you are, love. We all get scared the first time. Now, check the bag that Liam brought in and see if there is anything else that you need. We can bring it in to you tomorrow."

"Will you bring me in my hair curlers and my face cream? Oh, and a packet of biscuits and some sweets. The food here is terrible. I can't eat it and I'm starving." She looked pleadingly at her mother. "Will you come to visit me in the afternoons? Liam can come in the evenings."

They both nodded. Kathleen then became her usual chatty self, telling them about the women on either side of her and their situations. By the time they left, Kathleen was regaling the other women with stories of her acting career and all the famous people she had met.

Kathleen begged to be allowed home for Christmas but the doctor said no. She was very upset when Liam came in to visit her. He tried to persuade her that it was for the best.

"Will you come in here on Christmas Day?" she pleaded. "I don't want to be on my own."

"I don't think I would be allowed to stay all day. They're very strict about visiting hours. Your mother said she would visit you in the morning and I will visit in the afternoon, after I have Christmas dinner at my mother's."

Kathleen was enraged. "You're going to your mother's for Christmas dinner? What about me? I'll be on my own here with food I can't eat. You are very selfish!"

Liam tried to placate her, but she stubbornly remained

in a bad mood. He was glad when one of the nurses reminded him that visiting time was over.

Kathleen was still in the same mood when her mother visited her the next morning. Usually they didn't allow visitors in the morning but, because it was Christmas Day, she was allowed stay for half an hour. Many of the beds were empty on the ward because anyone who was able to had returned home for the holiday.

Kathleen's bad mood turned to tears when she saw her mother. "*I hate being here. I want to go home!*" She sounded like a small child.

Ellen talked gently to her and, by the time she left, Kathleen was sleeping.

CHAPTER 18

The summer had come and gone, and Joseph had hardly noticed as he immersed himself in his novel. Now it was Christmas again and he had the first draft finished. He knew that he needed to revise it but gave himself a week off to enjoy the festivities.

However, when the family gathered around the table for Christmas dinner the topic of conversation was far from festive initially.

De Valera, Taoiseach and leader of Fianna Fáil, had called a snap election.

"What on earth made him call another election so soon?" James wanted to know. "It's only ten months since the last one."

"Well, for the last ten months, Fianna Fáil has been dependent on the Labour Party for support in order to stay in power. He believes that his party will be returned with a good majority in the next election." Harry paused to take Maeve, who had been trying to attract his attention, onto his lap.

"Do you think he's right?" Joseph asked.

"He may very well be right. All the other parties,

including my own, were taken by surprise. They are not prepared. In my constituency it was particularly difficult. Paddy is still hanging on to life by a thread and the party couldn't decide whether to ask him to resign on the grounds of ill-health and put in another candidate – or do as they did in the last election which was to let Paddy run without making any public appearances."

"Do they have a suitable candidate to take over from Paddy? He was very popular, wasn't he?" Ellen had met Paddy and liked him.

Harry looked at his wife before answering.

"Yes, they have made a decision and asked me to be the candidate. I have resigned my commission in the army."

Ellen looked shocked. "Resigned your commission? But what will happen if you lose the election? Julia, have you agreed to this?"

"If it's what Harry wants, then I will support him," Julia said woodenly.

Joseph tried to support his brother. "I am sure Harry will be elected. He is an excellent candidate and is very well known in the constituency since the last election." He raised his glass. "Here's to Harry Devereux TD!"

The whole family raised their glasses and wished Harry the best of luck.

Then talk turned to more ordinary matters.

Ellen said that she had been to the hospital to see Kathleen that morning after Mass.

She didn't tell them but it hadn't been an easy visit. Kathleen was still furious that she wasn't allowed home for Christmas and behaved as though it were Ellen's fault. She was now huge and found walking difficult. Ellen had made her a special dinner of roast chicken and taken it to the hospital, but she had pushed it away when she realised it wasn't goose or turkey.

Now, Ellen simply told the family that Kathleen was finding things very difficult. Julia nodded sympathetically.

Joseph thought Harry and Julia seemed subdued as they looked after the needs of their children. Ellen was glancing anxiously at Harry and Julia from time to time and exchanging glances with James. He, on the other hand, was talking and laughing with a forced jollity and offering drinks to everyone. Only Mary was acting normally, helping their mother to serve the meal and chatting to the children. Joseph wondered whether the months of solitary writing had made him more sensitive to other people's moods or if there was something wrong.

People seemed to relax more as the meal progressed. The children made everyone laugh with their stories about what Santa had brought them. Maeve told them she had seen Santa as he put presents at the foot of her bed. Michael began to laugh at her but was quietened by his father's glance.

The trifle was served, a special one for the children and a sherry-laced one for the adults. Ellen would serve the Christmas pudding later.

Mary and Ellen were just beginning to clear the table when Violet and Ellie came in, as they usually did every Christmas Day.

There was a chorus of "Where's Essie?" from everyone. The twins were seldom apart.

Ellie and her mother looked at each other.

"Essie got engaged today to Matthew Clery. She's gone with him to show the ring to his family." Violet looked around with satisfaction at the reaction to her news.

"I didn't even know she was seeing him!" Mary said.

"Oh, we used to see him every morning on the way to work," Ellie said. "He's great fun. He asked us to a dance on Hallowe'en and that was when it all started. Then he got a promotion before Christmas and he asked Essie to marry him. The wedding will be in the summer."

"Well, I'm sure we all wish them all the happiness in the world," Ellen said, relieved that the decision had been made for Joseph.

Ellie came around the table to where Joseph was sitting. Harry got up to make space for her. "I don't know what I'm going to do without her, Joseph." She smiled into his eyes. "There is only me and you left now."

Joseph tried to still the panic he was feeling. He got to his feet. "Let's drink a toast to Essie and Matthew. He's a grand fellow. I'm sure he'll make her very happy."

He moved to the sideboard to get glasses for the newcomers, avoiding Ellie's entreating look.

During the night, Kathleen went into labour. The following day, St Stephen's Day, her daughter was born. When Liam came to see her and the baby, she was sitting up, putting on her make-up. Liam was delighted with the baby and said that she looked like Kathleen. She had the same blonde hair and fair skin. The nurse handed the baby to Liam and he cradled her, talking to her softly.

"What will we call her? I'd like to call her Breda, after my mother."

"I told you I don't like that name. We are going to call her Marlene."

"Marlene? What sort of name is that?"

"It's a German name. I'm calling her after Marlene Dietrich."

Ellen arrived to visit just then.

"Mrs Devereux, Kathleen wants to call the baby Marlene. I think it's a strange name for a little Irish girl. What do you think?

"Let me see the baby first. How are you, Kathleen? You look very well, love. Let me hold the baby for a while, Liam. Oh, isn't she beautiful? Just like her mam. Now, what's this about a name?"

"I want to call her Marlene," said Kathleen, "Liam doesn't like it. He wants to call her Breda. I don't like that name."

Ellen looked from one of them to the other. "Had you any other names in mind?"

"Well, I did consider Jean, you know, after Jean Harlow," Kathleen said, "but I prefer Marlene."

"Do you not think that Marlene might be a difficult name when she goes to school?" Ellen ventured to say. "And the priest will want to baptise her with a Christian name."

"All right so, we'll call her Jean, or perhaps, Jeanne," said Kathleen. "You know, after St Joan of Arc – her proper name was Jeanne. The priest should be happy with that. We will call her Jeanne Marie."

Liam looked relieved.

Ellen changed the subject. "When will you be allowed home?"

"In about a week. That means I'll be here for New Year's Eve. I can't wait to get home."

"Do you want to hold the baby, Kathleen?" Ellen rose and offered the baby to Kathleen.

"No, you hold her. I was holding her for hours this morning."

"Let me hold her." Liam smiled down at the baby.

"Isn't she beautiful? I can't believe she is mine. Thank you, Kathleen, for giving me such a beautiful daughter."

Kathleen smiled at the praise and settled back against the pillows.

Joseph arrived soon after to see the new baby. Kathleen was sitting up in bed, looking radiant. Liam was sitting at the side of the bed, holding the baby.

"Oh, you look so like Kathleen! Don't you, sweetheart?" Ellen took her grandchild from Liam and rocked her gently.

"What are you going to call her?" Joseph asked his sister.

"Jeanne Marie. I wanted to call her Marlene after Marlene Dietrich but Mam talked me out of it. I like Jean Harlow too, but I decided to use the French version. What do you think of the name?"

"I think it is a lovely romantic name. It suits her."

"Mam, they're letting me home on New Year's Eve after all. I'm dying to get home. Will you come to our flat and help me get Jeanne settled?"

"Of course I will, love. Liam, will you be able to manage to bring them home from the hospital?"

"Yes, Mrs Devereux. A friend of mine has a car and he'll come to collect us."

"I wish I could go to the New Year's Eve dance in the Guards Depot," said Kathleen. "Are you going, Joseph? I suppose you'll be going with Ellie? I heard all about Essie's engagement. It leaves the way clear for Ellie, doesn't it?"

Ellen saw Joseph's embarrassment at Kathleen's lack of tact and turned the conversation to Harry and his chances in the election.

* * *

It had been a tradition for many years that Joseph and the twins went to the New Year's Eve party in the Garda Barracks in the Phoenix Park. Joseph was friendly with a number of gardaí and always enjoyed the parties and dances which were a regular part of the local social scene. He could see no way out of going with Ellie so he called for her as usual at eight o'clock. She answered his knock immediately as though she had been waiting behind the door.

She looked radiant, her auburn curls gleaming, her eyes shining. She was wearing a new blue dress in the latest fashion which she showed off by twirling and pirouetting for his admiration. She looked beautiful.

"You look beautiful, Ellie. You'll be the belle of the ball."

"I'm so excited. I have you all to myself at last." She kissed him on the cheek.

Her mother watched benignly. "You make a lovely couple. Enjoy yourselves tonight. Take care of her, Joseph, and don't be too late."

"Oh, Mam, you know we can't leave until after midnight. We'll come straight home after that."

The night was cold but they warmed up as they walked briskly, Ellie clinging tightly to his arm. On the way they met other couples and groups of young men and girls, all making their way to the barracks. They could hear the band playing as they approached.

"Oh, I love that song 'Night and Day'! I hope they play it again later so we can dance to it. Doesn't the vocalist sound like Fred Astaire?"

The dance hall was full of happy people out for a good night. They left their coats in the cloakroom and Joseph waited while Ellie went to powder her nose.

"Joseph, how are you? I haven't seen you here in ages. Where have you been?"

It was Peter Daly, one of his school friends.

"How are you, Peter? I haven't been anywhere, just busy."

"I saw you coming in with Ellie, or was it Essie? You're usually with the two of them. Did I hear that one of them got engaged?"

"Yes, you did – Essie is engaged to Matthew Clery. Remember him? He was two years ahead of us in school."

"That leaves the way clear so for you and Ellie. Have you asked her yet?"

"Asked me what?" Ellie was standing beside him, smiling at Peter.

"Peter was asking if you would like a mineral."

"It's a bit early. I haven't even had a dance yet. Come on, Joseph, they're playing 'Where the Blue of the Night Meets the Gold of the Day'. Let's dance! See you later, Peter."

Ellie was a beautiful dancer. She and Essie practised frequently, pushing back the furniture in the kitchen and winding up the gramophone to play the tunes that they loved. She was steering him around the floor, holding him close, murmuring the romantic tune in his ear.

Joseph saw Peter standing on the edge of the floor with a girl who looked familiar. Peter nodded to them and leaned down to say something in her ear. No doubt he was telling her that he and Ellie would be the next engaged couple.

"*Ouch!* You stood on my foot. Pay attention, Joseph. You seem to be miles away."

He forced his mind back to the music and the dance and Ellie. It wasn't her fault that he felt the way he did.

"Sorry, Ellie. Now, is that better?" He held her close and twirled her around with the intricate steps that she had taught him.

"Much better! You're a good dancer when you pay attention."

People were watching them. He hoped it was because of their dancing and not because of gossip.

It should have been a wonderful evening but Joseph couldn't enjoy it. Yet he found himself trying to record it in his mind because he knew that it was the last time. The first draft of his novel was finished. He knew now that he wanted to spend the rest of his life writing. He had a plan but first he had to explain to Ellie that he could never marry her. Hopefully, she would meet someone else, as Essie had.

The band was playing "Auld Lang Syne". He and Ellie found themselves part of a boisterous circle, all holding hands and loudly singing the traditional song. After much clapping and cheering, punctuated by shrill whistles, the group took their partners for the last dance. Ellie snuggled close to him as the band played the opening bars of "Smoke Gets in Your Eyes". She was singing along and knew all the lyrics. It was apt for their final dance with its reference to a 'lovely flame' dying. He suddenly felt sick. He dreaded telling her. The thought made him hug her tight. She responded by reaching up to kiss him on the lips. He recoiled.

"What's wrong? Are you all right?"

"I just feel a bit sick. I need some air. Would you mind getting the coats?"

"You wait at the door. I'll just be a minute. Do you want some water?"

"No, I'll be fine once I'm out in the air."

The song had finished and the crowd was dispersing, some people chatting in groups, others making their way to the cloakroom.

Joseph waited a little way from the door, drawing in deep breaths.

"Here's your coat. Are you sure you're all right? There is a bench over there where we could sit until you feel better."

"No, I'd prefer to start walking."

They were now part of a procession of young people all walking through the park to get home. There was a full moon in the sky and a canopy of stars above them. The tips of the branches on the lovely old chestnut trees sparkled with frost. The footpath was slippery in places. Joseph walked fast so that Ellie could hardly keep up with him.

"Hey, slow down! These are my dancing shoes, not my walking shoes."

He stopped. "Sorry." He knew he had to do it now. "Ellie, there is something that I want to tell you. It's not easy and I don't know how to say it."

He could see the anticipation in her eyes.

"Yes?" she breathed.

"I can't marry you, Ellie. I don't want to settle down. I don't want to get married. I want to travel, see the world and, most of all, I want to write."

He started to walk again. He didn't want to meet her eyes.

She put out a hand to stop him and stepped around him to face him.

"*What?* How can you say that to me? All these years everyone thought that you would marry one of us. When Essie got engaged, I thought that you would surely marry me. Everyone thought that. What am I to say to them?" She began to cry. "You are very cruel."

His instinct was to comfort her, to put his arms around her and tell her that everything would be all right. But it wouldn't. He put his hands in his pockets.

"Come on, let's get home," he said. "It's getting very cold."

They walked home side by side in a silence only broken by Ellie's muted sobs. When they reached her front door, he watched her search for her key, insert it and open the door.

"I love you like a sister, Ellie, and I always will. I'm sorry for hurting you."

Like a child who has saved her real sorrow for when she got home, she burst out into a torrent of sobs.

He could hear her mother calling out, "*What's wrong, Ellie?*"

Then the door closed. A cloud passed over the moon as he turned to go home.

CHAPTER 19

Everyone in the family seemed to be very busy that January of 1933. Harry only took Christmas Day off from canvassing in his constituency. The family rallied behind him and Joseph and Mary found themselves at the constituency office most nights and every weekend. Ellen spent the evenings there when she wasn't helping Kathleen, making tea and sandwiches for the canvassers. Even James did some canvassing for his son. Julia pleaded that the children needed her since they saw so little of their father and managed to avoid any active part in the canvass. The one duty that she agreed to was appearing with Harry at Sunday Mass before he later addressed the crowd from the back of a lorry.

Joseph was glad of the distraction. From time to time he caught a glimpse of Ellie as they travelled to or from work. She looked pale and unhappy and it filled him with guilt. Her mother, Violet, and the rest of the family also gave him sorrowful looks whenever their paths crossed. Working with Harry took his mind off Ellie and also gave him an insight into politics. Unlike Harry, he had never been interested in party politics but now, as he canvassed and talked to people, he began to question the policies of Harry's party Cumann na nGaedhael.

Most evenings when he and Mary finished work in the constituency office, Harry joined them for a hot drink before they went home. Often, Joseph took the opportunity to question his brother about certain issues.

"Harry, when I was canvassing tonight, every door I knocked on had people inside who were worried about the high and rising unemployment rate," he said one night soon before the election. "Yet your party has reduced Social Welfare payments. Your party has done nothing to create new jobs. You have concentrated on a rural economy whereas De Valera and Fianna Fáil are promising to create new state companies to increase employment. De Valera seems very popular with the people."

Harry sighed. "Yes, you're right. But it is the world-wide recession causing higher unemployment, not our policies. We only reduced Social Welfare because we have to balance the books. De Valera is promising to increase Social Welfare payments and to introduce Widow and Orphans pensions and I don't know how his party will be able to afford it. He is also promising to remove the oath of allegiance and to do away with the office of Governor General. These policies are all very popular with the people. Now, we're all tired. Let's head for home. Thank you both for helping me."

The day of the election came. There was a high turnout and in the evening the streets were still thronged with people anxious to cast their vote. As soon as the polls closed, counting of the votes began. The count went on into the next day and evening. Finally, that night, it was announced that Harry had won his seat by a narrow majority. Joseph stayed for a while to celebrate with his brother. He was relieved to see that Julia had also arrived to join in the celebrations. Harry greeted her and steered her around the various senior figures in Cumann na nGaedhael. Joseph took advantage of Harry's preoccupation to leave the count centre. He was becoming increasingly uncomfortable with the party and the policies that Harry espoused.

He walked home wondering how he was going to occupy himself now that the election was over. He had just got to the Phoenix Park end of the North Circular Road when he heard shouting and screaming. As he drew closer he could see a large group of men, some of them wearing blue shirts, engaged in one-to-one struggles. Most of them were armed with hurleys or sticks. The screaming was coming from a group of women huddled on the outskirts of the group. Suddenly, a Garda van appeared. Gardaí poured out of the back and into the middle of the battle. They set upon the struggling men and dragged them one by one to the waiting van.

One of the men escaped and ran towards Joseph. He fell and cracked his head off the kerbstone. Blood flowed from his forehead and he lay on the road, groaning.

Joseph ran forward and knelt beside the man. He was barely conscious.

"Don't move. You have a bad head wound. I'll call an ambulance."

The nearest phone kiosk was at Kingsbridge Station. He started to run towards Infirmary Road when he tripped and fell. He realised that one of the gardaí had stuck his foot out and tripped him. Rough hands pulled him up.

"Here's another one, Jimmy. Put him in the van."

Joseph was dragged to the crowded van and thrown into it.

"*Wait!*" he shouted. "*What about the man on the ground? He has a bad head wound!*"

The door of the van slammed shut, the engine revved and the van lurched forward. The men inside it were thrown from side to side as it careered through the streets. When it stopped, the doors were pulled open and the men were manhandled out by the waiting Guards. Joseph realised that they were outside Mountjoy Square Garda Station. They were shoved in the door of the station.

"Now, lads, ye can cool off in there." A burly Garda Sergeant pushed them forward.

Joseph and two of the other men were thrown through the open door of a cell. It clanged shut and the sergeant disappeared. Joseph looked around the cell. There was a two-tiered narrow bunkbed on each side of the room. The mattresses on them were soiled. What looked like a large chamber pot was in the corner. Otherwise, the room was bare.

One of the men looked at Joseph and held out his hand

"They'll just keep us here for a few hours to let us cool off. Then they'll let us go. How'ya, my name is Des. This is Bertie. Haven't seen you around before. You're not one of them Fianna Fáilers, are you?"

"No. My name is Joseph. I was just walking by when I heard the commotion. Then I saw an injured man and tried to help him. That's when the Guards grabbed me. They didn't give me a chance to explain."

"They wouldn't. They probably thought that you were one of the Fianna Fáilers when you weren't wearing a blue shirt." Bertie lay down on the bottom bunk and stretched luxuriously. "I'm jacked. We left Tipperary this morning at seven. We had to cycle from our home place to Tipperary town and wait for the hired bus. Then we were dropped off in groups all over Dublin. Our group saw a bunch of Fíanna Fáil canvassers and we attacked them. We don't want them to take over the government. Someone called the Guards and here we are."

"I thought the Blueshirts were a rural-based organisation," Joseph said. "I've never seen any in Dublin."

"Oh, there are some of us in Dublin. But you're right. Our strength is in the country areas. Nearly everyone I know is a Blueshirt. It's a great organisation. Before I became a member, I had no life. There was nothing to do in my area. Then along came General Eoin O'Duffy organising us and he started all sorts of sports clubs and local dances. It's great! I cycle to at least one dance a week and I'm a member of a Gaelic football team and a hurling team, so it keeps me busy. I lost me best hurley in that little brawl."

Joseph was intrigued. He had heard of the Blueshirts but had never met one before.

"Tell me more about the Blueshirts. And tell me more about General O'Duffy. I know my brother met him. Isn't he the Head of the Garda Síochána?"

Des became animated. "Yes, he is but De Valera hates him and there are rumours that if Fianna Fáil win this election, O'Duffy will be out of a job. Did you know that he managed the Irish Olympic team in '32 in America where they won two Gold medals for athletics?"

"Yes, I remember that. It was a great achievement, but I didn't know that he was the manager."

"He's also very involved in the GAA. My older brother

is a garda and he told me that the General made sure that they played a lot of sport. People call us the Blueshirts but our official name is the Army Comrades Association. D'ye know, we have nearly 40,000 members now?"

They were interrupted by the opening of the cell door.

"Right, lads, ye can go home now."

Joseph followed the other two men out of the cell. He had to pass the other cells on the way out. They were still full – there were at least five men in every cell.

He waited until they got outside to ask, "Why did they not let the others out?"

Des looked at him. "Because they are all Fianna Fáil supporters or IRA men. Since De Valera lifted the ban on the IRA, they've been trying to break up our party's political meetings. They tried to disrupt a Cumann na nGaedhael meeting that we were policing. The Guards know we are Blueshirts but they had to bring us in as well since we were caught fighting. They must have known that you were an innocent bystander."

"Come on, Des, we'd better get going. I hope the bus doesn't leave without us. Good luck, Joseph. You should join the local Blueshirts. They're a great organisation."

The next day the full result of the election was confirmed. Fianna Fáil were short of a majority by one seat but had secured the support of the Labour Party. They would form the next government in coalition with Labour. Harry would now take his seat on the opposition side.

The new Dáil met on the eighth of February 1933. Harry invited his parents and Joseph to sit in the public gallery, to witness his first day as a TD. Mary couldn't get the day off and Kathleen was breastfeeding her baby.

James had a chest infection again and was disappointed to miss his son's first day as a TD in Leinster House but he encouraged Ellen to go with Joseph.

They arrived early because Ellen was anxious to get a good seat. She was dressed in her Sunday clothes and had even bought a new hat for the occasion. Joseph was keen to see the splendid building which had been designed by the acclaimed architect Richard Cassels for James Fitzgerald, the twentieth Earl of Kildare and the first Duke of Leinster.

Julia arrived before them with Harry and was waiting for them when they climbed the magnificent stairway. She greeted them warmly and complimented Ellen on her new hat. Ellen remarked that Julia looked lovely, almost back to her old self. Joseph took particular note of Julia's ensemble because Mary had asked him to. Julia had asked her dressmaker to copy a suit which Greta Garbo had worn in a recent film. The suit showed off her elegant figure perfectly. It had padded shoulders, a narrow waist and the skirt reached to mid-calf. It was in a fashionable shade of brown, with a cream blouse underneath. She wore a pillbox hat, also in cream, under which her auburn hair curled to her shoulders, and a matching handbag and T-bar shoes. She was the picture of elegance as befitted a TDs wife. Joseph was delighted that she seemed to be in good form.

From the public gallery they had a good view of the TDs as they entered the chamber. The Ceann Chomhairle took his seat first and the government TDs sat on his left with the main opposition party to his right. Harry was one of the last to enter and he acknowledged his family with a smile. Ellen was pointing out politicians that she recognised and Joseph had to shush her.

Éamon de Valera, the leader of the new government

and the Fianna Fáil Party, was a striking, tall figure with a lean, angular face. He began his speech in Irish and then switched to English. He was followed by the Leader of the Opposition and Leader of Cumann na nGaedhael, WT Cosgrave, who cut a much duller and more conservative figure than his rival.

Joseph was enjoying the theatricality of it all but, obviously, his mother wasn't. The public gallery was packed with people and had become unbearably hot. Ellen had removed her scarf and was looking flushed and uncomfortable.

"Mother, we can leave now if you wish," Joseph whispered to her. "It's getting very hot and Harry won't mind. When this speaker finishes, we'll make a quick exit."

She nodded to him and followed him out. It was cold outside and she replaced her scarf.

"Oh, I hope Harry doesn't mind. I was feeling overcome with the heat."

"He won't mind. Come on, let's go and get a cup of tea. There's a tea shop that I know just around the corner and they do lovely scones."

Joseph had just poured their second cup of tea from the large teapot when a young man came in through the door and came over to them.

"Joseph! I haven't seen you since school. How are you? What are you doing with yourself?"

"Brendan, it's good to see you! I'm working in the Civil Service now –Department of Agriculture. What about you? I heard that you went to London."

"Yes, I did. I spent two years there but decided to come back. I'm doing a bit of journalism, getting articles published here and there. Are you still writing?"

"Yes, I've had a few poems and short stories published and

I've just finished the first draft of a novel. The next step will be looking for an agent or publisher but I know how difficult it is to get accepted by one." He paused and gestured towards Ellen. "Sorry, I should have introduced you. This is my mother. Mother, this is Brendan O'Brien. Do you remember I used to go to his house sometimes to swop books?"

"Yes, of course I do. How is your mother, Brendan? I used to meet her occasionally when I went shopping in Moore Street."

"She's very well. My father died so that is why I came home really. Listen, Joseph, we must meet up and have a good talk about books and writing. How about next Saturday evening? We could meet in Ryan's on Parkgate Street."

"That would be great, Brendan. About eight o'clock?"

"Grand."

"See you then."

As Brendan left, Joseph reflected that it would be good to have a chat with someone interested in the same things as himself. Harry was always busy and he had lost touch with most of his school friends. Many had emigrated and others had got married and moved away. None of his colleagues seemed interested in books or writing. He was looking forward to seeing Brendan again.

His mother seemed to know what he was thinking. "He's a lovely lad. It will do you good to have someone who likes books like you do. You must miss spending time with Harry. He is always preoccupied these days. But I am glad to see Julia looking so much better."

Brendan was waiting for him at a corner table. "What'll you have? A pint of stout? Yes? The same as myself! I'll just go to the bar and get them."

They settled down and each took a long slug of his creamy pint.

"*Aah!* That's good!" said Brendan. "The stout isn't the same at all in London and they don't know how to pour it. Did I tell you that I'm thinking of going back over there? I was doing quite well with the writing before I came home. It's much easier than here – more papers and magazines and they don't care who you are if you can write. Also, there's not as much censorship there, unlike here."

"I know what you mean about censorship. It's very frustrating that any worthwhile book is banned in Ireland. We are left with what Frank O'Connor called 'the sugar-beet pulp of romances and cowboy novels'. I tried to get hold of his recent book *The Adventures of the Black Girl in Her Search for God* but, of course, it was banned as indecent. The book was actually a forceful argument against religion which is the real reason it was banned. People like Yeats and George Russell have argued against the banning of books, but it has had no effect. But, you're thinking of going back to London, you say?"

"Yes. My mother is trying to dissuade me, but I will probably go during the summer. In the meantime, you must come to some literary gatherings with me. Have you heard of the Republican Congress? You know the writer Peadar O'Donnell? He is one of the leaders. Frank Ryan is also involved. They are Marxist republicans but they care about literature as well as politics. You'd like them."

"There's just one problem. You know my brother has just been elected a Cumann na nGaedhael TD? He wouldn't be too pleased if he knew that I was consorting with Marxist republicans."

"You don't have to tell him. Besides, I only go to their meetings because some of them are writers and they all love to discuss literature. They also have good contacts with magazines which will publish the kind of thing you and I write. They got a few of my articles into *Reynold's News* which is a left-wing paper in England. Come to one meeting and see what you think. The next one is next Thursday. Their office is on Westland Row. I'll meet you there."

Joseph had misgivings during the week about the meeting but after days of boredom in his office he decided to go. When he got to Westland Row he spotted Brendan standing outside a building with a tall, well-built man. He waved and walked up to them.

"Frank, this is the man I was telling you about. Joseph Devereux, an excellent writer. He has already had a number of stories and poems published. Joseph, this is Frank Ryan, one of the founders of the Republican Congress. He is also editor of their newspaper, *An Phoblacht*."

The two men shook hands. As the other man leaned towards him and spoke, Joseph felt the intensity of his gaze.

"I hope you'll write some articles for us. We also have associations with other left-wing papers and magazines. We will always find space for a good writer."

"Thanks, sir. I usually write short stories and poems."

"That's all right. If your stories and poems are good and have a socialist slant, we will certainly publish them. And call me Frank. Everybody does. Now let's get in to the meeting."

As the meeting progressed, Joseph discovered that the members of the Republican Congress had all been

129

members of the IRA but had split from the parent organisation. They wished to set up a new left-wing republican organisation which would appeal to working-class people and small farmers. They were involved in supporting workers' strikes and worked in close cooperation with left-wing groups.

Joseph was struck by the energy and commitment of the men and women at the meeting. Frank Ryan had been imprisoned on a number of occasions for publishing what were termed "seditious" articles in *An Phoblacht*. Two of the women particularly impressed him, an older, very articulate woman called Nora Connolly O'Brien, the daughter of the 1916 leader James Connolly, and a younger woman, Cora Hughes, whose red hair reminded him of Ellie's. She was a university graduate but spent her time working with the poor in the slums and agitating on their behalf.

Peadar O'Donnell was a well-informed speaker who hated Fascism and tried to steer the Republican Congress to the left. He was a writer too and, in the following weeks, Joseph found him very encouraging about his own writing and his novel in particular. He read it and was very complimentary but suggested that it needed rewriting in certain places. Peadar gave him a few addresses and contacts of agents and publishers who might be interested in his novel.

The office of the Republican Congress had recently acquired a new typewriter and Joseph soon learned to use it. He typed pamphlets and letters for Peadar but then began to type the manuscript of his novel because Peadar had told him that agents and publishers would take a typed manuscript more seriously. He spent a lot of his money on typing paper, stamps and envelopes, and posted copies of his manuscript away in the vague hope that someone would like his writing. He got just one reply. It was from a small publisher in London and was complimentary but suggested various changes that need to be made in order to make it more marketable. Joseph was disappointed but resolved to put the manuscript away for a while before he tried to revise it.

Joseph's social life began to revolve around the Republican Congress. He not only went to meetings but also demonstrated with other left-wing groups. As far as his family was concerned, he was meeting with a writers' group. Normally, his mother would have been quick to notice his new activities but she was so taken up with Kathleen and the baby that she had little time for anything else. James was feeling the effects of the winter on his damaged lungs and spent much of his time in bed. Harry was so busy that the only time they saw him was on Sunday when he usually visited with Julia and the children.

No one in the family had any idea of Joseph's interest in socialism.

CHAPTER 20

Harry's first year as a TD was exhilarating. He soon found his way around Leinster House and became a popular figure within his party. There was a lot to learn about Dáil procedure and protocol.

Colm O'Brien, one of the older TDs, a veteran of the Civil War and now spokesman on defence for Cumann na nGaedhael, took him under his wing. Harry knew that his experience as an officer in the army was useful but was flattered by the attention. The older man often consulted him and asked him to do research and write reports for him. Harry also enjoyed his sessions in the constituency office or "clinic", as it was called. People came to the clinic with individual problems or difficulties, hoping their local TD could assist. Usually these were to do with getting a pension or being moved up the housing list or repairs to a school, but sometimes they were more interesting.

He took a particular interest in housing. He had a grudging admiration for the Fianna Fáil government which had undertaken a massive programme of slum clearance and building of social housing as soon as they were elected to government. Slum clearance had been a major issue in the recent election. The new government found some of the finance for this project from the money they saved when De Valera refused to pay the Land annuities to the British government. Harry did some reseach on the Land annuities and found that the origins of the annuities was confused. Lands purchased in Ireland under the 1891–1909 Acts had been financed by the issue of stocks. Irish purchasers repaid these stockholders and the money was collected and passed on by the Irish State. Under Article 5 of the 1921 Anglo-Irish Treaty, annuities were included in what the Irish Free State would pay to service the United Kingdom public debt. The Boundary Agreement of 1925 released the Free State from this obligation but the Cumann na nGaedheal government of 1926 had agreed that the Irish State would continue to pay it.

The annuities amounted to over £3 million per annum which was a substantial sum since the total revenue taken by the Irish Free State at that time was £25 million. Since the beginning of the new state, various groups had agitated to refuse to pay the land annuities to the British government, including one led by Peadar O'Donnell. Opposition was based on the argument that the British had no right to the money because it forced Irish people to pay for land which had been illegally taken from them in the first place. When the Fianna Fáil government withheld the money in 1932, the British swiftly imposed a tax on Irish imports. This provoked Irish tariffs on British imports and led to the Economic War which was bad for the newly emerging state.

However, De Valera's government forged ahead with their programme of slum clearance and social housing. They created a new post of Housing Architect for Dublin

Corporation which meant that there was a greater focus on home construction. An Englishman, Herbert Simms, was appointed to the role and revolutionised the architecture of inner-city blocks of flats. Harry went with an inter-party group to see some of the work of this remarkable man. Simms himself came to meet them and described how he favoured the Art Deco style and was influenced by the modern architecture of Berlin and Vienna. He also explained his approach to new housing schemes in the suburbs, places such as Crumlin and Cabra. Harry was fascinated by the man and his work. His own house and his mother's house seemed very old-fashioned in comparison.

He was also fascinated by the car which Herbert Simms drove. It was a Bentley, which Herbert described as a good family car, but which looked very luxurious to Harry. Some of the TDs drove cars though none of them were as beautiful as Herbert's. It made getting around the new suburbs much easier, Herbert explained. He took Harry for a drive one afternoon when they were going out to view a new housing scheme in Crumlin.

Harry was very taken with the car. He wondered whether he could afford to run one. He suggested it to Julia. She wasn't very enthusiastic, but he felt that it would help him get around his constituency more easily. He spent a few days looking at cars but eventually settled on the one which he could afford which was a Ford Anglia. The children were very excited when he brought it home but Julia seemed unimpressed.

The constituency office became a refuge for him. The relationship between him and Julia had deteriorated even further since he became a TD. She resented the amount of time he spent away from her, their home and their children. She didn't seem to realise how difficult it was for him to be with her and yet be afraid to touch her for fear of what it might lead to. When he saw her kissing and caressing the children, he wanted it to be him who was receiving the affection. Sometimes she tried to kiss or caress him, but he pulled away. They never really discussed their problem. It seemed insoluble.

His work in the constituency office was helped by a group of volunteers. Alice, the widow of Paddy Geoghegan, the TD whom he had replaced, was a regular. She was very knowledgeable about the area and knew most of the TDs in the Dáil. When her husband was a TD she had been his right arm and confidante so she had intimate knowledge of the workings of the constituency. When he needed advice about a constituency matter, he often turned to her. She was a woman of about forty, well dressed and attractive in a conservative style. She was very approachable and popular within the Party.

One evening, Harry and Alice were the last people remaining in the office and were just about to lock up when the door burst open. A distraught woman ran in and grabbed Alice by the arm.

"He's going to kill me! Please save me! The childer are at home – I tried to bring them with me but he was after me with the breadknife. Please help me!"

Harry ran to the door and tried to lock it but someone was pushing it in from the outside while shouting threats and abuse.

"Oh, don't let him in, don't let him in!"

The woman was cowering behind Alice.

Harry put his shoulder to the door and managed to close it. He could hear heavy breathing outside and then a heavy

135

blow and the door splintered. It was pushed in by a thickset, tall man who was cursing and swearing and wielding a breadknife. He fell on top of Harry. Harry grabbed him in a headlock and shouted to the two women.

"*Alice, get out! Get that woman out! I'll see to him!*"

The man wriggled out of the headlock and made a stab at Harry with the breadknife. Harry grabbed it and felt a searing pain in his hand. He held on and at the same time hit the man a glancing blow on the head with his fist. The man staggered back and fell, hitting his head on the corner of a desk. He lay on the floor, moaning, while blood gushed from under his head.

"*Alice, call an ambulance and the police!*"

Alice rushed back into the office and picked up the phone.

The woman followed her and knelt down beside her husband.

"*Oh, my God, you've kilt him! What am I going to do? Billy, Billy, get up before the Guards come!*"

The gardaí arrived before the ambulance. They recognised Billy immediately.

"Not you again, Billy! We'll have to take you into custody now that you have attacked someone and damaged property."

"He hit his head and is losing a lot of blood." Harry was wrapping his hand in a tea towel as he spoke. "The ambulance should be here shortly. He needs stitches, at least."

"What about yourself, sir? That looks like a bad cut."

"It's only a flesh wound. It looks worse than it is. Oh, that sounds like the ambulance now."

Two ambulance men came in with a stretcher. Billy had lost consciousness briefly but was now struggling to his feet with the aid of his wife.

"I don't want to go to hospital. I'm going home."

"It's either hospital or we take you into the station. You'll be charged with assault and criminal damage anyway, but it would be better for you if you get your injuries seen to first."

Billy's wife began to plead with the two gardaí who were now standing either side of Billy.

"Ah, let him home! I'll look after him. He just got a bang on the head. He'll be all right."

"Sorry, missus. He'll get jail for this."

"*This is all your fault, you bitch!*" Billy had moved threateningly towards his wife.

The gardaí held him back.

Billy turned to the ambulance men. "I want to go to the hospital. Me head is liftin' and I feel dizzy."

"All right, mister. Lie down on the stretcher there and we'll take you to the Meath hospital."

They arranged their patient on the stretcher and started out the door. The man's wife followed, talking incessantly, trying to placate her husband. The gardaí took some details from Harry and Alice about the incident.

"You seem to know him very well." Alice looked pale and shaken but composed.

"Yes, we have been called out a few times to the tenement where he lives. When he gets too much to drink he beats up his wife. The neighbours call us when the noise gets too much."

"Have you arrested him before then?"

"No, what goes on between a husband and wife is not our concern. We can't arrest him for beating up his wife."

"But you can arrest him for attacking me?" Harry interjected.

"Yes, we can. Now, we have to go. You may be called

to court to testify against him. Good evening, sir, ma'am."

Once the gardaí had gone, Harry started to clean up the office. The lock on the door was damaged and impossible to use.

"Harry, your hand is bleeding quite badly. It needs to be dressed and bandaged. I'll call Tim O'Dwyer and ask him to fix the door immediately. He always looks after any building work for us and he was a friend of my late husband. We can't leave it open."

She made a quick phone call and turned to Harry who was mopping the blood from the floor. "He said he'll come immediately. He'll probably do a temporary job until tomorrow. Now, we must see to your hand. We'd better go to the hospital."

"I'm not going to the hospital. It just needs to be cleaned and bandaged."

"All right, then at least let me do that for you. Come to my house and I'll clean you up. You don't want to go home in that state."

Harry looked at his jacket. The sleeves were blood-soaked and there were smears of blood down the front of his suit. "You are right. I don't want to frighten Julia. She's not very enthusiastic about me being a TD as it is."

Alice's house was only five minutes' walk from the office. He had been there the night during the previous election when Paddy won the seat. It was an old house, small but warm and comfortable inside. She led the way into the parlour.

"We always thought that we would move to a bigger house when the children came, but then that didn't happen, and it's so handy for the office and Leinster house that we stayed here. We have lovely neighbours and they were very good to me when Paddy was ill and later when he died. Now, sit down there and I will get some hot water and disinfectant and some bandages."

Harry's hand was throbbing and he felt quite dizzy. He removed his jacket and lowered himself onto the sofa. He wasn't as fit as he used to be when he was in the army. He rolled up his sleeve when Alice reappeared. She placed his hand in the bowl and gently wiped it. She took a clean towel and dried it before dabbing the wound with disinfectant. Then she carefully wrapped his hand in a bandage and secured it.

"There you are, all done. It's bleeding much less now. Is it painful?"

"Just a bit. You're very good at this."

"Oh, I did a couple of First Aid courses with the Red Cross. Would you like a cup of tea or something stronger?"

"A whiskey would be good. I feel a bit shaky."

When she came back with two large whiskeys, she sat beside him on the sofa.

"Won't Julia be worried when you don't come home at the usual time?"

"Not really. There is no usual time. I tend to work very late at the office and sometimes I go for a walk afterwards to clear my head. She is usually asleep and doesn't hear me when I come in."

Alice digested this information and what it implied. "Are things all right between you? I know it is none of my business but you can talk to me if you want to."

Harry thought for a few minutes. He hadn't talked to anyone since his conversation with Grace and that had been a while ago. "She's not very happy about me being a

TD. She thinks I spend too much time away from home and she's right. I'd better get going."

He started to put on his jacket. He was struggling to get his injured hand into the sleeve when Alice gently eased his hand in, turned him, adjusted the jacket on his shoulders, then straightened the front with a tug.

They were facing each other.

Suddenly, they were kissing, hungrily and passionately. With his good hand, he was caressing her.

"Harry, wait a minute." She helped him off with his jacket again and then slipped out of her dress. She was wearing a black silk slip. She removed his shirt and tie. He opened his belt with his good hand. She began to kiss him again while guiding him back onto the sofa.

"Are you sure you want to do this?" she asked.

"Yes, I'm sure."

Afterwards, they sat side by side and talked. She told him that Paddy had been ill for a long time and she had been his nurse rather than his wife. He couldn't bring himself to tell her the real reason for his difficulties with Julia because it felt disloyal, but simply said that they had drifted apart. They talked for a long time and then fell asleep. It was three o'clock in the morning when he eventually left. He had left his car outside the constituency office so he picked it up and drove home. His house was quiet when he went in. He looked in on the children and finally, at Julia. She was fast asleep, her arm thrown over his side of the bed. He undressed and wondered how he was going to explain his hand and bloodied clothes. An attempted break-in at the office was the best story that he could think of.

He didn't meet Alice again for two days. Then she came

to the constituency office in the evening. He felt awkward but she acted normally and soon they were talking about constituency matters.

When the others had left, Alice turned to him. "Do you regret what happened the other night? Because, if you do, we will never mention it again. I don't want to lose your friendship."

"I don't want to lose your friendship either. But, no, I don't regret it."

"Will you come back to my house tonight for a nightcap?"

"Yes, I can come for an hour or so, but then I'd better get home."

Most nights after that Harry went to Alice's house from the office. If he had a late night in the Dáil, he couldn't, but otherwise the office closed at nine so that gave him a few hours before he needed to return home.

His new car made it easier. He left it parked outside the constituency office while he visited Alice. They usually made love. He felt guilty but consoled himself with the thought that he didn't love her, not like he loved Julia. Alice was his friend and his confidante. He had always been close to Joseph and used to confide in him but, once Joseph began to develop left-wing ideas and to question the philosophy of his party, he found it difficult to talk to him. Alice filled the void in his life left by Joseph.

He also felt guilty about the small amount of time that he devoted to his family. He kept Sundays and most Saturdays for them, and they enjoyed the outings in his new car but he seldom saw them during the week. The children would be asleep anyway on weekday evenings by the time he got home, even if he left at nine o'clock. He seldom saw Julia alone. He had made an office for himself in their third bedroom and installed a daybed in it. That was where he slept. Sunday mornings were devoted to the children and most Sunday afternoons were spent with his family or hers. Their relationship became distant.

He knew that his family noticed. His parents watched him anxiously but didn't say anything. Mary knew that Julia was unhappy and had mentioned it to him, wondering if she could help in any way. He had just shook his head, unable to explain.

CHAPTER 21

Joseph began to learn more about the Blueshirts, who were a military wing of Cumann na nGaedhael. At a meeting in Limerick, their leader, General O'Duffy, declared "What the Blackshirts did for Italy and the Brownshirts did for Germany, the Blueshirts will do for Ireland".

Joseph had been reading about what Hitler's Brownshirts had been doing in Germany and was appalled that anyone would want a similar organisation in Ireland. O'Duffy, who had been dismissed as head of the Garda Síochána shortly after De Valera came to power, organised a march on Leinster House for the thirteenth of August 1933. The march was prohibited by the government but the Blueshirts still swarmed to Dublin. The IRA leadership did nothing except warn their followers to avoid party politics but many republicans and socialists were in the streets to counter Blueshirt demonstrations. De Valera's government saw the Blueshirts' action as defying his ban and they outlawed the organisation. In response to the ban, Cumann na nGaedhaell and the National Centre Party merged to form a new party, Fine Gael, on the third of September 1933.

Eoin O'Duffy became its first president.

The policy of isolation from the class struggle adopted by the IRA caused discontent among the socialists and republicans. A special conference at Athlone in April 1934 was attended by prominent socialists, republicans and former IRA leaders. It was agreed that Republican Congress branches should be established throughout the country. The conference received support from a conference of trade unionists in Belfast.

In June1934, Joseph went with friends to take part in the annual Wolfe Tone commemoration in Bodenstown, County Kildare. A party of five hundred had also travelled from Belfast to take part. They were prevented from following the Republican Congress contingent by a huge group of IRA who did not want them to unfurl their banners. The Belfast men fought their way through to join the Republican Congress as they marched through the village of Sallins behind the Workers Union of Ireland whose band was playing the Red Flag. The next day the *Irish Times* commented on the irony of Ulster Protestants being prevented from honouring Wolfe Tone by Catholics.

A meeting of the Republican Congress was held on the twenty-ninth to the thirtieth of September in Rathmines. The Congress was split in two on the central issue which was whether the Congress should become a new revolutionary Socialist Party or remain as a united front for all progressive forces against Fascism. Peadar O'Donnell and Frank Ryan led a vote of 99 for a united front. The Connollys, Nora and Roddy, were for a new Socialist Party. They got a vote of 84. The Connollys and their supporters joined the Labour Party and trade union support for the Republican Congress melted away slowly.

Joseph marched with the Republican Congress on the eleventh of November 1934, Armistice Day, in a demonstration against war and poverty, and was delighted to see a contingent of British ex-servicemen, proudly wearing their medals, marching with them through a cheering crowd of Dubliners. He remembered the loneliness of his father, who had worn his medals proudly on every Armistice Day, being mocked by his own countrymen as a traitor. He regretted that he could not invite his father to join him in the march. His friend Brendan O'Brien had refused to join the march because, he said, the Republican Congress had moved too far towards the left and was condemned by the Catholic Church. They had a major row about it before the march.

Joseph was incensed. "This march is against war and poverty. It is not about Communism. There is terrible poverty here in Dublin, but the two main political parties are doing nothing about it. Every week in our paper, *An Phoblacht*, we carry articles about the slum conditions that our people live in. Have you even read any of them? Last week's article showed that forty-nine per cent of the city's housing is unfit for human habitation. The previous week, the article showed that as many as twelve people can be living in one room. Can you believe that there were forty-nine people living in a small house in Holles Street? Neither the Fianna Fáil government nor the previous Cumann na nGaedhael government have done anything about it. This is not the republic people fought for in 1916. We have to mobilise all the socialist groups to achieve that."

"I don't want to consort with Communists. I am not going to come to these meetings any more. Goodbye, Joseph. I'm sorry we have to part like this."

145

The Congress however, continued to fight tenants' battles and also for the right of workers to join a union. With the restraining influence of Brendan gone, Joseph became more involved in leading workers' marches, demonstrations and pickets. He also continued to write for the Congress newspaper. Activists were often harassed by the police.

In December 1934, Joseph was arrested for supporting workers on a picket who were striking for the right to join a union. He was sentenced to four weeks in Mountjoy Prison. The first his family knew of this was when he failed to come home one night and Harry found out where he was.

Harry arrived at the prison to see Joseph and to look for his release. He was allowed to see him alone in a visitors' room. When he embraced his brother he noticed how thin and bony he had become.

"My God, Joseph, what have you been doing? Our parents are distraught. What about your job? Do they know where you are?"

"I resigned from my job three months ago. I hated it anyway. I kept waiting for an opportunity to tell our parents, but I never seemed to find one with all the comings and goings in our house. Kathleen is always there with the baby and, if she is not, then Julia and your children are there. I've been working full-time with the Republican Congress, editing their paper and attending meetings and demonstrations. They pay me a small wage and I am much happier there. I feel I'm doing something worthwhile and helping to change society. I'm sorry, I should have told you all before this."

Harry had been staring at his brother in disbelief during all of his explanation.

"You've given up your job? Without discussing it with anyone? Do you know how lucky you were to have a safe Civil Service job when unemployment is so high?"

"I told you I hated my job. I am much happier now and I have made some good friends among the Republican Congress. I also have a few publishers looking at my novel."

"Your novel! Do you really think you can make any sort of a living as a writer in this country?"

"No, I don't, not while people like you are banning any decent book that is published."

"People like me? What do you mean, people like me?"

"Your party and your private army, the Blueshirts, are against any progressive ideas. Fianna Fáil are in cahoots with the Church. All of you have labelled any socialist group communists, just because they fight for the people's rights in employment and housing."

Harry looked at his brother in disbelief. "Joseph, this is me, your brother, you are talking to. My party, Fine Gael, or Cumann na nGaedhael as it was then, has kept this country on a safe and steady course since Independence. I agree, they were a bit too conservative at times and they could have done more for the poor, but without them this country would have descended into chaos."

"The country is descending into chaos anyway. Have you not noticed the marches and protests about housing, rent, unemployment, low wages and the right to belong to a union?"

Harry could see that his brother was in no mood to listen. "I'm going to see what I can do about getting you out of here. It shouldn't take too long. Here, I brought you in some Mars bars and a bottle of red lemonade."

Joseph smiled at the Mars Bars. They were his favourites.

"Thanks, Harry. Are Mother and Father all right?"

"Yes, they're just worried about you. Right, I'll see you in a couple of hours."

Harry went directly to see the Minister for Justice, Noel Galligan, whom he knew slightly. He was shown into the ministerial office in Leinster House as soon as he arrived.

"Harry – what can I do for you?"

"Thanks for seeing me, minister. I have a favour to ask. I'm sure you heard about a group of picketers in the Liberties last week who were jailed for four weeks for supporting a strike for the right to join a union?"

"To be honest, there are so many of these incidents these days that I lose track of them. What's your interest in them?"

"My younger brother was one of the picketers and is in Mountjoy Prison now. He is easily led and got in with the wrong crowd. He is a good man and was never in trouble before. I'm asking you to get him released. I will guarantee his good behaviour."

The minister rose and gathered some files from his desk.

"I'll see what I can do, Harry. Come back this afternoon. Now, I have a meeting. As it happens, one item on the agenda is public order and the rising incidence of demonstrations."

Meanwhile, Joseph was enjoying his first day in prison. He had been on picket lines many times, supporting the strikers, and had always found it an education. It was tedious, walking up and down in the cold, but the tedium was relieved by the lively political discussions that took place among the strikers. Prison was similar. It was cold, crowded and uncomfortable but he relished the feeling that he was helping to change things. It was an education for him. He realized that he had been living in a different world before this, cocooned in the relative comfort of his parents' home and absorbed in the imaginary world of his novel.

In the late afternoon, he was surprised to be brought to the visitors' room again. Harry was waiting for him.

"Good news. I've managed to get an order for your immediate release."

Joseph thought quickly. The thought of his warm home was tempting but if he went with Harry now he would lose all credibility with the strikers, and, more importantly, his comrades in the Republican Congress.

"No, Harry. I'm not leaving until my comrades are freed too. I'm sorry, I was a bit dazed this morning and didn't realise what you were going to do. Thanks for everything. I'll see you in four weeks."

Harry was almost speechless with disbelief. "But you can't want to stay here – it's – it's cold, it's dirty, it's crowded!"

"Just like the homes and working conditions that many of my comrades endure."

"Mother and Father will be distraught when they hear where you are. What will the neighbours say?"

"I'm sorry to upset our parents but I don't think they care what the neighbours say, any more than I do."

"You'll miss Christmas with the family! And what will my boys think when they hear where their Uncle Joseph is?"

"I am sure you will explain it to them. Thanks, Harry. I know you mean well." He held out his hand to say goodbye.

Harry ignored it and called the prison officer to let him out. He left without looking back.

At the end of January Joseph was released from prison. He went straight home to his parents' house. They were in the kitchen when he arrived, sitting either side of the table, a bowl of porridge in front of each of them.

His mother sprang to her feet and embraced him.

"Oh, my poor boy! You look so thin! Sit down now and I'll get you some breakfast. We weren't sure what time you would get home. Would you like some porridge? Will I do you a fry?"

"I'd murder a fry, Mother. But finish your own breakfast first."

James moved slowly to sit down beside his son and put his arm around him.

"I'm glad you're home safe, son. We were worried about you. Let me pour you a cup of tea while you are waiting for your fry."

Ellen bustled about, her own breakfast forgotten.

"There's some home-made strawberry jam and soda bread. Have some while you're waiting. Mary told us that you didn't want us to visit you. That's why we didn't come to the prison."

"I know. I didn't want you being upset and, anyway, it was only for four weeks. Mary was great, she came in every week with the newspapers and biscuits and chocolate you sent. Thanks, they kept me and some of the other lads going. The food is terrible in there. That fry smells lovely, Mother." He looked appreciatively at the frying pan and its contents.

"What happened between you and Harry, son? He

wouldn't say anything except that you'd be released at the end of January and that you didn't want any visitors."

Joseph noticed how much older his father was looking. "Oh, we just had a bit of a disagreement. His politics are very different to mine. He was upset because I wouldn't allow him to get me released. How do you think my comrades would feel if I was allowed home and they weren't, just because my brother is a TD? Anyway, we'll make up again when we meet – we always do."

He settled down to eat the fry which his mother placed before him and turned the conversation to the doings of the rest of the family. He didn't have to wait long before some of them arrived to see him. Kathleen was the first to arrive with baby Jeanne. She hugged him and then gave him the baby to hold while she sorted out all the baby equipment which she had in the pushchair.

"You look well, Joseph, in spite of being in jail. Did you meet any interesting criminals there? You've lost weight – I only wish I could. I'm half a stone heavier now than I was before I had the baby. I'm so bored at home that I eat all the time. No, Jeanne, don't be struggling like that. She wants to get down and walk, Joseph. She loves running around. She has me worn out."

Joseph smiled at his niece and stood her on the ground. She immediately found her ball at the side of the pushchair and threw it to Joseph. He caught it just before it hit an ornament on the mantelpiece. She then retrieved her doll and presented it to him.

"What's your dolly's name, Jeanne?"

"June. Do you want to see my other dolls?"

"Oh, I'd love to. How many have you got?"

"Lots," the little girl said before gathering an armful of

small dolls and bringing them to Joseph. "I have a tea-set too but it's at home."

It was clear that normal conversation would not take place as long as Kathleen and Jeanne were there.

Half an hour later, Julia arrived with her youngest two. "I have to collect Michael from school at two o'clock so I can't stay long. How are you, Joseph? You look well. Glad to be home?"

She smiled at him as she removed the children's coats. Pádraig climbed onto Joseph's knee and Maeve held up her arms to be lifted onto the other. Jeanne began to cry. Kathleen picked her up and gave her a biscuit.

"My, every time I see you two children, you have got bigger. How are you, Julia?"

A shadow crossed Julia's face. "I'm fine. It's you we're all worried about. What's this I hear about you being a member of the Republican Congress? They are always in trouble with the law."

Joseph looked pointedly over at his parents and then back at Julia. He didn't know what Harry had told her, but he didn't want to discuss the topic in front of his parents. "I was demonstrating with a group of workers who want to be allowed to join a trade union. That's why I was arrested. It was nothing to do with the Republican Congress." Pádraig was bouncing up and down on his knee. "Do you want to play horsey, Pádraig? How about you, Maeve? All right, here we go!"

He began to sing "The Galloping Major", the song his father used to sing to him and Harry. James took Jeanne from Kathleen, sat her on his knee and joined in and then all three children sang as they were bounced up and down in rhythm to the tune.

When Julia started to prepare to leave, Kathleen said she would walk part of the way with her. "A friend from the Gate is calling in later – Liam will be out at a school meeting – so we'll be able to have a good chat, that's if Jeanne behaves herself and doesn't start crying."

Ellen kissed the baby. "Jeanne is usually very good. She just gets a bit overtired. She uses up a lot of energy, don't you, sweetheart? Now, give Grandad and Uncle Joseph a kiss."

James picked Maeve up. "Are you going to give Grandad a kiss? Oh, that's a lovely one. How about you, Pádraig?" He leaned down and the little boy hugged him. "We'll see you as usual on Sunday. Bye, Julia."

The house seemed suddenly very quiet without the children. Joseph realised that he was exhausted. "I think I'll go up to bed and have a sleep for a few hours. I didn't sleep very well for the last few weeks. The mattress was hard as a rock and very uncomfortable. Call me when Mary gets home."

It seemed the height of luxury to have fresh bedlinen and warm blankets as well as a comfortable bed. He was thinking of the many people in the city who spent all their lives in crowded, uncomfortable and unsanitary conditions as he drifted off to sleep.

CHAPTER 22

Kathleen and Julia chatted comfortably as they walked down Infirmary Road together, Jeanne in her pushchair and Julia with a child held by each hand. "How are you feeling these days, Kathleen? I know you were feeling a bit down the last time we met. It must be easier now that Jeanne is a bit older."

"Oh, it's not so much that Jeanne is the problem. She's very good really and Liam is great with her when he gets home. It's just that I feel so bored and lonely at home. The flat is small and other people in the building are much older. I just feel that life is passing me by."

"Maybe you'll feel better when you have another baby."

Kathleen reacted fiercely. "I don't want another baby! I'm terrified of having another, just when Jeanne has become easier to look after."

"Really? I must say I was delighted when I found out that I was expecting each of my three and wanted to have more. But now I know that another pregnancy could kill me. It's very hard. Anyway, it's not likely to happen. I hardly see Harry these days. The Dáil sits for very long hours and many evenings he goes to meetings or has advice sessions in his local office. With three children, I don't have time to be bored but I certainly get lonely. Only for my sisters I don't know what I would do."

"Well, my sister hates me and never talks to me."

"She doesn't hate you. Give her time. Mary is kind and I know that she loves Jeanne. She will forgive you eventually, as soon as she meets another man. Well, here we are. Say goodbye to Auntie Kathleen, children."

The two women embraced and went their separate ways.

Kathleen could feel tears pricking her eyes. She didn't know what was wrong with her. She often felt like crying. Sometimes, when she put Jeanne down for her afternoon nap, she lay on her bed and cried. But she wouldn't do that today because her friend Frances was coming to see her. They had worked together in the wardrobe department in the Gate Theatre.

Frances was standing on the doorstep, waiting for her when she got home. She looked radiant in an elegant coat with a fur collar and a small cloche hat.

"Frances! I'm delighted to see you. I should have asked you over before this but you are always so busy in the theatre and you live so far away now. You look wonderful! Come on in. I'll just put Jeanne down for her nap and then we can have a chat."

Frances admired Jeanne, said how much like Kathleen she looked and put the kettle on while Kathleen was in the bedroom. She had a pot of tea waiting when Kathleen returned.

"You still remember where everything is in the flat, I see." Kathleen put cups and saucers on the table and opened a packet of Nice biscuits.

"Yes, I do. I loved this little flat and I missed it when

we moved out to Collinstown."

"We were very lucky that you told me you were leaving the flat. It's impossible to find a decent place to live in Dublin now and the rents are very high. Anyway, how are you keeping? You look marvellous. Is that a new coat and hat?"

"Yes, it is. Denis got a promotion to supervisor so he bought me this outfit to celebrate. And we have something else to celebrate. I'm expecting a baby!"

Kathleen knew about her friend's efforts to conceive since she had married five years previously.

"Oh, Frances! I am so happy for you. When is it due?"

"In five months. I didn't tell anyone until we were sure. I wasn't very well for the first two months and I thought I was losing the baby, but everything is all right now. Anyway, one of the reasons I came to see you was to tell you that I am leaving the Gate at the end of this week. I have been off sick a lot and Mr Edwards is not too pleased. Anyway, Denis thinks it would be safer for me to stay at home. You told me that you would love to get back into the Gate. But would you want to return to the wardrobe department?"

Kathleen could feel a cloud lifting and a door opening. "Thanks for telling me, Frances. I'd love to get back into the Gate, even in the wardrobe department. Has Mr Edwards anyone in mind to replace you?"

"I haven't told him I am leaving yet. I'll tell him first thing in the morning. I wanted to tell you first. But how would you manage with Jeanne?"

"Well, she's three now. Liam is home every evening and if I have to do the odd morning or afternoon for matinées or fittings, then I'd ask my mother to help. I'm sure she would because she's been very worried about me. I have been a bit down in the dumps lately."

"You've no reason to feel like that with a good husband and a lovely baby. I used to envy you. I can't wait to stay at home with my baby."

Kathleen thought that the reality of staying home in a tiny flat with a crying baby was very different to Frances' romantic notions, but she said nothing. Her mind was racing ahead. Liam would need a bit of persuading, but she knew she could do it. Her mother would agree to help because she seldom refused her anything. She would have to go through her wardrobe to see what still fitted her. Everyone who worked at the Gate looked glamorous, even the backroom staff. She hadn't bothered much lately because she didn't go anywhere except to her mother's. Her hair was looking a bit dull, but she would get a bottle of Stayblonde and restyle it, maybe like Jean Harlow in *Saratoga*. Her mind was brought back to the present by Frances' voice.

"I think I hear Jeanne crying."

Kathleen went into the bedroom. Jeanne was reaching through the bars of her cot for her teddy which had fallen on the ground.

"Here's Teddy, love." She settled her back down and covered her up. "Now, go back to sleep."

The little girl smiled sleepily as she lay back, clutched her teddy and closed her eyes.

Frances was tidying up the tea things when Kathleen returned.

"I'll have to go soon. It's a long way home and I want to be there when Denis gets home for his tea. I'm telling Mr Edwards first thing tomorrow so the sooner you see him after that the better. Good luck with it. I'll pop in to the theatre to see you in a few weeks."

Kathleen stroked the fur collar of Frances' coat as she

157

helped her into it. "What is it? It's beautiful, so soft and silky."

She couldn't afford to buy any new clothes since she gave up her job at the Gate. Liam's salary just about covered the necessities.

"It's musquash. It was expensive but Denis insisted. Bye, love. See you soon."

Ellen called Joseph at five o'clock when Mary arrived home from school. Mary gave him a hug and they sat down beside James at the fire. Ellen made a pot of tea and joined them. James was the one who broached the subject of Joseph's job, a topic that had been hanging in the air like a raincloud.

"Harry told us that you've given up your job in the Civil Service. Is there any chance that you could get it back?"

Joseph tried to keep the exasperation that he felt in check. "I don't want it back, Father. I want to do other things. For the moment, I am happy working for the Republican Congress and doing some writing."

Ellen looked anxious. "But that's not very steady or well paid, is it?"

"No, but I'm happy doing it. I hated the Civil Service."

Ellen looked at her husband. "We just want the best for you, that's all."

James nodded and smiled at Joseph. "It sounds like you have made up your mind anyway, son."

Mary supported her brother. "Joseph wants to write. He has a chance of having his novel published and he has written some really good articles recently. You should read them. I admire his writing."

Ellen and James then thought that if their sensible

daughter supported Joseph in his ambitions, then it must be the right thing to do.

"Where's Jeanne?" Liam asked when he arrived home.

"She's still asleep. I didn't wake her because I want to have a talk with you. Frances was here today."

"Frances? Oh yes, your friend from the wardrobe department."

"Well, she's going to have a baby and –"

"That's good. Listen, I think I'll wake Jeanne – she won't sleep tonight otherwise."

"No, wait for a few minutes. Listen to me – Frances is leaving her job at the Gate. She thought I might be interested."

"Interested? How do you mean?"

"Interested in going back to work at the Gate."

"But what about Jeanne?"

"Jeanne is three. She's not a baby. I would be working at night. You would be home. If I have to work mornings or afternoons, I'm sure my mother would help out."

"But won't you miss being with Jeanne? She will miss you. I don't want you to go back to work. We can live on what I earn."

"Just about! And what about what I want? I hate being at home alone all the time. I am very lonely and bored. I love Jeanne but she doesn't need me as much now."

"We could have another baby and –"

"*I don't want another baby!* I thought I made that clear."

"Yes, every night you make that clear." Liam collapsed onto the couch. "We should be very happy. We have a lovely daughter, I have a good job. I know this flat is small but in time we will have a better one. I love you but you won't let me show it."

"I'm returning to the Gate, whether you like it or not."

"All right, I won't try to stop you. Now, I am going to wake Jeanne. No doubt I will be the one who has to cope if she doesn't sleep tonight."

Kathleen waited until Liam emerged from the bedroom with a rather grumpy, sleepy Jeanne. She tried to take the child from Liam's arms but Jeanne clung on to him.

"*Want Daddy! Want Daddy!*"

"All right, you can have Daddy!"

She went into the bedroom and studied herself in the mirror. She would wash her hair and put curlers in later. Now, she had to find something suitable to wear.

Liam didn't speak to her at all that night. The next morning, he left without having any breakfast. Kathleen gave Jeanne her porridge, washed and dressed her and left her to play while she dressed herself. She was satisfied with what she saw in the mirror at the end of her preparations. Her skirt waistband was only slightly too tight but was covered by her jacket. Her blouse, in a pale blue, flattered her and her hair was shiny and just curly enough. She put on some mascara and lipstick and pouted at her reflection. She was pleased with what she saw. When she was putting on her little girl's coat she had a moment of regret.

"I'm going to miss you, my sweetheart. Give Mammy a kiss."

Jeanne gave her a very wet kiss and climbed into her pushchair.

"Right then, off we go to Granny's!"

Her mother was surprised to see her so early in the day. Kathleen explained the reason for her visit.

"They're looking for someone to work in the wardrobe department at the Gate. I am going to see them about it today. Would you mind looking after Jeanne until I get back?"

Ellen didn't answer immediately. She lifted her grandchild onto her knee and removed the little girl's coat. Then she looked directly at her daughter.

"I hope that you have thought about this, Kathleen. What does Liam think about it? Are you sure you want to leave Jeanne every night? Do you realise that you will hardly see your husband if you are out every night? And what happens if you have to work in the day, for matinées, for example? Who will look after Jeanne?"

"I was hoping that you would, Mam. Liam has agreed to it and he will be there most of the time. Please say that you will help. I am going mad at home with nothing to do. The money will help, too. We just about manage on Liam's money."

"Of course I'll help you. But I just want you to think about those questions. Now, do you want a cup of tea before you set off?"

"No, thanks, Mam. And thanks for understanding." She hugged her mother and Jeanne and left.

She didn't see her mother shaking her head with a look of concern on her face.

Hilton Edwards was in his office when she arrived at the Gate. She knocked on his door and looked in.

"Mr Edwards, may I have a word with you?"

"Of course, Kay. I haven't seen you for a long time. How are you?"

"I'm very well, Mr Edwards. I heard that you might be looking for someone to work in the wardrobe department. I would like to apply."

"Well, news does travel fast. I only heard that Frances is leaving an hour ago! Are you sure you want to come back full-time? What about your baby? I don't want to take on someone who might be unable to work at times."

"My baby is over two, almost three. My mother and my husband will look after her when I'm working. I won't miss any time at work, I promise you."

"All right, I'll take you on for a three-month trial period, starting tomorrow. Don't let me down."

Kathleen could hardly contain her excitement. Back at the Gate, even if it was only in the wardrobe department! She would do her best to find a way back into acting.

"Oh, thank you, Mr Edwards! I promise that I won't let you down." She smiled at him but he was already frowning at a page which he had picked up from his desk.

CHAPTER 23

With the outbreak of the Spanish Civil War in July 1936, the Republican Congress found a new focus. Cardinal McRory started raising funds at church collections to support Franco and the Fascists. Stories about atrocities against Catholic nuns and priests by the Spanish republicans appeared in all the newspapers. The stories were largely untrue, but the Catholic Church encouraged anti-communism and anti-Semitic propaganda at the time. Harry and Joseph avoided the subject of the Spanish Civil War when they met in their parents' house.

The Republican Congress sent Peadar O'Donnell to Spain to report on what was really happening. He reported back that the Republicans were the legitimate government of Spain, having been elected by the people whereas the Nationalists, led by Franco and some other army officers who did not want a socialist government, were part of a growing fascist movement in other parts of Europe such as Germany and Italy. When Eoin O'Duffy, who had faded into relative obscurity after being dismissed as head of the Garda Síochána by De Valera, made a comeback by organising an Irish Brigade to travel to Spain to fight on the side of Franco's Fascists, the Congress members were incensed and they began to hold meetings to publicise the Spanish Republican cause.

By the time winter came, O'Duffy had several thousand volunteers and seven hundred of them set off for Spain. They were seen as religious crusaders and given a tremendous send-off.

By early December, Frank Ryan had organised the first groups of Irish volunteers to fight on the Spanish Republican side. Joseph found himself caught up on the roller coaster of republican emotion and was one of the first volunteers.

The first problem to be overcome by the Irishmen planning to fight in Spain on the Republican side was the need for passports. Few of the volunteers possessed a passport. By the time applications were made to the Ministry of External Affairs, because of the Irish Government's non-intervention agreements, Spain had been struck off the list of countries to which passports gave access and normal protection. Applications were scrutinised by the authorities. Those who could not get a passport simply travelled to England and thence to Paris on a weekend ticket which did not require a passport. From Paris it was easy to travel to Spain. Joseph simply said that he was travelling to Paris to study French and immediately received his passport.

He could not decide on when and how to tell his parents. He confided in Mary and, although she was upset, she had some sympathy with his reasons for volunteering. She suggested that it would be best to tell them when other members of the family were present.

When all the family gathered in his parents' house on

the following Sunday for dinner, he waited for the meal to be over and then said that he had something to tell them.

"I have volunteered to go to Spain to join the International Brigade, fighting on the side of the Republicans," he told them.

His parents were visibly shocked.

His mother asked, "When?"

"In the next few weeks."

Ellen burst into tears.

His father simply said, "But why, son?"

Harry was angry. "Why would you do that? All the people who are going to fight on the Republican side are communists. How do you think this will look for me? My own brother consorting with communists and IRA men!"

Joseph tried to stay calm. "They are not communists. None of the people I know in the Republican Congress are communists. They are socialists, which is a different matter. Some of them are ex-IRA but they have been expelled by the IRA because they are going to Spain. The men who are going to Spain with O'Duffy are supporting Fascism. The Church is preaching that Franco is fighting for Catholicism but he is not. He is fighting for Fascism."

Harry went white. "You are very selfish. You've upset our parents and you'll make me look like a fool. Get the children ready, Julia. We're going home."

Julia looked apologetically at Joseph but started to put the children's outdoor clothes on.

"Why is Daddy cross with Uncle Joseph?" Michael asked.

Mary shushed him and helped Julia put on his coat. Maeve started to cry. Kathleen had her arms around her mother while Liam looked sympathetically at Joseph but said nothing.

* * *

Nothing more was said about Joseph leaving for Spain until only he and his parents were left in the room.

His father pleaded, "Don't go for the moment, son. Give yourself more time to think about it. I'm not saying that you are wrong but war, any war, is a terrible thing. Wait a few weeks before you decide."

"I've already decided, Father. I won't change my mind."

His mother bowed her head. "Then we can only pray to God to keep you safe."

When she hugged and kissed him, he could feel the tears on her face.

He left soon after to go to a meeting of the Republican Congress. Before he closed the door, he looked back at them sitting either side of the fire and realised the pain that he had caused them.

At the meeting it was decided that, since almost all of the group had received their passports, they could depart as soon as possible for Spain. On Friday the eleventh of December about forty men stepped on board one of the few Liverpool-bound ships not full of O'Duffy's volunteers. This was reported widely in the papers that weekend, but no attempt was made by the authorities to stop them.

At the quayside, Frank Ryan made a speech to the assembled press.

"Our commitment to the Republican cause in Spain is a demonstration of the sympathy of revolutionary Ireland with the Spanish people in their fight against international Fascism. It is also a reply to the intervention of Irish

Fascism in the war against the Spanish Republic which, if unchallenged, would remain a disgrace on our people."

Joseph was standing beside Frank Ryan as he spoke. A crowd had gathered on the quayside – some were supporters of the men who were departing, some were hecklers who were sympathetic to O'Duffy and the Blueshirts.

To the side of the crowd, he saw a familiar figure. It was Harry.

Harry moved forward to meet Joseph as Frank finished speaking.

"I couldn't let you leave without saying goodbye."

The two men embraced.

"Take care of yourself, JoJo."

His use of the childhood nickname brought tears to Joseph's eyes.

"I will. Please look after Mother and Father. I'll write as soon as I can."

The last thing that Joseph saw through a blur of tears as the ship moved away from the quayside was Harry waving.

The Irish Sea was rough that night but the men were in good spirits. Other passengers were largely emigrants, hoping for a better life in England. They looked with curiosity at the group of volunteers. Frank Ryan and Kit Conway led their party to the bar where a singsong had already begun. They had a few drinks and joined in some of the rebel songs but, mindful of the likely hardships ahead of them, soon settled down to sleep wherever they could find a chair or a space on the floor.

From Liverpool they took the train to Victoria, on to

the coast, across the channel and a train onwards to Paris. From there they made their way to the Spanish border at Roussillon. They broke up into small groups to cross the Pyrenees at night with the help of local guides. It was a hazardous, difficult journey and they were ill-equipped for it.

The groups met up again in the Catalan town of Figueras. They reached Albacete, headquarters of the International Brigades, a week after leaving Dublin. They were immediately assigned to the XV Brigade or *La Quinta Brigada,* who were predominantly English-speaking and allocated the nearby village of Madrigueras as their training ground.

In November Franco's troops had launched a major attack on Madrid which failed but the elected Republican government had been forced to shift from Madrid to Valencia on the coast. Albacete was strategically important because it was between Valencia and Madrid which was now under siege from Franco and his experienced North African troops.

Joseph and a few of the young men he was billeted with explored Albacete whenever they had any free time. They were surprised at the poverty of the town. Apart from a few municipal buildings, it consisted mainly of one-storey hovels. The local people were delighted to see the international volunteers and they were offered food and drink wherever they went. The food was very different to what they were used to, but the wine was good and it helped them to sleep in their primitive quarters.

The XV Brigade, largely British but with a large number of Irish, was regarded by the Republican leaders as being made up of battle-hardened veterans of the First

World War, unlike the Spanish, who were largely inexperienced in war. In reality, although some of the British and Irish had been involved in the First World War, and also in the War of Independence in Ireland, many of the volunteers, like Joseph, were too young to have been involved in either.

Just before Christmas, the British battalion was called on to assist the French-speaking XIV Brigade in an attack on Andújar in the south of Spain. A company of one hundred men, forty of them Irish, set off in railway wagons on Christmas Eve. Joseph was one of them even though they had supposedly been selected for their experience in the battlefield. They were led by Captain George Nathan, a British Army veteran. Kit Conway, an experienced soldier who fought in the Black and Tan War and had led a Flying Column on the anti-Treaty side in the Civil War, led the Irish section.

They moved forward into what seemed like a good position, the village of Lopera, west of Andúcar, but soon found that they had actually attacked the strongest part of the enemy line. They were also being strafed from the air. The attack failed and they suffered heavy casualties, among them eight of the Irishmen. Nevertheless, the company was considered to have fought bravely.

Then relations between the Irish volunteers and the British officers began to deteriorate. Many of the Irishmen wanted to form an exclusively Irish battalion. They resented being under the command of British officers who were ex-professionals and similar to the very men that they had fought in the War of Independence in Ireland. But Joseph had heard from the group of Irish who had gone to Lopera to fight under Captain Nathan that he was a good officer and always looked after his men. His own experience of Nathan was that he was friendly and approachable, so he was shocked to hear adverse comments about him.

"Did you know that Nathan was a Black and Tan officer?" Paddy Gaynor asked him. "He was a member of a hit squad directed by Dublin Castle. He was responsible for the killing of two Sinn Féin leaders in Limerick in 1920. I'm not serving under scum like him."

Rumours began to circulate about other British officers. Frank Ryan tried to diffuse the situation by announcing that a recognised Irish section was to be formed within No.1 Company.

The rumours about Captain Nathan proved to be true and he was removed from his command and given an administrative job. Kit Conway succeeded him as Commander of No. 1 Company.

Then the British newspaper, *The Daily Worker*, ran a report on the actions of the British at Lopera, but without mentioning the Irish unit or the Irishmen who died there. This further incensed the Irish. They were aware that the American Battalion, called the Lincolns, were stationed only twelve kilometres away. One faction within the Irish group was keen to join the Americans. It was decided to put it to the vote.

Joseph did not know which way to vote. Frank Ryan, his mentor, seemed to be for joining the Americans but he couldn't be sure. Another group, led by Charlie Donnelly, with whom he had become friendly, maintained that class solidarity was more important than old enmities. In the end, the majority were in favour of joining the American Abraham Lincoln Battalion. The Irish were accepted by the Americans and assigned to the second section of Company 1 and were joined by volunteers of Irish descent from the US and Canada to make up their numbers.

While this drama was being played out, the two sides in the war were preparing for a massive offensive in the valley of the Jarama river, south-east of Madrid. Franco's Nationalist troops had failed to capture Madrid during the winter so they resolved to cut off the capital from the temporary capital Valencia, from where it was getting supplies and reinforcements. To do this, they had to cross the River Jarama to the south-east. The Nationalists had 25,000 men, well-trained regular troops as well as experienced North African soldiers who were fierce in battle and showed no mercy to captives. They were supported by German troops, including two heavy machine-gun battalions and a tank corps.

The ill-equipped XV Brigade and the Abraham Lincoln Battalion were assigned to prevent Franco's troops from crossing the river.

Frank Ryan had been sent on a mission to Madrid but returned in time to brief the men. He told them that the attack from the Fascists would come at nightfall and to get all the rest they could. The men sat on blankets on the ground and shared whatever cigarettes and food they had, joking that they might as well finish off everything since they might not be alive to enjoy them in the morning. Joseph looked at the men around him and realised that they were poorly equipped to go into battle. Most of the Irish volunteers were from inner-city backgrounds and were still wearing clothes and boots more suited to city streets than the rough terrain that they found themselves in now. They had been issued with an assortment of automatic pistols and Russian rifles but had very little training in their use. Many of them were very young and had no experience of warfare.

"I heard that the men who fought at Lopera were given the wrong ammunition for their guns," a young lad from Waterford said to Joseph. "They had to face tanks and had no anti-tank guns. No wonder so many of them died."

Joseph shushed him. "There is no point in thinking like that. We have good officers and right is on our side. We will be all right."

The nationalist offensive had begun on the fifth of February with assaults on the Republican positions on the west bank of the Jarama. The Republicans were taken by surprise and lost almost 2,000 men during the following days. However, reinforcements arrived and they managed to prevent the Nationalists from crossing the river. The Nationalists regrouped but were battle weary.

Nightfall saw the advance of Franco's Moroccan troops and the beginning of three days of close-quarter combat. The three battalions of the XV Brigade were hurriedly put into the line and were all that stood against Franco's crack troops. The British and Irish field officers and men had no idea of what they were actually facing. They thought that they were supporting other troops, not mounting the main attack.

Company No. 1, under Kit Conway, was the first to engage the enemy. Having taken the Pingarrón hills, the Nationalist troops assaulted the Pajares heights to the north which was defended by the International Brigade. Conway's Company quickly realised that they were greatly outnumbered by well-armed troops. Joseph was behind Conway and he saw men falling left and right as shells were exploding all around them. The noise was deafening. Tanks were advancing towards them. They had no anti-tank guns. Conway told him to convey instructions to the section on their left to move to the ridge covering their left flank.

Joseph was looking through Conway's field glasses at the Moroccans advancing on them when he felt a searing pain in his thigh.

Kit Conway was hit at about the same time. He fell down beside Joseph. He whispered, "Don't leave me for the Fascists."

Joseph passed out. When he came to, orderlies were putting Kit Conway on a stretcher. They moved quickly back down the hill. One of them said to Joseph, "We'll be back for you. Hold on."

He must have passed out again because he woke up feeling very cold. He had no idea how long he had been unconscious. He had thought that Spain would be warm even in January. But though the days were usually sunny, the nights were very cold. He strained to look around him. It was getting dark. There was no one in sight. He could see a blur of olive trees and hear the explosion of shells and the whistle of bullets. He knew he should try to get to shelter, even the shelter of an olive tree. Painfully, he turned on his stomach. With his arms, he pulled himself along the ground. His right leg was very painful and he gritted his teeth to prevent himself groaning. He could see a grove of old, gnarled olive trees ahead of him. Their branches reached to the ground and would give him some sort of shelter. At times he almost passed out again but he inched along, resting when the pain got bad. He reached the grove and crawled in against the base of the tree in the centre. The ground was wet with rain that had fallen earlier in the night. He was already wet with sweat and rain but his throat was like sandpaper and his mouth was burning with thirst. He lowered his head to drink from a pool of muddy water at the base of the tree. It tasted muddy and brackish and made him feel ill, but it slaked his thirst. He could hear the battle still raging.

He felt himself drifting off again but was pulled back to consciousness by a noise close to him. He tried to focus on where it was coming from. It sounded like something being pulled along. It seemed to be coming from somewhere behind the tree under which he was hiding. He held his breath and tried to peer through the leaves. A face became clear, a young face with brown skin and frightened black eyes. Could it be one of the Moroccans? He felt for his gun but he had lost it somewhere when he was pulling himself along the ground. The face got closer.

"Hello. I'm an American with the International Brigade. My name is Max. Are you English?"

Joseph could hardly speak. "No, I'm Irish. I'm with the Lincolns. My name is Joseph. I got shot in the thigh. Are you all right?"

"Yes, I am. A bullet grazed my head and knocked me out. I also took a bullet in my right arm. When I came round, everyone had gone. I've been hiding here for quite a while. I saw you approaching but I knew you weren't Moroccan or Spanish. Your skin is too pale."

"I thought you were the enemy when I saw your face."

"With my dark skin? My father is Jewish and my mother is Italian. Do you mind if I come a bit closer?"

He moved over until he was lying parallel to Joseph.

"Can you walk?" he said. "No? I didn't think so. I can but I don't think I could carry you. Anyway, I don't know how to get back to our lines in the dark. If we wait until morning we have a better chance. They may send stretcher parties out then looking for survivors."

Joseph was having trouble focusing on his new friend but was glad of the company. Maybe two of them together stood a better chance of finding their way back to their lines.

Dawn was breaking when Joseph woke up, momentarily startled on feeling the American beside him. They must have drawn close to each other for warmth during the cold night. Max was lying on his good side, his wounded right arm held in an awkward position on his chest. Joseph was lying on his back. He needed to change his position but found it too painful when he moved his leg.

He watched the sun as it rose, creating shards of pink light in the sky. The birds had started singing. It was a beautiful morning but, apart from the birds, there was an eerie silence. Where were the recue parties?

He realised that Max had opened his eyes and was looking at him. He smiled at Joseph and suddenly leaned forward, kissing him on the lips. Joseph was startled but didn't try to move away. They continued to look at each other and then Joseph was the one who leaned towards Max and kissed him.

He groaned as he lay back down again.

Max looked concerned. "Let me have a look at your leg. I had a bit of medical training before I came out here."

He felt Joseph's leg with his good hand. The trouser leg was stuck to the leg in a black sticky mess.

"It's not bleeding any more. That's a good sign. The bullet missed the artery. It may have chipped the bone. We need to try to get back to our own lines now that it is daylight."

"I don't think I can get up."

"OK, I'm going to put my good arm under your shoulder and help you sit up. Then we can try to get you to your feet. When I say go, use your arms to push yourself up into a sitting position. Right – *go*!"

With a great effort Joseph levered himself up using his hands and the pressure of Max's arm.

"Great! Now let's try to get you to your feet. OK, hold on to my arm, put your good foot on the ground and push yourself up. Make sure you keep the other leg off the ground."

Joseph tried to stifle his groans as he followed Max's instructions. He could feel the wound beginning to bleed again with the pressure. At last he was on one foot, leaning on the tree trunk on one side and Max on the other.

"Now put the arm on your wounded side around my neck and I will try to support you. Can you put your other foot to the ground to steady yourself?"

Joseph had his teeth clenched against the pain and didn't answer. Max was taller and much stronger than he was, he realised. Unsteadily, they inched along until they were free of the overhanging branches. They stopped to look around and get their bearings. They could see all sorts of debris on the ground, items of clothing and books, probably jettisoned by the men from their knapsacks as they ran down the hill. Further down the hill there were bodies, too far away for them to be able to recognise anyone but they could tell from the colour of the clothes that they were Republicans and not Franco's Moroccans.

"I think we should try to get further down the hill where the bodies are. Search parties will be out looking for wounded and dead. Do you think you can make it?"

Joseph nodded. He didn't really think he could make it. He couldn't even talk but he didn't want to be left alone.

Again they started on their slow ascent, staggering from tree to tree, stopping occasionally for Joseph to rest. They tried to ignore the bodies they passed and particularly the parts of bodies.

Eventually, Joseph had to admit that he could go no further.

"You go on, Max. If you find help you can bring them back to me. I'll wait here beside this tree, close to the bridge. It'll be easy to find me."

Max was reluctant to leave him but knew it was the only way they would get help. He kept his gun in his left hand as he climbed further up. He didn't look back.

Joseph lay down at the base of the tree. His mouth and throat were burning with thirst but there wasn't even a dirty pool of water in sight. The sun had probably dried up the pools of rain. He wished he had written a note to his parents before they went into battle. He could feel himself drifting off into unconsciousness. He tried to stay awake by reciting poetry to himself but eventually drifted off again.

The sun was going down when he woke. Someone was shaking him. He tried to open his eyes but he couldn't. The blackness kept pulling him back.

In the distance he could hear someone saying, "He's

unconscious. Be careful how you lift him. He's lost a lot of blood."

He felt himself being lifted and then put down gently. Something warm was wrapped around him. His mother was tucking him in. He always kicked the bedclothes off and she would come in before she went to bed and tuck them in again. He was smiling as he went to sleep.

The noise woke him. He could hear men screaming, moaning, cursing and crying. It took him a while to focus. He strained to lift his head and look around him. There were rows of men on stretchers or on beds all around him. Doctors were moving around between the beds, sometimes stopping to examine someone. An occasional nurse hurried by. He was in a field hospital.

Max! Where was Max? As if in answer to his question, Max appeared beside him. He had his arm in a sling and a bandage around his head.

"Max! I am glad to see you. How did I get here? Are you all right?"

"Yes, I'm fine. I got a flesh wound in my arm and cuts and burns on my head where the bullet grazed me but they have taken care of me. How are you feeling?"

"Thirsty and my head is aching."

Max found a beaker of water beside the bed and helped Joseph to drink from it.

"Were you with the people who brought me here?"

"Yeah. I met a stretcher party looking for wounded and dead. They carried you back here to the hospital. The doctors took the bullet out of your leg, cleaned it, stitched you up and here you are. You'll have to stay here for a few weeks because you have an infection in your leg but, once that heals, you'll be fine. I can't go back into combat for a while because my arm is useless, so I'll come to see you every day."

The infection was slow to heal so Joseph had to stay in the hospital for longer than he expected. The hospital was now organised and those who had been in the field hospital when he first woke up were now recuperating or had died. Kit Conway had died almost as soon as he got to the field hospital. Charlie Donnelly, a poet with whom Joseph had become friendly had also died. The battle was deemed to be a success for the Republicans because they had prevented Franco's troops from crossing the river. Madrid was still withstanding the siege. However, they had lost thousands of men. It was no consolation that the Nationalists had lost a similar number.

Frank Ryan was also in the hospital with a serious wound. Joseph visited him as often as he could. Many of the men were much more badly wounded than he. Once he began to recover, he tried to help them. Sometimes he wrote letters home for them. At times he read to them, sometimes poetry that he chose himself but usually any novels that were available in the hospital.

Max came to visit every day as he had promised, and Joseph discovered that they had similar tastes in literature. Eventually he revealed that he had written a novel and also had a number of poems and short stories published. Max was impressed.

"Gee, I was a medical student for two years but gave it up because I wanted to write," he said. "Then I decided to volunteer for Spain. I hate Fascism and especially their attitude to Jews. Fascism seems to spreading through

Europe like wildfire and needs to be stopped. Maybe when the war in Spain is over, the way to stop it is by writing about it rather than fighting."

As Joseph's leg began to heal he was encouraged to take walks to strengthen the muscles. Max accompanied him on these walks which were short at first. He had got to know the surrounding countryside quite well and was delighted to show Joseph his favourite places. Then, as soon as Joseph was able, he took him into the hills to show him the caves where shepherds used to live.

They sat in the entrance to one of the caves and admired the countryside around them. It was spring and the wildflowers were in bloom. Later on, the terrain would be arid and burnt from the heat of the sun but, for the moment, it was green and dotted with the subtle colours of wildflowers. It reminded Joseph of the Wicklow hills.

Max put his arm around Joseph's shoulders. "You don't regret what happened when I found you under the olive tree?"

"No, not at all," Joseph said. "I felt that I had been waiting for you all my life."

He turned to embrace Max and they kissed.

Joseph drew him further into the cave. "Weren't we lucky to find each other?" he said.

CHAPTER 24

At the end of March Joseph was called to see his commanding officer, John Scott, who was the commander of the First Company in the Lincoln Battalion.

"Sit down, Devereux. I have something to ask you. You know that Frank Ryan was badly injured at the Battle of Jarama. He has somewhat recovered but we are sending him home to Ireland to recuperate. We need a couple of reliable men to accompany him and look after him. You need to recover yourself so we thought that you might be willing to go with him. We will also send someone with medical experience to go with you because it is an arduous journey."

"Thank you, sir. Yes, I will be glad to accompany Frank Ryan. I'd be honoured to look after him. How long will we be staying in Ireland?"

"That depends on his health. I know he wants to return as soon as possible. You will be leaving in two days' time and we will give you an escort to the French border. After that you will have to manage as best you can."

Joseph immediately went to see Max.

"Max, I have been asked to accompany Frank Ryan

home to Ireland to recover from the injuries that he got at Jarama. They want someone with medical experience to come with us. If you see the commander now, he might let you come with us. We'll be coming back to Spain as soon as Frank is well enough."

"It's worth a try. I'm fed up hanging round here anyway. My arm is slow to heal and they won't let me return to normal duties until it does."

One hour later, Max came back with a smile on his face. "I'm going with you! Commander Scott was surprised at me volunteering but since I'm useless here anyway and I have some medical training, he is letting me go. I'm looking forward to seeing Dublin!"

Joseph sent a letter to his parents, telling them that he was coming home for a visit with a friend. It probably wouldn't arrive much before him but at least they had some warning. He wondered what they would make of Max.

Two days later they set out for the French border with an armed escort. There were five of them returning to Ireland, all of them with one kind of injury or another. John Doyle from Waterford and Mick Boland from Dublin were the other two. Mick also had some medical experience.

It seemed an easier journey than when they were coming in the opposite direction, probably because they knew what it was going to be like. The difficult part was crossing the Pyrenees. Joseph's leg ached and throbbed as they negotiated the steep slopes and at times he had to lean on Max.

Their guide was excellent and suggested that they put Frank on a donkey for some of the journey. Frank was feeling quite weak and was a big man so it seemed like a good idea. The guide also gave Joseph a stout stick which he could lean on. The donkey was surefooted and knew the route but Frank hardly had the energy to hold on to the primitive saddle as they descended the narrow paths and it was only the secure grip of Max and Mick that kept him from falling off. When they got to the French side, the guide bade them farewell and returned to Spain with the donkey.

They all rested for a while and then, with one man on each side of Frank, they took it in turns to help him along until they got to the train station. There they managed to buy water, coffee, bread and cheese which they devoured while they waited for the train to arrive. Then they all sank into their seats and slept intermittently until they reached Calais and the ferry.

The channel was rough but they hardly noticed and slept again until they reached Dover. Another train journey took them to Liverpool and the ferry to Dublin.

They were all excited to be finally on the ferry. As the ship made its way down the Mersey to the sea they gathered on the deck and stayed there until they were on the open sea. Eventually the cold wind drove them to seek shelter in the cabins. They woke up in time to see the Kish lighthouse as they headed into Dublin Bay and the Docks. They had half expected that the authorities would take them into custody when they arrived. However, no one seemed interested in them as they came through customs.

Friends of Frank's were waiting for them. Two of them settled Frank into a car and drove away. Another man, whom Joseph vaguely knew, took the four remaining men in his car. John was going to stay with Mick in Stoneybatter until he could get the train to Waterford the next day. Joseph asked for Max and him to be taken to the end of Infirmary Road. Tears came to his eyes when he saw the familiar hill leading up to Aberdeen Street. They thanked the driver and set off up the hill.

Ellen, James and Mary were all having breakfast when they arrived. Ellen burst into tears when she saw her son and ran forward to embrace him.

"Joseph! Thank God you're safe and in one piece!"

James cleared his throat. "We didn't get your letter until yesterday so we weren't expecting you for a few days. Sit down now and make yourselves comfortable."

"Mother, Father, this is my friend Max who looked after me when I was in hospital. Max, meet my father and mother and my sister Mary."

"Delighted to meet you, sir, ma'am, and Mary. I'm Max Coen and I'm from New York." He gave them all a warm handshake.

"Oh, so you are from the American Lincoln Battalion that the Irish joined," James said. "I'm delighted to meet you. Sit down here now and have some breakfast. You must be starving after that long journey. Are you cold?" He jumped up and started to riddle the range and put some turf on it.

"I'll put the pan on. You must be dying for a good fry." Ellen was opening bags of rashers and sausages.

"Mother, Max is Jewish. He doesn't eat rashers and sausages. You could cook him a few eggs and, if you have some of your lovely soda bread, he would enjoy that."

Ellen looked nonplussed but put some eggs on the pan. She cut up some soda bread and put it with butter and jam on the table.

"I'll make a pot of tea now. Are you sure, Max, that that will be enough for you?"

"That looks great, ma'am. We didn't get butter or jam in Spain so I'll enjoy it."

Joseph's mouth was watering as he waited for his fry. "We were quite well fed in Spain, though. The people were very generous and often brought us stews or fish. The wine wasn't bad either. But I often dreamed of a bottle of porter and some bacon and cabbage."

The two young men ate heartily.

"This bread is delicious," said Max. "So is the jelly, I mean jam. Is it all homemade?"

Ellen nodded.

"I thought so. My mom makes delicious bread and sometimes jams. She's Italian and she loves cooking. My dad and mom have a small restaurant in Brooklyn."

Joseph could see that his parents were charmed by Max.

So was Mary who had been smiling at Max since he arrived.

"It's great to meet you, Max," she said at last. "I have to go to work now but I'll see you later."

The four of them chatted while the two young men ate their fill. Joseph was careful not to tell them too much about the action they had seen in Spain or the comrades they had lost. Instead, they talked about the camaraderie of the International Brigade and the bravery of the men they had fought with.

Ellen stood up and began to clear the table. "You boys must be very tired. That was a long journey. The bed in the front bedroom is made up. Sleep as long as you like. I'll call you for your dinner. Sleep well, the two of you."

Joseph led the way to the outside toilet in the yard and then up the stairs to his old bedroom and the double bed which he and Harry used to share.

"I could sleep for a week. Which side would you like?"

Joseph lay awake for a while, listening to the familiar sounds of factory horns calling people to work, children on their way to school and the shunting of the steam engines in Kingsbridge Station. Max had fallen asleep with his good arm around him. Joseph turned carefully so as not to wake his friend and settled comfortably with his back to Max and Max's arm still holding him in an embrace.

Downstairs, Ellen was preparing dinner. She bustled around, putting a rabbit in the oven with roast potatoes and parsnips. James had gone out for his usual walk. He returned about one o'clock, the paper under his arm.

"James, will you go up and call the boys? Dinner is ready and, if they sleep any later, they won't sleep tonight."

James hung up his coat and climbed the stairs. There was no sound at all from the bedroom. He turned the handle gently and opened the door just a crack. He could see the two young men inside, in a deep sleep. They looked so innocent. Max had his arm around Joseph in an embrace. Joseph was nestled with his back against Max's chest. They were both bare-chested.

James looked at them for a few minutes. They reminded him of something, something that he had seen in the trenches: young men, afraid of dying, giving comfort and love to each other. He backed out of the room and closed the door. Then he knocked very loudly and called, "*Dinner is on the table, lads! Come down when you are ready!*"

He didn't say anything to Ellen when he came down. There was no point in worrying her and, anyway, he didn't think she would know what he was talking about.

CHAPTER 25

Kathleen had thrown herself into her work at the Gate Theatre. The wardrobe department was always busy, but nothing was too much trouble for her. She often took work home with her, garments that needed to be altered in some way. If extra fittings were needed, she was the first to volunteer for the job. Her mother didn't seem to mind looking after Jeanne for a morning occasionally. When she had a spare moment, she spent her time in the wings, watching rehearsals and imagining that she was playing the lead role. She enjoyed the time she spent with Jeanne more, now that she was no longer bored at home. Her time with Liam was very limited because she was at the theatre six nights a week. They spent her free day, Sunday, with her family so they were seldom alone.

When Joseph arrived home from Spain with his friend Max she felt envious of their experiences and wondered whether she would ever get the chance to travel somewhere exciting herself.

Then in early April, she heard that the company would be taking their latest production, Ibsen's *Hedda Gabler,* to the US in June. It had always been her dream to travel to

America with an Irish theatre company. She watched the rehearsals and as many of the performances as she could and wished that she had a chance to play the eponymous heroine. She would certainly be able to play the bored housewife with understanding!

In May, Eileen, the actress playing Hedda, became ill during a matinée performance and was taken to hospital. Later, they heard that she had a ruptured appendix. Her understudy played the role that evening and was not very good. She missed cues and fluffed lines and some members of the audience were seen to leave the theatre at the interval, an unheard-of happening in the Gate. Then they heard that Eileen would be unable to travel to New York. The understudy was immediately involved in intense rehearsals to bring her acting up to the required standard. After a few performances, Hilton Edwards let it be known that he was not happy with the result.

Kathleen could not believe it. Here was her chance!

At the first opportunity, she approached Hilton Edwards.

"Mr Edwards, I have watched every rehearsal and performance of *Hedda Gabler*. I know the part of Hedda inside out. I know that I could play her successfully. I have only had small parts up to this but please give me an opportunity to show what I can do."

He considered what she was proposing for a few minutes. "You can take the part of Hedda next Saturday for the matinée. After that, I'll make a final decision."

She didn't tell anyone in her family about the audition, partly because it would make her more nervous if they were in the audience and partly because she didn't want them to know about the possibility of her going to

America. They would only try to talk her out of it.

At the matinée, Hilton Edwards was sitting in the front row of the stalls with Micheál MacLiammóir beside him. Kathleen was trembling with nerves before the performance but, once the curtain opened, she found that she was just concentrating on being Hedda and had forgotten her nerves. When the final curtain closed there was silence and then, rapturous applause. She took five curtain calls.

Both Hilton and Micheál came backstage to congratulate her.

"You have the part, my dear. Are you sure you can get away for two months?" Hilton was looking anxious.

"Definitely, Mr Edwards. My mother is happy to look after my daughter, and my husband is a teacher so he will be free for the summer."

"Good. Do you have a passport?"

"Oh my God! I never thought about that. No, I haven't."

"Don't worry. I know someone at the passport office who will deliver one quickly to you. I have an application form in my office. Fill it in, get a photograph taken and get them back to me as soon as possible. You are going to make a splendid Hedda, my dear."

Kathleen hurried home that evening, trying to decide how to break the news of this wonderful opportunity to Liam and her mother. Breaking it to her mother was probably easier than persuading Liam. She decided to go straight to her parents' house rather than home.

She was glad to see that her parents were on their own. Joseph and Max were out somewhere. They were surprised to see her – she always worked on a Saturday evening.

"Kathleen, is there something wrong? Is Jeanne all right?" Her mother looked anxiously at her.

"Don't worry, Mam, everything is fine. I just wanted to tell you and Dad some good news. I played the lead role in *Hedda Gabler* this afternoon. The actress who should have played her took ill during the matinée last week and I replaced her this week."

"Oh, the poor girl! What happened to her? Is she all right?"

"She'll be fine. She had a ruptured appendix so it was lucky that they got her to the hospital so quickly. It will take her a while to recover."

"For how long will you be playing the part?" Her father usually didn't take much interest in what was going on at the theatre.

"For as long as the production lasts." She was hoping that her father would go out for his usual walk after tea. She wanted to talk to her mother alone.

They chatted on and eventually, to her relief, her father said, "Well, I'm off now for a bit of a walk before the rain comes. God bless."

After he had left, Kathleen sat down by the fire.

Ellen joined her. "Was there something that you wanted to talk to me about, love?" Her mother always knew when she wanted something.

"Yes, Mam, there is. The play that I was talking about, the one I got the lead role in, *Hedda Gabler*, well, the company are travelling to America with it. In June."

Ellen looked at her in alarm. "That poor girl will have recovered by then, won't she?"

"No, Mam, she won't be able to go. I'll have to go in her place."

190

"What? But how long would you be gone for?"

"If the play goes well, two months."

"*Two months!* You'd be away from Jeanne for two months?" Her mother fell silent for a while. "It's a long time. How do you feel about that? Surely you would miss her?"

"Yes, of course I would. But this is my big chance. I've been dreaming of a chance like this. It's only two months! Jeanne loves being with you and Dad. Liam will be there at the weekends and he will be completely free from mid-July. Please say you'll help me, Mam, please."

"Have you told Liam yet? I don't think he'll be happy about it."

"No, I haven't and I know he won't be happy but I have to do it. If I turn down this chance, I may never get another. *Please, Mam, help me.*"

Ellen looked at her daughter's pleading face. She could never refuse her anything. "All right, love. If Liam agrees to it, then I will too."

Kathleen burst into tears and hugged her mother. "Oh, thank you, Mam. You don't know how much this means to me."

Now she just had to persuade Liam.

When she got home, he had just put Jeanne to bed. The little girl was just nodding off to sleep after her bedtime story when Kathleen crept in.

"God bless, sweetheart. Sleep well." She kissed her and breathed in her sweet scent. She would miss her daughter but she knew that the little girl would be well looked after.

Liam was surprised to see her home so early on a Saturday night. He was moving about the flat, gathering toys and books and putting them away.

"I was just going to make a ham sandwich for myself.

Would you like one? Jeanne and I had dinner with my parents today so I'm not very hungry."

"Yes, a sandwich would be lovely. But, Liam, I have something to tell you. I played the lead role in *Hedda Gabler* this afternoon. Eileen, who had been playing the part, became ill during the week – appendix. The understudy took over but wasn't very good, so I got the chance to audition for it at the matinée this afternoon. I got the part and I am very happy. My performance got five curtain calls!"

Liam continued to make the sandwiches. "I'm happy for you. How long will the play run for? I suppose it won't take up much more time than working in the wardrobe department?"

"It'll be running in Dublin until the beginning of June. Then they'll be taking it to New York."

"New York!" He stopped, butter-knife poised, and stared at her. "But surely Eileen won't be fit to travel by then?"

"No, she won't. So they've asked me to go with them."

"Well, that's not possible. Looking after Jeanne is more important. Working in the wardrobe department was one thing – I could even put up with you acting again. But going to New York! I don't know how you could even think of it!"

"My mother is happy to look after Jeanne and you'll be on holiday from mid-July. I'll be home by mid-August, long before you have to go back to school."

"No, Kathleen, I don't want you to go."

"Well, I'm going, whether you like it or not! You can't stop me."

She ran into the bedroom and lay on the bed, sobbing.

Liam came in after her and sat on the side of the bed. He smoothed her hair.

"I'm just concerned about Jeanne. She would miss you. So would I."

"I know that. But I can't miss this opportunity. I may never get another one."

Liam was silent for a while.

"All right. If your mother is willing to look after Jeanne while I'm at school, I'll agree to you going."

"Oh, thank you, Liam! This means so much to me. I will make you proud of me. I can't believe it! I'm going to New York!" She hugged Liam and looked up at him. "You are the best husband a girl could wish for!"

He buried his face in her hair and whispered, "I hope I am not the most foolish husband a girl could wish for."

She didn't hear him.

Kathleen had two weeks of performances in Dublin before they were due to go to New York. All of the family, with the exception of Mary, came to see her perform. Her parents were the first, accompanied by Joseph and Max. They were all very impressed when Hilton and Micheál came to meet them at the interval. Hilton told her parents how delighted he was with Kathleen's performance. Ellen felt a glow of pride and was glad that she had supported her daughter.

Micheál was very friendly and chatted to Joseph and Max about their experiences in the Spanish Civil War.

Before they left, as people were returning to their seats for the Second Act, he gave the two young men an appraising look.

"You must come to one of our parties here at the theatre sometime. I'm sure you would enjoy it."

James looked at Micheál and then at Max and Joseph. He said nothing.

Harry and Julia attended the last show before the company set off for New York. It was a wonderful performance and the cast received a standing ovation while Kathleen was presented with a huge bouquet of flowers. When she joined her brother and his wife who were waiting for her at the bar, she had to make her way through groups of admirers who wanted to congratulate her on her performance. Eventually, Harry came to her rescue and brought her to join Julia.

"My God, that was such a great send-off. I hope the audiences in New York are as appreciative."

Julia hugged her. "They will be. You gave a wonderful performance. We are very proud of you."

Then Harry hugged her. "Yes, I am proud of my little sister. Are you all ready for the journey?"

"Yes, I am. We have just one day's rest before we head down on the train to Cobh. Then it's about a week until we get to New York. We'll have a chance to rehearse and get to know the theatre before our first performance."

"Better get home quickly then. Has Liam been to see your performance?"

"Yes, he came with his parents last week. They don't approve of me going to New York at all, but I think they enjoyed the play."

"We'll drop you home. I have my car outside. Don't forget the flowers."

When Kathleen arrived home, Liam was waiting for her. "Oh, you are earlier than I expected. How did it go?"

Kathleen took off her coat and hat and looked around

for a vase. "Harry and Julia brought me home. It was an absolutely wonderful tonight. I was presented with these flowers during the curtain calls. Aren't they beautiful? There was a great atmosphere in the theatre and the cast really rose to the occasion. There is really something special about the final night of a successful play. I can't describe the feeling I get when the audience rises to their feet in appreciation."

She finished putting the flowers in a large jug, placed them on the table and sat down.

Liam was standing, looking at her. "I can't believe that you will be gone for two months. Jeanne and I will miss you so much."

"I'll miss you both too. I'll think of you every day. Thanks for giving me the opportunity to do this." She smiled up at him.

Liam moved over to sit beside her on the sofa. He put his arms around her and kissed her passionately. Kathleen responded and put her arms around him. He moved his mouth down her throat and held her close to him.

"Don't do that." She stood up. "I have to go to bed now. I'm very tired and I have a lot to do tomorrow."

"Of course. You go ahead. I'll come to bed later."

He opened a book and began to read. When he eventually went to bed, Kathleen was already asleep.

The next day was Sunday. Kathleen woke early. She left Liam sleeping and started to sort out Jeanne's clothes. She planned to leave some of them permanently in her mother's because the little girl would be spending a lot of time there. Her own packing was almost complete with only a few last-minute things to be added.

Jeanne woke up as the bells for nine o'clock Mass were ringing. She dressed her, gave her breakfast and left her to play.

Liam came in, looking as though he hadn't slept.

"It's a lovely morning, Liam. I thought that we could take Jeanne to the park to feed the ducks. You'd like that, wouldn't you, sweetheart?"

"But I said that I'd take her to my mother's today. I thought that you would be too busy for us."

"I did most of my packing during the week. I want to spend my last day at home with Jeanne. I won't see her for a long time."

"You won't see either of us for a long time. All right, I'll get dressed and we'll go to the park."

"Come on, Jeanne – let's get some bread for the ducks."

The park was busy with families taking a walk or bringing younger children to the duck pond. Jeanne squirmed to get down from Liam's arms. Kathleen gave her the bag of bread and they both watched as she broke off pieces and aimed each piece at a selected duck. Soon she was surrounded by a cacophony of hungry ducks.

"The three of you make a lovely picture. Your little girl is beautiful. She looks just like you. You must be very happy." The woman had been watching Jeanne and her antics with the ducks.

"Yes, we are happy." Kathleen smiled at her.

Liam said nothing.

The following morning Kathleen woke up with a feeling of dread. It took her a while to shake it off. Was she doing the right thing by going to New York? What if Jeanne became ill? Would Jeanne pine for her? She had never been parted from her daughter for more than a day. How would she endure two months without her?

As if on cue, Jeanne began to cry. "*Mama! Mama!*"

Kathleen rushed to her.

Jeanne was red-faced and distressed. Kathleen felt her forehead.

"Liam! Jeanne has a high temperature! What will we do?"

Liam came quickly and picked up his daughter. He cradled her against him.

"She feels quite hot. I don't think she slept very well last night. She was very restless. Your mother will be here any minute now. She'll know what to do."

Kathleen took her daughter and soothed her. "It's all right, darling. My poor baby."

She looked at the clock. She was supposed to be leaving in an hour's time. Maybe she should cancel the trip. But if she let the company down at this late stage, she would never get an acting job in Ireland again.

Ellen arrived a minute or so later. She came hurrying into the bedroom.

"Mother, thank God you're here. I think Jeanne has a temperature and seems to be in pain."

Ellen came and looked closely at Jeanne who snuffled a bit and stopped crying.

"Yes, she has a bit of a temperature," she said as she laid a hand on the little girl's forehead. "I think she just has a cold. I'll make her a honey-and-lemon drink."

"Thank God it's only a cold!" Kathleen said. "I was beginning to think of all sorts of things that it could be."

Kathleen took Jeanne from her mother and began to

rock her gently in her arms. The little girl was falling asleep.

"I'll put her down as soon as she falls asleep," Kathleen said to Liam. "Don't come to the station with me. Stay here with Jeanne."

"I'll go with Kathleen, Liam," said Ellen. "Joseph said that he and Max would call here and they can walk with us. You'd better get your bag, Kathleen."

Kathleen settled her daughter and watched her sleeping peacefully for a few minutes before she went downstairs.

"We'll wait outside for the boys, Mother. I don't want them to wake her. Bye, Liam. I'll write as soon as I get there. Take care of Jeanne." Her voice broke on the last few words.

"Take care of yourself, Kathleen, and enjoy the experience." He kissed her quickly on the cheek and opened the door.

Joseph and Max were just coming down the street.

"Are Liam and Jeanne not coming?" Joseph asked.

"No, Joseph, Jeanne has a cold and is not feeling very well. She's sleeping now." She wiped away tears.

Joseph put his arm around his sister. "Come on, we'd better get going or you'll miss the train. Don't worry about Jeanne. The whole family will look after her."

"I know you will but I am going to miss her so much."

At the station she embraced her mother, kissed her brother and gave Max a hug. She was the last member of the cast to arrive. They saw her tears and fussed around her, helping to stow her bag and making space in the carriage for her.

The whistle blew and the train pulled away. She felt empty, as though she had left her heart behind.

CHAPTER 26

The SS *Olympic* looked huge when they saw it from the docks at Cobh. It was far out in the bay and passengers were taken out to it by tender – a boat which could dock in the harbour, unlike the large ship which had to anchor out at sea. They were helped from the quayside onto the tender which set off as soon as it had its full complement of passengers. When they reached the ship they were met by a steward who showed them to their cabin.

Kathleen was to share a cabin with Claire Kelly who played the part of Thea Elvsted in the play. She was a lively young woman from Wicklow and she and Kathleen had become friends. They were travelling tourist third class. Their cabin was on a lower deck with no sea view. It had two bunks with crisp white linen, a wash basin and some storage for their clothes. The luxurious upper deck cabins with sea views were for the wealthy passengers whom they had seen earlier, boarding a different tender.

The two young women were very excited and started to unpack. When they heard two long, sonorous blasts on the ship's horn, they realised that they must be leaving port and went on deck to join their friends.

As the ship pulled away from the docks into the open sea, people were waving from the shore. They all waved back and saw Cobh harbour become smaller and smaller until it looked like a picture on a postcard. There was a stiff breeze but the sun was shining and they stayed on deck for a long time. The air was invigorating with the salt smell of the sea which almost masked the smell of the ship's fuel.

An old man who had been watching the receding shoreline of Ireland turned to them. "Do you see those seven fingers of land sticking out into the Atlantic?" he said. "That's the last piece of Ireland that you will see for a while. It's the Seven Heads peninsula in West Cork. In the days of the potato famine, parents used to go there to see the last glimpse of their children as they emigrated to America. Often they lit bonfires so that their children on board the ship would see that last farewell. Both parents and children realised that they would probably never see each other again. Sad, wasn't it?"

His words made Kathleen think of Jeanne. She could feel her eyes filling up with tears.

"Kay, are you all right? Do you want to go down to our cabin?"

"No. Let's take a little walk around the deck. I'll be fine in a few minutes."

She pushed all thoughts of Jeanne and home out of her mind and made herself think of the adventure ahead.

Later, when they joined the rest of the cast in the restaurant for dinner, she felt she was taking part in a production. There was an abandoned, holiday mood among her friends and she threw herself into the gaiety.

"Have you ever had a cocktail, Kay?" David O'Leary,

who played her husband, George Tesman, in the play, was smiling at her.

"No. I haven't."

"You have to drink cocktails in New York. Everybody does. Would you like a Manhattan?"

"It sounds lovely. What is it?"

"It is made with a shot of bourbon whiskey, sweet vermouth and a dash of angostura bitters all shaken up and served over ice with a cherry and a twist of orange."

"You sound like an expert cocktail-maker."

"On my first visit to New York I was introduced to a Manhattan. It is the essence of New York."

David returned with two Manhattans for the girls. They were joined by other members of their party, all of them trying out a variety of cocktails.

The meal that followed was excellent, beautifully cooked and presented. There was a bewildering array of cutlery on the table, white china plates and crisp linen napkins.

Claire was impressed. "If our whole trip is as good as this, we're going to have a wonderful time."

Later, when they went to their cabin, they found that the ship had begun to roll alarmingly.

Claire looked apprehensive. "The sea is so rough. I didn't think it would be like this in June. I hope that I can sleep tonight."

Kathleen didn't think she would sleep either, now that there were no distractions from her thoughts of Jeanne. However, the cocktail and the glass of wine she had drunk with dinner put her to sleep quite quickly.

They were woken by the noise of people talking as they passed their cabin door.

"It must be time for breakfast. I'm starving." Claire was struggling into her clothes as fast as she could.

Breakfast was served again in the dining saloon on an upper deck.

While they ate, they chatted to the others about the amenities on board. There was a smoking room and a lounge where one could play board games or borrow a book from the library. There were also games organised on the deck.

"I'll definitely borrow some books but I don't think I'll bother with board games. I think they're for the older passengers." Claire laughed. "I'm more interested in getting a suntan."

The two young women fell into a pattern over the next few days. After breakfast they walked on the deck for an hour or so. Later, after lunch, they sat on the deck and sunbathed. It was possible to hire deckchairs but they felt it was a waste of money and sat on the deck instead.

"We'll be as suntanned as any of the Hollywood stars if we keep doing this," Claire observed. "Isn't it funny how it suddenly became fashionable to be suntanned? My mother would be shocked if she saw me exposing my skin to the sun."

"My mother lived in India for seven years, you know," said Kathleen, "and never exposed her skin to the sun. They thought that only people who had to do manual work outdoors should have tanned skin. We have Coco Chanel to thank for the suntan craze."

"I can't wait to see New York. David says that where we'll be staying is very central. West Forty-Sixth Street and Seventh Avenue, I think he said."

Evenings were spent with the rest of the cast in the restaurant. Kathleen, or Kay as everyone called her, fell asleep every evening thinking of her daughter. Liam occasionally came into her mind but only in association with Jeanne. She wrote to her parents and Liam, telling them about the voyage and the new experiences.

One morning, a week later, word came that they were approaching New York harbour and would be disembarking in a few hours. They had already filled in all the necessary forms for immigration and customs.

All the members of the cast were on deck. As they approached the mouth of the harbour and the Hudson River, the unmistakeable Statue of Liberty rose dramatically from the sea. They marvelled at the size and height of it. It was a scene that was familiar from the movies and they could hardly believe that they were seeing it in reality.

"That must be Ellis Island," Kay realised.

As she pointed to the small island, they all thought about the millions of Irish who had landed there over the centuries, hoping for a new life. Then the panorama of the skyline of Manhattan rose majestically before them. The variety of the modern buildings was stunning. Sunlight glinted off the glass in the millions of windows in the skyscrapers.

"Do you see that building with the spire on top? That's the Empire State Building," David said.

Soon they were disembarking. It took a while to get through immigration. Then the boxes containing props and costumes and their suitcases were loaded into a few taxis with the stage manager and some older members of the cast. The rest of them decided to walk since they had been told that it was no distance to their rooming house. It would also give them a chance to stretch their legs and to look around.

David took the lead since he had been to New York previously. He pointed out landmarks and advised them about the way to find places.

"Finding your way around New York is very easy. The main thing to remember is that the avenues run north to south in a straight line. The streets run east to west also in a straight line. We should be able to walk to our rooming house in about half an hour."

They craned their necks to look up at the height of the buildings as they walked. They could hear various languages being spoken by the people around. Kay recognised Italian but most of the languages were unfamiliar. She had never seen such a variety of people – white, black, brown, young and old. Some of them were sitting chatting on the steps leading up to the buildings. Others were hanging out of the windows, talking loudly to those below. Cooking smells were in the air, spicy, aromatic and enticing. Music could be heard from some of the houses – jazz, opera and some rhythmic music which was unfamiliar. Children were playing up and down the street. It reminded her of the streets in Dublin where people lived in tenements, except here the houses were in fairly good repair and the people better dressed.

Their rooming house was at the end of the street. Their bags had been left there while the props and costumes had been taken to the theatre. They climbed the steps to the hall door which was opened by the landlady. She introduced herself as Mrs Braun, speaking in a heavy German accent. The rooms were strictly segregated, she told them, men on the lower two floors and women on the third and fourth. She began to lead the group up the stairs to their rooms.

Their bags had been left in the hall and Kay and Claire were out of breath by the time they hauled them up the stairs. Their room overlooked the street and was sparsely but adequately furnished with heavy, old-fashioned furniture. There was a double bed, one sagging armchair, a basin and ewer, a dressing-table with a mottled mirror and a large wardrobe. It didn't match their expectations of New York. However, it was clean.

Mrs Braun gave them a key. "The first rule is, no men in the room. If you come home later than midnight, the door will be locked, and you must knock for me to open the door. I will not be pleased."

The two young women looked at each other. It was beginning to sound like a boarding school.

"If you want to wash some clothes, you may do it here – there is always hot water. You may hang them in the yard. The bathroom is down the hall, shared by all the women on this floor. You may have a bath once a week. Please do not use too much hot water. Do you have any questions?"

"Yes. What time is breakfast? And where can we get something to eat now?" Kay was starving.

Mrs Braun looked displeased. "If you want something to eat now, you must go out. No food must be kept in the room. Breakfast is between eight and nine o'clock only. Good evening."

As soon as she left the room, Kay and Claire burst into laughter.

"She's a right old battle-axe, isn't she?" said Claire.

"Yes, she makes the place sound like an institution. I'm

hungry. I'm sure the others are too. Let's go down and join them."

They found a diner in the next street. It was cheerful and bright with red check tablecloths. There was a strong smell of coffee. It reminded her of Sven. She dismissed the thought as quickly as it came. She turned to Claire.

"I don't imagine we will get tea here, but the coffee smells good."

"I could eat a horse. I can smell bacon and eggs anyway. Oh, here's a menu."

They ordered bacon and eggs and were bemused when they were asked "Sunny side up or over easy?"

Claire tasted the food and then ate enthusiastically. "This pancake and maple syrup is delicious. And so is the coffee. I think we should come here every day to eat."

When the bill came it was very reasonable. Bruno, the Italian owner, introduced himself and his wife Gina. He recognised their accents.

"I have many Irish friends here. I hope you will come to my restaurant often."

It was a good beginning. They were to start rehearsals the next day, Monday, so they took a walk to familiarise themselves with the location of the theatre.

The Cherry Lane Theatre was located in the West Village near 7th Avenue. It was quite a long walk and they got lost on the way because that part of New York had not been built in the grid system of avenues and streets. It was an old area of beautiful brownstone houses, small cafés and interesting streets. The theatre itself was situated down a leafy lane.

Next day, they took the Number 6 bus and found their

way to the theatre quite easily. The manager of the theatre, Marco Mercadante, greeted them in the foyer. He looked Italian but spoke with a strong New York accent.

"Welcome, everyone, to Cherry Lane Theatre! We're looking forward to hosting your production. There's a lot of interest in it already and good advance ticket sales. Make yourselves at home and, if you have any questions, I will be happy to answer them. The props and costumes were delivered yesterday and are all backstage. Now, I'll take you on a tour of the building."

The theatre was comfortable and soon they began to feel at home in it. It was smaller than the Gate but well planned. The cast and backstage staff soon got to work, hanging up costumes, placing props and examining the lighting. The actors had brought wigs and small items of their costumes with them.

They had their first rehearsal that afternoon and it went very well. Marco was standing in the wings, watching. Kay was conscious of his presence. Afterwards, he spoke to her.

"I know the play quite well, but you bring something extra to it, a wistfulness and a sadness that gives the character extra depth. I'm looking forward to the first performance."

Although he was dark and fairly ordinary-looking, something about him, maybe his self-confidence, reminded her of Sven and made her mistrust him.

"Thank you." She turned her back and joined her friends.

CHAPTER 27

The first night of the play in New York was a great success. They had a full house and many of the local Irish Americans attended. After the final curtain there was rapturous applause and repeated curtain calls. Marco Mercadante brought a few members of the audience backstage to meet the cast. They were mostly people from the theatrical community, actors and directors and writers, many of them his friends. He brought all of them to meet Kay, introducing her as an up-and-coming young Irish actress.

Afterwards, they went for drinks in a local bar. Marco was good company, full of stories and anecdotes about his experiences as a theatre manager.

When the group began to disperse, Kay asked him if he had ever done any acting.

"Oh, you thought that I was always a theatre manager? No, I started out as an actor but then developed an interest in directing. I was lucky. I got the opportunity to direct a number of off-Broadway plays which were pretty successful."

"Why are you working as a manager here at the Cherry Lane Theatre then?"

"A friend of mine is the manager here. I didn't want to

take on a long run as director because I am planning to go to Hollywood very soon. My friend wanted to take a vacation and asked me to fill in for him while you guys were here."

Kay was immediately interested in his plans when he mentioned Hollywood. She asked him tentatively whether he knew the actor, Sven Olsen. He didn't but wanted to know how she knew Sven. She told him about Sven playing in the Gate and his departure for Hollywood, but didn't reveal her relationship with him.

She was so involved in the conversation with Marco that she didn't notice that most of her friends had left the bar. Then she looked around for Claire.

"Oh, they all seem to have left. I suppose they were tired. It's been an exciting day. I'd better go too."

"Let me see you back to where you're staying. It's the least I can do. If I hadn't been talking so much, you would have left with your friends. We can take a cab if you're tired."

Kay smiled at him. She had changed her mind about Marco. "Thank you, that's very kind of you. I wouldn't like to take a taxi on my own."

They were some of the last people to leave. Marco whistled and waved at a passing cab. On the journey, he told her a little bit more about himself. He was thirty-five and divorced. His wife had been an actress too. She had got tired of the unpredictable lifestyle and wanted to settle down and have a family. He wanted to continue acting. When they parted, he started directing and had some success. She was now married to someone else and had two children.

When they got out of the cab, he asked the cab driver to wait.

"I can't ask you in, I'm afraid," Kay said. "No men allowed by the landlady."

"That's OK. I'd like to see you again so that we can talk some more. Would you like to go to Coney Island with me on Sunday?"

Kay had heard of Coney Island. "That would be lovely. I want to see as many of the sights of New York as possible while I'm here."

"Good. I'll see you tomorrow at the theatre." He kissed her quickly on the cheek and got back into the cab.

Claire was still awake when she got to their room. "You seem to have made a conquest there. I was watching the two of you talking and he couldn't take his eyes off you."

"Oh, don't be silly. I'm a married woman. He was just being kind. He had to take me home in a taxi because everyone left without me. He wants to show me Coney Island on Sunday."

"Be careful. I think he wants more than that."

The following week was too busy for Kay and Marco to be able to spend much time together but, when she was on stage, she was conscious of him watching from the wings.

It became the custom for the whole cast to go to the nearby bar for a drink after the show and Marco usually joined them. Kay then went home on the bus with Claire – she was always tired after the show. She had never played such a major role before and it was exhausting, playing night after night, with two matinées. She had no understudy so she dare not become ill. Besides, she didn't want any gossip about her relationship with Marco. He was a friend, that was all, and he was fun to be with. She was looking forward to going to Coney Island with him.

They met early on Sunday morning and took the subway

to Coney Island. Kay had no idea what to expect except that she had heard about the famous rides and the beach. They found themselves part of a huge throng of people all making their way to the sandy beach. Kay was overwhelmed by the number of people around her. They seemed mostly to be working-class young men and women and families with young children, as well as a sprinkling of people who looked middle class, judging by their clothes and demeanour. There didn't seem to be any black people.

There was scarcely a spare inch on the beach. Many people were in swimming costumes, and some of the women's costumes were quite daring. Men and women lounged and sunbathed together in a way that was new to Kay.

"I didn't bring a swimming costume with me," Kay said when Marco asked her if she wanted to swim.

"I should have warned you but you can hire one from that shop over there if you want to," Marco said and began to open his bag and take out his towel and costume.

Kay looked at the skimpiness of some of the women's costumes around her. "I don't really feel like a swim," she lied.

She thought that Marco was going to change right there in front of everyone but he went over to a changing hut and came back all ready for a swim. His body was very tanned and muscular.

"Here, sit down on my towel. I'll just have a quick swim."

He ran down to the sea and dived in. He was a good swimmer. She kept her eyes on him all the time he was in the water. Then he was back beside her.

She got up and shook out the towel. "Here's your towel. Did you enjoy that?"

"It was great. Pity you didn't swim. It really washes off all the stresses of the week. Maybe next time. I'll just go and change and then we'll see the other attractions."

There was a long boardwalk leading to the beach and it was lined with hot-dog stands, ice-cream vendors and amusement arcades. Marco bought ice creams and they ate them as they walked.

"This is gelato, Italian ice cream. It's the best in the world."

"Oh, Irish ice cream is pretty good. I used to love getting a wafer or a cone as we walked to the park when I was a child. We live near the Phoenix Park, one of the biggest parks in Europe but there isn't a funfair in it."

They were leaving the beach behind.

"You know," she said, "I thought that Coney Island was an island and that we would have to cross by boat to get to it."

"Well, it was once an island separated from the rest of Brooklyn by Coney Island Creek but gradually it was filled in by landowners and very recently when the Belt Parkway was constructed, so it is now a peninsula."

Kay was looking around her, fascinated by the strangeness of the buildings and the variety of amusements on offer. "Look at that huge building over there. What is it?" It was a steel-and-glass building in the shape of a pavilion.

"That's Steeplechase Park. Inside it you can visit the Barrel of Fun where you are tossed around on top of other people that you don't know. After that you can visit the Blow-Hole Theatre where a gust of air blows up women's dresses and all the men are highly amused."

Kay looked shocked.

"No, I didn't think you would like either of those. I'm

taking you to Luna Park which is really beautiful. You get the full effect at night when it is all lit up. It's like fairyland because every structure in it is lit up and the architecture is beautiful. There is also a food area and that's where we are going for lunch."

They queued up for hot dogs and Coca Cola and then sat at a table to enjoy them.

Baby elephants and camels were being led around. Kay saw a circus tent nearby.

"Oh, I love a circus. Can we go?"

Marco went to get the tickets and they spent two hours watching the amazing acts.

"Would you like to go on one of the rides?" Marco asked as they emerged. "We could go to Dreamland Park or Shoot the-Chutes lagoon."

Kay looked nervously around. "I'd prefer to just walk around and see everything."

"That's fine. We'll walk some more and then get a coffee and have a chat."

Kay had to link Marco as they walked around because the crowds had increased as the day went on and she was afraid of being knocked over or losing sight of him. They found a place which sold coffee and delicious-looking cakes.

"You know all about me now," Marco said. "Tell me about you. I hardly know anything about you." He was looking at her intently.

Kay suddenly found herself talking. She told him about Sven, how he had broken her heart. She told him about Liam, that he was a good man but she shouldn't have married him. And then it poured out: her hopes for Sven and her, her anguish at finding herself pregnant, the way she tricked Liam into marrying her, how she took her sister's boyfriend, the birth of her beautiful daughter and how she hated the life that she was then expected to live. By the end of the recital she was in tears.

"You must think that I am a horrible woman to do things like that," she sobbed.

Marco gave her his handkerchief. He came around the table and sat beside her, holding her close. Her sobbing increased and she buried her head in his jacket.

"You poor kid! You really made a mess of things, didn't you? But you're older and wiser now. You can make things better. Liam sounds like a good guy. He agreed to you coming to New York, didn't he? Maybe he will agree to you continuing your career."

Kay wiped her eyes and blew her nose. "I don't know. Maybe he will. Thanks for listening to me. I haven't talked to anyone about it before. In fact, no one at all knows. Not a soul. Please don't tell anyone."

"Don't worry, Kay. Have no fears on that account. I won't tell anyone."

She could see the sincerity in his eyes.

"Right, it's time to go home," he said. "If we wait any later, the subway will be packed." He kissed her on the nose. "You look like Rudolph. You might want to powder your nose. There's a restroom right over there."

In the restroom, Kay looked in the mirror. Her nose was red and shiny. She took out her compact. She felt better for having told someone. Marco was a good listener and she trusted him not to betray her secrets.

Over the next few weeks, Marco took Kay to see many of the sights of New York. They visited the recently constructed Rockefeller Centre, the Empire State Building and climbed the many steps inside the Statue of Liberty to get the wonderful view of the harbour and the skyline of Manhattan. Kay looked out at a ship just making its way into the harbour and remembered her first sight of New York. It seemed a long time ago. Ireland seemed very far away.

CHAPTER 28

The way his father looked at him after Micheál invited him and Max to a party had not escaped Joseph. He wondered whether his father was aware of their relationship. He doubted it but, then, maybe he was wrong – after all, his father had been in the army and at war for four years. His mother had no idea, he was sure of that. Maybe it was time for them to go back to Spain. His leg was almost healed and he had regained his strength. Max's arm was much better and Frank Ryan also seemed on the road to recovery.

He decided to take Max to meet Frank and plan their return to Spain.

His parents had been very upset when Kathleen set off for New York but they didn't have time to miss her because Jeanne was in their house every weekday. Liam brought her to the house in the morning before he went to school and took her home in the evening, after they had both had their tea with the family. Mary was home earlier than Liam and spent an hour every day playing with the little girl. The house began to revolve around Jeanne and her needs. At first, she seemed to miss her mother but after a few days she grew used to the routine.

Relations between Mary and Liam had been very strained but now they were forced into a more friendly relationship. When they got their holidays in mid-July, their relationship was cordial enough for Liam to invite Mary to join him and Jeanne for a trip to the Zoo in Phoenix Park. Joseph understood Mary's hesitation and quickly asked whether he and Max could come too.

They took a picnic and bought some nuts for the monkeys at the entrance. Max had been in the park with Joseph many times but never in the zoo. He looked around him with delight at the wonderful old trees and the lush lawns.

"It reminds me of Central Park except that there are not so many people."

Jeanne wanted to get out of her pushchair and walk as soon as they got inside the gates. The Zoo was busy because it was school holidays and there were a lot of families around. They could hear deep roars coming from the lion house where the animals were being fed. They looked in but the smell was appalling so they moved on to the monkey house. Jeanne was delighted with the antics of the monkeys and wouldn't leave until all the nuts were gone.

The highlight of the visit was to the sea lions' pool. They too were being fed. The keepers threw fish up in the air and the sleek sea lions caught them. All the while they kept up a loud honking. Their faces looked almost human. Jeanne kept holding out her arms to them as though she wanted to hug them.

Then they ate their picnic on the lawn and watched the little ponies which were taking children for rides around the perimeter.

"Hey, look at the elephant!" Max was as excited as a child.

An enormous elephant was walking by with a howdah on his back. People sat balanced on benches either side of the howdah as the animal swayed ponderously along the path. A keeper walked ahead of him.

"*I want a ride on the efelant! Want a ride on the efelant!*" Jeanne was jumping up and down with excitement.

"I'll go and buy five tickets," said Joseph.

Liam wanted to pay but Joseph insisted that he would.

He returned in a few minutes. "We have to queue now over there."

When it came to their turn, they stood on a platform from which the keeper helped them onto the howdah. The elephant waited patiently. When there were no more seats left, the keeper gave the signal and the elephant began to walk. The howdah swayed alarmingly and Jeanne was shrieking with excitement. Liam and Mary were either side of her, each with an arm around her. Joseph and Max were on the other side. When their ride finished, Jeanne didn't want to get down. Only the promise of an ice-cream cone persuaded her.

They all sat on the grass and licked their cones. Liam looked around. They were surrounded by families. This should have been his life, he reflected, family outings with Mary and their children. Instead he had fallen for the glamour and excitement of Kathleen. He had really made a mess of his life.

Mary was wiping Jeanne's mouth with her handkerchief. "I think Jeanne is getting very tired. We'd better head home."

Liam picked up his sleepy daughter and put her in the

pushchair. "Thanks for a lovely day, Mary. And thanks to you two lads. It was a real family outing."

"Thank you. I enjoyed being with Jeanne." Mary avoided looking at him.

"We really enjoyed it too, didn't we, Max?" said Joseph.

Joseph made sure to walk with Mary, and Max walked beside Liam as they made their way home.

When Ellen saw Jeanne fast asleep at an awkward angle in the pushchair, she picked her up immediately. "I'll put her down to sleep upstairs, Liam. You can collect her tomorrow. Have a free evening, for a change. Go out and have a few pints."

Few men would have put up with the life Liam was leading, she thought, working by day, looking after Jeanne in the evenings and weekends.

"Thanks, Mrs Devereux. I might pop into Ryan's for a while." He paused for a minute and turned to Joseph and Max. "Will you two join me? And would you like to come, Mary?"

Mary didn't look at him. "No, thanks, Liam. I'm going to have an early night."

"We're off to to meet Frank Ryan," Joseph replied, "but we have time to join you for a pint first."

Ellen looked at her daughter. It was very difficult for Mary having Liam around so much of the time. Since Jeanne was born, their relationship had improved but it was still awkward. There was no doubt, though, that Mary loved Jeanne.

Joseph and Max returned later that evening from their meeting. They found Ellen sitting alone by the fire. James was already in bed as his chest hadn't been too good that day.

"Have you any news, Joseph? How is Frank Ryan?" Ellen asked.

She dreaded the thought of them returning to Spain. They had been lucky the first time and had recovered from their wounds. Would they be so lucky a second time? There was no point in trying to talk them out of it. She and James had tried a number of times with no success.

"Frank is nearly back to himself. We had a good chat with him. Would you believe that he managed to start another publishing house since he came home? He advised us not to go back to Spain, although he plans to return there himself. Apparently, soon after we left Spain, the Nationalists abandoned any attempt to take Madrid. He said that the International Brigade played an important part in defending Madrid and we should be proud of ourselves, but he has heard that the International Brigade is to be disbanded soon. The Republicans needed us in the beginning because they had a very inexperienced army, but they are better organised now."

"Probably we were good for propaganda purposes too," Max added.

"Do you mean that you might not go back?" Ellen asked, hardly daring to hope.

"Probably not, even though Frank is going back."

"Oh, that's great news! You must stay. Your father will be delighted. You can stay here as long as you like, Max. Joseph, you might be able to get your old job back. Harry would put in a word for you."

"I don't want my old job back, Mother. I haven't decided what I want to do."

"Thanks for your hospitality, Mrs Devereux, but I

think I will be heading back to New York quite soon. My parents miss me a lot."

"I'm sure they do. Well, I'm off to bed. Jeanne is asleep up there too, so be quiet when you're coming up to bed. Well, that was great news. God bless you!"

Joseph threw a log on the fire and sat back down opposite Max.

"Are you disappointed about not returning to Spain?" Max asked.

"Not really. To be truthful, I was feeling nervous about it. We were lucky once. We might not be so lucky the second time. But at least when we were there, we weren't worrying about the future all the time and wondering about what we should do with our lives. We only had to worry about staying alive."

"I know what you mean. It seemed like a great adventure when I started out and I even thought that I might write while I was there but of course I never got the time to do that. As you say, we mostly thought about where the next meal was coming from and just staying alive. I don't regret going though. We stood up for something we believe in and that's important. And, we met each other. I'm very grateful for that."

Joseph leaned over and took his hand. "And so am I. Are you serious about going back to New York soon?"

"Yes, I am. I can't sponge off your family for much longer. I hoped that I might persuade you to come with me. You want to write, and you need to find a publisher for your book. New York is a good place to do both those things."

"But how would I earn a living? Even if I got my book published, it would take a while to bring in money and then probably not enough to live on."

"It's easy to get work in New York. If you want to concentrate on your writing, you could work as a waiter at night and write by day. That's what I plan to do. Come with me. At least give it a try."

"I suppose I could ask Harry for a loan to pay my fare. He wasn't enthusiastic about me going to Spain, but he will see the point in this."

"So you will come? That's great! We can start making plans tomorrow."

The two young men embraced. Max kissed Joseph and looked into his eyes.

"It'll be a whole new life for us. I know it's not an easy decision to make, but I know it is the right one. It'll be easier for us to be together in New York. There are areas of New York City where a lot of creative people like writers, artists and actors live and they are not judgemental."

"I want to be with you. It's just that I hate the thought of leaving my parents and family. But I can't stay here either. I'll talk to Harry about it as soon as I can."

CHAPTER 29

Mary had been shocked when Kathleen left Jeanne and went to New York for two months. She reflected that if she had a beautiful little girl she would never leave her and certainly not for two long months.

The energetic little four-year-old was really too much for her mother to look after so she did her best to help. She loved Jeanne already but now she was becoming very attached to her.

Every day, she took the little girl for a walk in her pushchair or played with her. She prepared and fed her an evening meal while Liam ate his. She packed her belongings when it was time for her to go home with Liam. In spite of the hurt he had caused her, she found a new regard for Liam as she watched the loving way he looked after his child. When he invited her to go to the Zoo with Jeanne and him, her initial reaction had been to refuse. But when Joseph asked if he and Max could come too, she accepted. They had a lovely family day and her relationship with Liam became more relaxed. She saw him watching the other families with their children and wondered whether he was thinking the same thing as she was: that he and she could have had a normal family life just like them if Kathleen hadn't got in the way. She would never forgive Kathleen but began to understand that Liam was as much a victim as she was.

When the weather became very warm in July, they took Jeanne to the seaside at Bray. She loved the train and waved out of the window at all the stations along the way. They swam from the beach and held Jeanne's hands while she paddled, they sunbathed, walked the promenade with her and bought candy floss and ice-cream cones.

By the end of the day, the little girl was sleepy from all the fresh air and activity and Liam had to carry her from the train while Mary looked after the pushchair. They decided that it would be easier to go straight to Liam's flat rather than to her mother's.

Mary had never been in the flat before. It was small and looked even smaller because it was so untidy with children's toys everywhere. While Liam put Jeanne to bed, Mary tidied up and put things away.

He returned within a few minutes.

"She's fast asleep already – it was a long day for her. She had a great time. Thanks for coming with us, Mary."

"I enjoyed it, Liam. Now, I'd better get home. Mam and Dad feel lonely if there's no one coming home in the evening."

Liam had felt happier that day than he had in a long time. He watched from the window as Mary walked down the street and the feeling began to evaporate.

Joseph waited until the following Sunday before he approached Harry. He knew he would be at home with the family so he made his way there after dinner. Max wanted to come with him.

"No, Max. You stay here. Make some excuse why you didn't come with me. This won't be an easy meeting. Harry won't want me to go to New York. I don't know whether he realises what my relationship with you is but, one way or another, he won't want me to leave. Then I have to ask him for the loan of the fare. It's better if I see him alone."

When he got to the house, Julia answered the door.

"Joseph, it's good to see you! You just missed Harry and the boys. They're gone up to the Park to practise hurling. I was feeling a bit tired so Maeve and I are having a quiet afternoon. Come on in, they should be back in about half an hour."

"Thanks, Julia, but I think I'll walk up to meet them. I want to have a chat with Harry. I'll come back with them then."

He walked quickly to the place where he knew they usually went to practise football or hurling. He could see the three figures from a distance away. Michael had his mother's auburn hair and Harry was taller than average.

Harry saw him approaching.

"Joseph, this is a nice surprise! Boys, you two practise. I'm going to have a chat with Uncle Joseph."

The two boys waved to Joseph and returned to their game.

There was a bench nearby and they sat on it.

"Max didn't come with you?"

"No, I wanted to talk to you alone. We went to see Frank Ryan last week. He advised us not to go back to Spain. He has been told that they are going to disband the International Brigade. They don't need us anymore."

"You're not going back? That's great news. Mother and Father must be delighted. Are you going to look for another job? Maybe I could help? I know some –"

Joseph cut him off. "I am going to New York with Max. I told you that I want to travel and write. We can stay with Max's parents initially but then we will get jobs at night, maybe as waiters or in a bar, so that we can write in the daytime. I can also look for a publisher for my novel."

Harry looked stunned. "I had no idea that you were planning anything like this. Did Max persuade you? Is it because of him that you're going?"

"Yes, it is, in a way. I wouldn't have the courage to do it on my own. We get on very well together, we are both writers and we see the world in the same way."

"I did wonder about you two. I can see that you're very close, but I thought that it was because of your shared experiences in Spain. Now I see that there is more to it. You want to be with him, don't you?"

"Yes, we want to be together. I have never felt so strongly about anything before. Can you understand that?"

"I can't say that I do. But you are my brother and I want you to be happy. If Max makes you happy then I wish you both the best of luck. I can see why you are keen to go to New York. Life will be much easier for you if you are away from the prejudices of Ireland."

"Thanks, Harry. That means a lot to me. I didn't expect you to be so understanding."

"Well, maybe I have learned over the past couple of years that life is not as black-and-white as we were brought up to believe. Julia and I are having difficulties, some of them caused by the rules of Church and State and some of them caused by my selfishness and stupidity."

Joseph looked surprised. He had never heard his brother talk like this. "What kind of difficulties?"

"Well, since Julia lost the baby we haven't been able to have relations for fear of putting Julia's life at risk if she became pregnant. It put a great strain on our marriage. I escaped to my work and … and a friend."

The problem was becoming clear to Joseph. "I did notice that things seemed strained between you and Julia. To be honest, Julia looks quite miserable at times. Surely there is something you can do to make things better?"

"Yes, you are right. There are things I can do, and I am going to try. I love Julia very much and I'm afraid I just shut her out of my life. She deserves better. Now, that's enough about my problems."

"Harry, do you think Mother and Father suspect anything about Max and me?"

"No – they haven't a clue. You know what the Church and the State say about such relationships. According to them, you are condemned to hellfire. Our parents are traditional Catholics. It would break their hearts if they knew. As far as they are concerned, say you are going to New York to write. They will be glad that you have a good friend like Max for company. Now, we'd better get home. Julia will be wondering where we are. I'll call the boys."

Julia had tea waiting for them when they got home. Joseph observed how distant they were with each other. The boys chatted to Joseph and Maeve insisted on sitting on his knee while they ate. While Julia put the children to bed, Harry said that he would walk a part of the way with Joseph. It gave Joseph the opportunity to ask Harry about a loan of some money.

"How much do you need? I'd better give you enough to keep you for a few weeks as well as the fare."

"I couldn't –"

"No, I insist. You can pay me back whenever you can."

Joseph stopped in the street and hugged his brother. "Thanks, Harry. You have made things so much easier for me. I'm not looking forward to telling Mother and Father. They can't understand why I don't want a regular job and they certainly won't understand why I want to leave Ireland."

"I think you'll find that they understand more than you realise. Now, I'd better turn back. I'll see you next week."

Joseph and Max spent the next few days researching dates and fares for ships travelling to New York. Harry brought the money he was loaning to Joseph a few days later, some of it already converted into dollars. When Joseph opened the envelope and saw the unfamiliar currency, it brought home to him the finality of what he was about to do.

Max talked to him about his concerns and assured him that he was doing the right thing. They eventually selected a ship that left Cobh on the sixth of August and made their bookings.

Joseph was dreading telling his parents. They had always taken pride in the fact that all of their children were at home and had good jobs. Too many families had seen their children leave, one by one, for England or America, leaving their parents facing a lonely old age. At least, he thought, he was the only one leaving. Harry and Mary were happy in their careers and Kathleen would be home soon from New York. She was due to return two weeks after they left but he felt that if he delayed by two weeks to see her, he might not go at all.

He would wait until Sunday to tell his parents. Harry

and Julia and their children would be coming for dinner and Mary would be home as usual.

When Ellen and James left for eleven o'clock Mass in Aughrim Street, leaving Mary looking after the dinner, Joseph offered to help her prepare the vegetables. Max was still in bed.

It took some time before he worked up the courage to speak.

"Mary, I have something to tell you. Max and I are leaving for New York next week. I'm going to tell Mother and Father after dinner. It will be easier for them if you and Harry are here when I tell them."

Mary stopped what she was doing and turned to face him. She was visibly shocked.

"Leaving for New York! Next week! Joseph, how could you do this to them? It was bad enough when you went to Spain. They were ill from worrying about you. And now you're off again with a week's notice. You are very selfish!" She buried her face in the tea towel she was holding and began to sob.

"Mary, I didn't take this decision lightly. I just can't return to my job in the Civil Service or any job like it. I want to write but I wouldn't be able to make a living doing that here in Ireland. In New York, Max tells me that it is easy to get a job as a waiter or barman in the evenings so that I could write during the day. Maybe I'll return to Ireland if I establish myself as a writer. I hate telling Mother and Father but it's my life and I am going to live it the way I want."

This was a Joseph Mary had never seen before, a Joseph who was confident and knew what he wanted from life. In a way, she envied him.

"I'm sorry. It was just such a shock to hear that you're leaving. It will be even more of a shock for Mother and Father. Does Harry know about this?"

"Yes, he does. He would prefer that I didn't go but he understands my reasons."

"We'll miss you and you will be lonely for us, I'm sure, but at least you will have a friend in Max."

They could hear their parents returning from Mass.

"Do you know, Mass is getting shorter and shorter. They seem to rattle through the responses at a great pace," Ellen was saying as she took off her coat. "Oh, good, you have the dinner well under way, Mary. Harry and his family should be here soon."

"Yes, the vegetables are cooking and the chicken is nearly done. Joseph has been helping me. Would you like a cup of tea while the dinner is cooking?"

"Thanks, Mary. That would be lovely."

They had just finished setting the table when Harry and Julia arrived with the children. The children were in boisterous form but settled down when they all sat at the table.

Ellen looked around at her family. She loved Sundays when she often had them all for dinner. Harry and Joseph were teasing each other about incidents in their childhood, Julia was cutting up Maeve's chicken and the boys were chatting to Max about their football practice that morning. Mary, however, was very subdued.

Mary got up to serve dessert – it was jelly and custard which the children loved. As soon as they had gobbled it up, they were allowed to leave the table, while the adults finished eating.

Joseph suddenly spoke up. A few minutes before, he had been laughing with Harry. Now he looked nervous.

"Mother, Father, I …"

"What is it, son?" James had noticed Joseph's nervousness.

"I'm going to America, to New York." The bald sentence hung in the air like a raincloud.

Ellen turned white.

James looked at Max. Then he looked back at Joseph. "When, son?"

Joseph choked out the words. "Next week."

Ellen began to cry silently. Rivers of tears ran down her face but she made no attempt to wipe them away.

Mary moved to her mother's side and put her arm around her. "Mam, are you all right? Will I get you a glass of water?"

Ellen shook her head. She rose from the table, leaning on Mary's arm. She suddenly looked old. "It's just the shock. I'll lie down for a while. I'll be all right."

Mary helped her mother up the stairs. Joseph watched them go, his eyes filling with tears. He felt sick to his stomach. James was sitting with his head in his hands.

Harry moved to sit beside his father. "I know it's a shock, Father, but Joseph wants to be a writer, and this is the best option for him. He can stay with Max and his family for a while, so he won't be on his own."

James looked directly at him and Harry suddenly realised that his father understood the relationship between the two young men.

"Yes, I'm glad he won't be on his own, but we will miss him." He reached over to where Joseph was sitting and grasped his hand. "We will miss you, son. Now, I think I'll just see if your mother is all right."

He made his way to the stairs. Joseph watched and tried to blink back the tears which were blinding him. Max wanted to go to him, to comfort him but couldn't.

Mary came down the stairs. "She'll sleep for a while now, I think. Father is staying with her."

Julia had been warned by Harry but even so she felt exhausted by the heartbreak of it. I didn't take much these days to make her cry. She could imagine what it must be like for your children to emigrate. She hurried the children into their coats. Harry was having a word with Joseph and Max.

Julia gave Mary a hug. The children were asking where their grandparents were as she pushed them out the door and into the car.

Mary put some water on the range and began to collect the plates. She kept her back to Joseph and Max. There was a long silence only broken by the clatter of dishes.

Joseph turned to Max. "Let's go down to Ryan's for an hour or two, Max."

Mary waited until they left to let the tears come. She couldn't bear to see her parents so upset.

Harry drew up outside their house and said he had some urgent things that he had to do in the office. Julia looked resigned and said nothing. He watched them as they went inside and then he started the car again.

Alice was surprised to see him when she answered the door. He never called on Sundays.

"Harry, what a nice surprise!

"Alice, there's something I have to tell you.

She studied his face. "Come inside and sit down."

He followed her into the parlour and they both sat down.

"What is it, Harry? Has something happened?

"In a way, yes, something has happened. I have faced the truth about what I am doing. I'm taking advantage of your loneliness and destroying my marriage. I'm not going to see you anymore, Alice, at least, not like this. I'm sorry if I hurt you. I love you … but not in the way I love Julia."

There was a long pause while Alice visibly composed herself. "I'm sorry to hear that, Harry. You mean a lot to me but I know your heart has always belonged to Julia. I hope we can remain friends, at least."

"Of course we will, Alice. We bump into each other a lot in the constituency office, anyway. I'm sorry, Alice. "

They both stood up and moved towards each other. They embraced. Harry kissed the top of her head.

"Goodbye, Alice."

He turned and moved quickly into the hall without seeing the tears running down her face.

Julia was in bed when he got home. The light was still on in the bedroom. She was sitting up, reading. She looked at his face when he came in.

"Harry, is there something wrong? Is it your mother?"

"No, love, there's nothing wrong – at least there was but I hope I can fix it."

He came over, sat on the side of the bed and took her hand.

"Julia, things have not been good between us since, since …"

"Since we lost the baby. Harry, you don't touch me anymore. It's been so long since you slept beside me. We hardly talk. The children are beginning to notice. What are we going to do?"

"That's what I want to talk to you about. We have decisions to make but we have to make them together. I love you, Julia. No matter what we decide, I will always love you."

The following week dragged by. Each member of the family tried to behave normally but the tension in the house rose with every day that brought their departure nearer. On their last evening, the whole family gathered to say goodbye. Mary had heard about "American wakes" but had never realised how close to a real wake they were. There was sadness and a forced jollity, optimism for a better life and the knowledge that an old life was ending. Anecdotes were told about the emigrants, provoking hysterical laughter. The evening eventually ended in tears and pleas not to leave.

Joseph promised that he would come home to Dublin as often as he could, that it was not like years ago when emigrants to America were never seen again by their families. The others simply nodded.

Joseph felt as though all the emotion had been wrung out of him, leaving him limp and dazed.

Eventually, all the tears and pleas were exhausted.

Max had looked on at the anguish of the family and had felt helpless. Joseph lay in bed that night, dry-eyed and sleepless. Max tried to comfort him but he was unresponsive.

His mother called them when it was time to get up. She was pale but composed and controlled and served breakfast as though it was an ordinary day. His father busied himself getting the fire going. Harry arrived to drive them to the railway station. He waited while they finished breakfast and then hurried them to the door.

Ellen and James didn't trust themselves to speak. They simply hugged their son and then Max. Joseph didn't look back as the car pulled away. He was trying to hold back tears and his breakfast which felt as though it would erupt into his mouth at any minute.

At the station, it was a normal workday. Harry parked and went on to the platform with them. He hugged Joseph for a long time.

"Take care of yourself, Joseph. I am going to miss you. Make a good life for yourself in New York." He turned to Max and embraced him. "Max, look after him."

CHAPTER 30

All too soon it was the last week of the play. The cast members started making preparations for returning home, going to Macy's to buy small gifts and visiting their favourite places for the last time. Kay found some beautiful clothes for Jeanne and a small, lifelike doll. She bought a book of American short stories for Liam, a silk scarf for her mother and some sweet-smelling American plug tobacco for her father. As she wrapped and packed these items, she thought about her life in Ireland. Would she have to be content with small parts or even return to the wardrobe department when she got back? She had been happy there but that was before she tasted the heady cocktail of success on the New York stage. She thought about their small, cramped flat and Liam and his expectations of her. She wished that she could talk to her mother. Jeanne filled her thoughts, her sweet baby scent and her gurgling laugh. She wondered whether her daughter missed her or if she even remembered her. She tried to imagine how the little girl might have changed in the two months she had been away. Sometimes she couldn't bring Jeanne's face into focus and that terrified her.

Liam and her mother had written frequently and kept her up to date on everything about Jeanne. Ellen wrote about Mary and how good she was with Jeanne. She took her out for walks frequently and they had been for a visit to the Zoo with Joseph and Max and Liam. Kay was surprised at that. Mary was obviously more forgiving than she herself would be in similar circumstances. They all seemed to be getting on very well without her.

Her own letters home were less frequent. She had never liked writing letters. She wrote to her mother and asked her to share her news with the rest of the family. She wrote to Liam a couple of times but found it difficult and awkward. What could she write to him about? How she loved New York and had been escorted around the sights by Marco? How she revelled in the feeling she got at the final curtain every night, when the audience applauded and even gave her several curtain calls? It was an intoxicating feeling and she felt more at home on the stage than anywhere else. In the circumstances, Liam wouldn't be interested in that.

The final night of the play was very emotional. Some members of the audience had come a second time to see it. New friends that they had made were also in the audience and the applause at the end was rapturous. Kay could not believe that it was her last performance in New York. She felt the tears running down her face as she bowed and smiled. Finally, the curtain came down and the exhausted cast went backstage to change.

Kay was taking off her make-up when Marco knocked and came into the dressing room she shared with Claire. He congratulated them and asked if they were going to the bar with the other members of the cast.

"Of course we are, Marco!" said Claire. "We're tired but delighted with the response tonight. I'm excited as well at the prospect of going home. I feel like a party." She was packing up her costume.

"You go ahead, Claire. I'll follow you to the bar."

As Claire left Kay wiped the last of the cold cream from her face and looked at Marco in the mirror.

"I wasn't going to go tonight," she said. "I'm exhausted and I have to finish packing. Claire and the others are delighted to be going home but I'm not. Of course, I want to see Jeanne but the idea of going back to my old life terrifies me. I love New York. I love the buzz of the city and the wonderful places to go. I can see the opportunities and the possibilities here. I hate leaving all that behind me."

"OK. We could go to the bar and meet the others for just one drink. Then, if you like, we can have a quiet drink somewhere ourselves and I'll drop you home in a cab. What do you say?"

"That sounds good. I'll be ready in a minute."

When they got to the bar, the others had already broken up into small groups. Kay went around some of the groups and was greeted by kisses and hugs. She returned to Marco.

"They won't miss us at all. Let's leave now."

Marco knew a small Italian restaurant which was not very far away. He said he was hungry, and Kay realised that she was too. She hadn't eaten all day. They ordered a bottle of Chianti and studied the menu.

"I'm going to have Veal Saltimbocca," Kay said. "It will be a long time until I taste it again."

"I'll have Osso Buco. Can you not get veal in Ireland?"

"No, not much. The meat is very good there but it tends to be cooked very plainly, not with sauces like Italians do it."

They ordered and then chatted about the evening.

When they finished their main course, Marco ordered dessert.

"Tiramisu for me. How about you, Kay?

"Nothing, thanks. I'll just have a coffee."

"Tomorrow is your last Sunday here. I'd love to take you somewhere special."

"I'll see how I'm feeling in the morning. I'm exhausted at the moment but I suppose I could do with something to take my mind off things."

Marco paid the bill and they left. It was a beautiful warm night. Couples sauntered by, enjoying the summer evening.

Marco tucked Kay's arm under his. "Let's have a walk. I need to walk off that Osso Buco."

They chatted easily as they walked. They passed a row of brownstone houses and Marco paused.

"That's where I live. Want to come in for a few minutes?"

Kay thought for a minute. "OK, but not for long. I still have to do the rest of my packing and I'll be out with you tomorrow."

They climbed to the third floor and Marco showed her around. Kay was impressed. The apartment was small but well planned with a good-sized living-room-cum-kitchen, two small bedrooms and a bathroom.

"I've lived here for four years. My friend Bill shares with me. He is going to keep on the apartment when I go to Hollywood and look for another person to share with. Bill is away at the moment, visiting his folks in Wisconsin.

Now, can I get you a drink? How about wine? Or would you like a beer? That's all I have to offer."

Kay removed her jacket and sat down on the sofa. "A glass of wine would be lovely."

Marco bustled around, getting glasses and opening the bottle. He put two glasses of wine on the small coffee table and sat down beside her.

"I'm glad you are coming out with me tomorrow, Kay. I want to show you Central Park. It's the heart of New York. They have done a lot of work on it over the last few years and it is really lovely with beautiful trees and shrubs and great walks. My favourite time there is the Fall, when the leaves are turning but summer is good there too."

"I'm glad I am going to be with you tomorrow, my last day. I'm going to miss you."

He turned towards her. "Y'know, I'm really going to miss you too."

He leaned forward and kissed her, gently at first but when she responded his kiss became hungry.

"Marco, what are we doing?" She pulled away.

"You don't want it?"

"Yes, I do, but it is only going to be heartache for both of us. It's time for me to go."

"I'm sorry, Kay. I didn't plan to do that. I don't want to ruin our last night. Have your wine and we will just talk."

"All right, but I really will have to go soon. Tell me some more about Central Park. "

Later, they walked part of the way and then got a cab to her boarding house.

"I'll see you in the morning at about ten o'clock," he said. "Thanks for a lovely evening."

She found it difficult to sleep that night. Images from her time in New York kept flashing through her mind: the musty smell of the theatre during rehearsals, the first night and the rapturous applause, the visit to Coney Island, climbing the steps in the Statue of Liberty hand-in-hand with Marco, drinking coffee at a sidewalk café and watching the passing parade of fashionable New Yorkers, the last night at the theatre and the emotion she had felt at the audience response. His kiss.

She tried to banish these images by conjuring up images from home: her parents sitting chatting by the fireside, Jeanne holding up her arms to be lifted, her friends at the Gate Theatre, Jeanne red-faced, crying and teething, her job in the wardrobe department. In the end the images became a nightmare jumble from which she kept waking.

The next morning when she looked in the mirror, she was pale-faced with black circles under her eyes. It was a good thing that she knew how to use make-up.

Marco arrived. He had brought a picnic from a deli with him and also a bottle of Italian wine.

The weather was warm and sunny. They set off for Central Park and joined the throngs that had the same idea. The Park was beautiful with an amazing variety of trees, some of them already delicately touched with autumn colours, colourful shrubs and smooth green lawns. It reminded her of the Phoenix Park – and her dates with Liam when they secretly met there.

She tried to concentrate on what Marco was saying about the history of Central Park.

"Y'know, this park was constructed in the mid-nineteenth-century but it was allowed to fall into disrepair. One guy is responsible for restoring the Park and making it even better than before and that is Robert Moses. He and Mayor La Guardia cleaned it up in a single year, between '34 and '35. There used to be sheep grazing over there on Sheep Meadow and there was a shantytown on what is now the Great Lawn. He also had walls and bridges repaired and playgrounds, ball fields and handball courts constructed. That's why there are so many people using it now. It's a great amenity for the city."

Marco was very proud of his city.

"Yes, it is lovely. Let's have a look at one of the ball games. I've never seen a baseball game or an American football game."

There was a football game in progress and they watched it for a while. Kay hadn't an idea what it was all about but she pretended to enjoy it and was amused at Marco's shouts at the players. She tried to explain to him about the rules of Gaelic football which her brothers had played but Marco didn't understand her explanation at all.

All around, families were sitting on rugs on the grass and enjoying their picnics.

"Let's go to somewhere quieter for our picnic," Marco said. "I know a place not too far away."

They crossed a beautiful low bridge made of granite, which reminded Kay of Dublin. So many buildings in Dublin featured granite – even her mother's house had windowsills and doorsteps made of granite.

Their picnic spot was under a huge tree.

"Oh, it's a blue tree!" Kay looked up into the branches.

"Yes, it's a Colorado Blue Spruce. You often see small ones used as Christmas trees."

Marco opened his bag and produced a rug, wrapped sandwiches, two small glasses and the bottle of wine.

"They're baloney sandwiches. I hope you like them."

Kay bit into a sandwich. "Yes, I do. Thanks for bringing the picnic."

As they ate and drank Kay became lost in her thoughts.

"A penny for them!"

"What? Oh sorry, I was just thinking about tomorrow. It seems to have come so fast. Let's walk a little more. I want to see Park Avenue. Isn't that where all the wealthy people live?"

They set off and as they walked Kay stumbled and Marco put his arm around her. She leaned into him and they stopped.

Marco gazed into her eyes. "Kay, I don't want you to go. I don't think you want to go either. Come to Hollywood with me. I love you, Kay. We're good together."

"I have to go, Marco. I can't leave my daughter."

"I understand. Well, I had to ask. I won't mention it again. Let's start walking back to the subway. I'll see you home. Do you want me to come and see you off in the morning?"

"Yes, I do. Thanks, Marco, for everything."

Claire was asleep when she got in.

That night, Kay hardly slept. She imagined returning home and holding Jeanne in her arms. She couldn't see Jeanne's face clearly. Each time she brought it into focus, it blurred and faded. She thought about Liam and what their relationship had become. She thought about her parents. Tossing and turning, she tried to imagine what the coming years would be like. Then she had a nightmare. She was trying to find Jeanne in a big house with a labyrinth of rooms. Each room she went into was empty but she could hear Jeanne crying. She woke up, sweating and crying. By dawn, she was exhausted. She got up quietly and did the rest of her packing. Then she left the house. She had to wait for a while before a cruising cab came by.

Marco was surprised to see her so early. He was rumpled with sleep and wearing a bathrobe. "It's only five o'clock!"

She walked into the hall and turned to face him, her face white and tearstained.

"Marco, I'm not going back to Ireland. I want to be with you, either here in New York or I will go to Hollywood with you. I can't go home. I'm heartbroken that I won't be with Jeanne but I think she is better off without me. I can't live with Liam anymore because I don't love him and he doesn't love me. He wants me to be someone that I'm not. I can't just leave him and take Jeanne. He loves her and will never give her up. I've thought about it all night and I've made up my mind. It's breaking my heart but I can't go."

Marco took her into his arms and soothed her like a child. She began to sob, long racking sobs that shook her body. When they had subsided a little, he led her up the stairs and sat beside her on the sofa.

"Here, let me wipe your tears. I want to be with you too. Just be sure that you are making the right decision."

"I don't know about it being the right decision but it is the only one that I can make. If I went back, after this taste of freedom and success, I would be more depressed than ever and more difficult to live with. It would be bound to affect Jeanne. All I've done for Liam is make his life miserable. My parents will miss me but they have other children who love them."

"Have you told Claire or any of the others?"

"No. I'll go back and see Claire and try to explain to her. She can tell the others. I'll write to Liam and my parents."

"OK. I'll come with you. Now, I'm going to make you some eggs and coffee before we go."

Claire woke up when Kay entered the room.

"Kay! I woke up earlier and there was no sign of you. What's wrong?"

"Claire, I have something to tell you."

Claire sat up. "What is it?"

"I am not going home."

"Not coming home? What do you mean?"

"I mean I'm not returning to Ireland. I've decided to stay here."

"*What?* But, your daughter, your husband! You can't mean it!"

"I've made up my mind. I haven't been happy and I've been making my husband and my family miserable. They are better off without me."

"You will break your parents' hearts! How could you do that to them? How could you leave your daughter? You are being very selfish. Is this all about Marco?"

"No, it's all about me. Marco understands me and has been there for me, but it is about what I want."

"I don't believe it. This is like something in a bad melodrama. Kay, we're friends. You can talk to me. Please talk to me. You are making a terrible mistake."

"Will you tell the others? I can't face telling them."

"But you might change your mind. There are still a few

hours before we leave. Think about it again. I won't say anything to the others until we are leaving."

"Thanks, Claire, but I won't change my mind. There's something else you can do for me. I have some presents for my family. Will you deliver them for me when you get to Dublin?"

Claire was crying now and looking at her in disbelief. Kay took the wrapped presents from her suitcase and left them on the bed.

"Take care of yourself. I'll write to you."

She embraced Claire, took her suitcase and moved quickly to the door and down the stairs. Marco was waiting in the hall. They walked back to his place in silence.

The ship was departing at ten o'clock. Kay sat and watched the clock for the next few hours. At ten o'clock, she turned away, silent tears running down her face.

Marco left her to her private grief for a while. Then he came and took her hand.

"Kay, I promise I'll do my best to make you happy. You and I are two of a kind so I think I understand you. When you're ready we'll talk about our plans for the future. Until then, we'll stay here and I'll look after you."

Kay took his other hand. "Thanks, Marco. You are very good to me. I just need a bit of time."

Marco held her close to him. "Just remember that I love you."

CHAPTER 31

Kathleen was due home in the middle of August.

One morning in the second week of August, Mary was in the kitchen when she heard the post being delivered. She went into the hall to retrieve the letters. Her parents had gone to ten o'clock Mass so she sorted through the post. There were a couple of bills and a letter from America. It was addressed to her mother. She recognised Kathleen's writing. She turned over the airmail envelope. There was no return address. Kathleen was due home in a few days so they wouldn't have expected a letter. Why then had she written? Her letters had been few enough during the previous seven weeks. She stared at the envelope for a few minutes, then some premonition caused her to open the letter. It was brief.

New York
7th August 1932

Dear Mam and Dad,
This is a very difficult letter for me to write. I am
not coming back to Dublin. It was a hard decision

to make but I think it is the best one for everyone. I have done nothing but cause worry for you and Dad since I was young. I have made Liam miserable since I have been married to him. He is better off without me. I am sorry for the hurt I caused Mary. She deserves to be happy and I hope she will be, one day.

You will wonder how I can leave my beautiful daughter, Jeanne, like this. It seems cruel but it is the best thing I can do for her. I am too selfish to be a good mother although I love her with all my heart. I know that she will be well looked after by Liam and all the family and especially Dad and you.

I'm sorry for the heartbreak that I know this letter will cause you.

I will write again as soon as I am able and give you my new address. Don't worry about me. I have friends in New York who will look after me.

Your loving daughter,
Kathleen

Mary felt behind her for a chair and sat down heavily. This news would devastate her parents. And what would it do to Liam? How was he going to manage with school term starting in two weeks? Kathleen had always put herself first, but this was unbelievable. How could she abandon Jeanne?

She looked at the clock. Her parents would be home soon. What should she do? She needed support. With Joseph gone, there was only Harry. She could run down to Kingsbridge station where there was a phone. Harry would be in the Dáil chambers and she could get a message to him.

* * *

Harry was surprised when an usher came to find him. He was in a committee meeting so he excused himself and went to the phone. Mary had left a number for him. She immediately picked up. Her voice sounded agitated.

"Harry, please come as soon as you can to Mam and Dad's house. A letter just came from Kathleen. She's not coming home."

"What do you mean, 'Not coming home'? Is she staying longer than planned?"

"No, Harry. She's not coming home at all. Mam and Dad haven't seen the letter yet. I think you should be here when I give it to them. Coming so soon after Joseph leaving, I think it will have a terrible effect on them."

"I don't believe it. How could she do this to them? What about Jeanne? Is she going to leave her here? Does Liam know yet?"

"I don't know. I imagine he must have got a letter at the same time. In any case, he and Jeanne are due to come here this afternoon."

"I'll just explain to my colleagues that it is a family emergency and I'll come straight away. Don't say anything to them until then."

Mary hurried home but her parents had just arrived when she got there. They were surprised when she came in the door after them.

"I had to run down to May's shop for something I needed. I'll be down in a minute."

Upstairs she got her breath back and sat on the bed. She could hear her parents discussing the electricity bill.

"It's so expensive. We were quite happy with the gas. I

don't know why we had to change to electricity. It's a much harder light too. It gives me a headache when it's on."

"Ellen, we have to move with the times. I like the electric light. Me oul' eyes aren't as good as they used to be and I can read better with the electric light. And the electric fire is great. What would we do without it?"

The exchange sounded so ordinary and everyday. They were just getting back to normal life after Joseph's departure and now this!

Half an hour later, Harry arrived in his car. His parents were surprised to see him mid-week. He usually only came on a Sunday with Julia and the children.

"Harry! We didn't expect to see you today," said James.

Ellen's expression changed to one of anxiety. "Is there something wrong?"

Mary handed the letter to Harry. He read it quickly and nodded to Mary.

"What is that you're reading?" said Ellen.

"Mother, there is something we have to tell you," Harry said.

"Oh my God, is it Joseph? Has something happened to him?"

"No, Mam. Joseph is fine," said Mary. "A letter came for you this morning and I opened it. It's from Kathleen."

"Kathleen? But she's on her way home now. She'll be here on Saturday." James moved to stand beside his wife.

"That's just it, Dad. She's not coming home. That's what the letter says."

"Not coming home? Until when?" Ellen asked.

"Not coming home at all," Harry said.

There was silence in the room only broken by the ticking of the clock.

"But she has to!" Ellen said in great agitation "What about Jeanne?

"She'd never leave her little girl." James turned to look pleadingly at Mary. "There must be some mistake."

Ellen put her hand out. "Give me the letter, Harry." She took the letter and read it twice. "There's no mistake, James. She's not coming home." Her voice broke. "It's all my fault. I shouldn't have listened to her. I shouldn't have agreed to look after Jeanne. But I thought that the break would do her good – she had been so depressed and I wanted to help her . . ."

Her voice faded on the last few words and she lurched forward. Harry moved quickly and caught her before she hit the ground. He held her for a minute and then lowered her into an armchair.

"Quick, Mary. Get some water. It's all right, I think she just fainted. Mother, can you hear me?"

Ellen opened her eyes. "What happened? I don't …"

James was leaning over her. He held her hand. "It's all right, love."

Mary held a cup to her lips. "Here, Mam, drink some water. You got a shock and fainted." She turned to Harry. "We'd better send for the doctor. It's probably just the shock but it's better to be sure."

"All right. I'll go and get him. Should we help her up to bed?"

"No, she's better off by the fire. I'll just put a blanket around her."

While Harry was gone Mary got a blanket from upstairs and tucked it around her mother. She could see the colour returning to her face.

"Would you like a cup of tea, Mam? What about you, Dad?"

They both nodded. James looked as pale as his wife. He was still standing there, holding her hand.

"Dad, I'll move the armchair over beside Mam for you. It will be more comfortable."

James waited wordlessly while she moved the chair, then sat down and resumed his grasp of Ellen's hand.

Mary looked over at them while she made the tea. They looked old and broken in a way she had never seen before. Her heart bled for them but she managed to hold back the tears.

Half an hour later, Harry arrived back. The doctor arrived soon after. Doctor O'Brien was their family doctor and had known them all for years. He immediately went to Ellen and looked into her face.

"Mrs Devereux, I am just going to take your blood pressure and listen to your heart. Harry told me that you had some bad news so that is probably what caused you to faint. But we have to be careful and make sure that is the case."

"I'm grand, doctor. I just got a shock. I'll be fine. There was no need to drag you all the way here." She looked reproachfully at Harry.

The doctor got out his stethoscope. "Harry did the right thing. Now, I'll just listen to your heart."

He listened for a few minutes.

"It's a bit fast but that's probably from the stress. Now I'll test your blood pressure." He put his fingers on the pulse-point on her wrist and kept them there while he looked at his watch for a few minutes. He paused. "The pressure is a bit high. We'll keep an eye on it. In the meantime, Mrs Devereux, you need to take it easy. Stay in bed for a few days and try not to worry. I know that's easier said than done."

252

"Thanks, doctor. I feel a bit better now."

Harry saw the doctor to the door and out to his car.

"Will she be all right, doctor? That's the second bad shock that she has had in a couple of weeks."

"Your mother is a resilient woman, Harry. She has a tendency to high blood pressure but we will keep an eye on that."

Harry decided to stay with his parents for the rest of the day. The arrival of Liam and Jeanne would be just as stressful as the morning's revelations, so he wanted to be there to support his parents and to help Mary. None of them felt like eating their usual dinner so Mary simply heated up some soup and they all made an effort to eat it.

Two o'clock came and went and there was no sign of Liam.

By four o'clock Harry had decided to go to Liam's flat when there was a knock on the door.

Liam stood outside with Jeanne in her pushchair. He was grey and drawn. He looked from one of their faces to another.

"I see that you got a letter too."

Jeanne was clamouring to get out of her pushchair. She held her arms up to Harry, who lifted her up and kissed her.

"*Uncle Harry, Uncle Harry!*"

Mary took her from him and brought her inside. "Do you want to come upstairs and play with your dollies?"

Once his daughter was out of the room, Liam collapsed into a chair with his face in his hands. He cried silently for a while and they all waited, not knowing what to say to him. At last he lifted his head, mopped his tears with his handkerchief and blew his nose.

"I thought I had cried myself out his morning. What

am I going to do? I can't believe that Kathleen could do this to us. How could she leave her child? How am I going to manage? I have to go back to school in two weeks. Do you think she really means it? Maybe she'll change her mind in a week or so." He sobbed again. "This is all my fault. I should never have agreed to her going to New York."

"I don't think she'll change her mind," said Harry. "Anyway, she has no ticket now and would have to borrow the money to get home. One way or another, you will have to make plans to manage on your own for the foreseeable future." Harry was being practical and was speaking from experience. He knew his sister.

Ellen spoke for the first time. "Liam, it's not your fault. Kathleen was always very headstrong. We all love Jeanne and we'll help to look after her. We'll just continue as we were before you got school holidays. You can bring Jeanne here every morning and collect her in the evening. James and I will be happy to look after her, won't we, James?"

James looked doubtfully at his wife. "Yes, of course, as long as you are able for it."

Nobody mentioned the doctor's visit.

"You are all so good. I haven't told my own parents yet. They won't be very surprised. I'm afraid they never approved of Kathleen."

Mary came back down the stairs, carrying an armful of dolls, with Jeanne by the hand.

"I'll make tea now, Mam."

"I'd better go home," Harry said. "Liam, Julia and I will do whatever we can to help. I'll call in tomorrow evening to see how you all are. Mother, look after yourself." He embraced her and touched his father on the shoulder.

"God bless, Harry. See you tomorrow."

There was silence for a while after he left, broken only by the clatter of crockery and Jeanne's conversation with her dolls.

They all sat around the table when Mary asked them to.

"I'll give Jeanne her tea when we're finished. She doesn't seem interested at the moment."

Ellen drank her tea but ate nothing.

Mary turned to Liam. "Liam, you two had better stay here tonight. You're exhausted and Jeanne is a bit unsettled. Eat something and go to bed. We can make plans in the morning."

"Yes, you're right. I haven't the energy to walk home and put Jeanne to bed. You are all very good. I'm not hungry so, if you don't mind, I'll head off to bed."

Jeanne looked after him as he left but continued to play with her dolls.

"Do your dollies want their tea?" Mary said to her. "You can feed them while I feed you, wouldn't that be a good idea?"

Jeanne got her little tea set and put it on the table. Mary lifted her up and sat beside her. The little girl allowed herself to be fed while she offered spoonfuls to her dolls. She looked thoughtful.

"I want Mammy Kathleen to play tea parties with me. Where's Mammy?"

The three adults were startled. Jeanne had taken in more of the conversation than the adults realised.

Mary said, "Mammy's in the theatre."

Jeanne nodded and returned to her game.

CHAPTER 32

While Liam and Mary were still on holiday from school, they took care of Jeanne together in Liam's flat. Ellen wanted to help but her blood pressure was still high so the doctor told her that she must continue to rest. She did so reluctantly. She was worried – not just about Jeanne, but also about the growing relationship between Mary and Liam. She saw how in tune with each other they were, how relaxed they were together, the way they confided in each other and the way they looked at each other.

Mary went to Liam's every afternoon and they either took Jeanne out for a walk or played with her in the flat. Later, Mary gave her something to eat and got her ready for bed while Liam cooked a meal for them both. When she came home, usually about nine o'clock, there was a glow about her which had been missing for a long time. Ellen was glad that the school holidays were coming to an end.

Liam was still looking for someone to look after Jeanne while he returned to work. He rejected a number of possible people until Julia visited one day and made a suggestion.

"You know, Liam, Lily Dempsey has been helping me with the children since I was ill. You met her, Mary, didn't you? She's wonderful with them. I'm better now and all three are at school so I don't need her help as much. If she came to you to look after Jeanne, she could still do a bit of cleaning for me and babysit in the evenings when I have to accompany Harry somewhere. I spoke to her about it and she is happy to do that. All her own children are grown up and have left home now."

Mary had met Lily in Julia's house and had seen how good she was with the children. "That's a great idea, Julia, isn't it, Liam? Won't you miss her, though, Julia?"

"I will, a bit. But Liam's need is greater."

"Thanks, Julia. She sounds ideal. Can you give me an idea of how much she expects to be paid?" Liam was always worried about money these days.

"We will still be asking her to babysit and to do some cleaning for us so we will share the expense. We can talk about it later."

Mary suspected that Harry and Julia had discussed this and were going to subsidise the arrangement. Liam was insistent so Julia named a weekly sum that he could just about afford. He insisted that Lily continue to meet their Maeve from school as she always did which meant she would have to leave his flat at two o'clock. Mary immediately offered to be at the flat at two and wait until Liam came home. Lily then came to the flat one day to meet Jeanne who took to her immediately.

Now that arrangements had been made for the care of Jeanne, Liam and Mary could concentrate on their own preparations for the new term.

On the first day of term, Mary went to Liam's flat before school to ensure that everything was left ready for Lily.

Jeanne cried when Mary and Liam were leaving and it was hard to leave the crying little girl but they had to hurry or they would be late. They arrived together just as the bell was ringing for the start of class. There were some curious looks as they hurried through the door. Mary was looking forward to meeting her new group of High Babies but she was also a bit nervous – it was only her second year teaching. Liam was anxious about his sixth class because he'd had little time to prepare.

At breaktime, Mary was on duty in the playground with another young teacher called Carmel. The children were noisy and excited on their first day and the two young women were kept busy. When there was a quiet lull, Carmel came over to Mary.

"Did you hear about Liam O'Broin's wife?" she asked. "She went to America to act, if you don't mind, and didn't come back. Isn't it awful?"

So the news had got around. People loved a good gossip. Mary avoided answering by rushing to the rescue of a boy who had fallen. Carmel obviously didn't realise that she was Liam's sister-in-law. Then the bell for the end of break went and she walked back to the school in the midst of a group of pupils.

At lunchtime, she saw Liam in the staffroom. Some of the other teachers were giving him pitying looks. One or two spoke briefly to him. He looked extremely uncomfortable.

Soon, it was the end of Mary's working day and she hurried to the flat so that Lily could leave. All was quiet when she got there. Jeanne was playing school with her dolls, Lily sitting beside her and the flat was clean and tidy.

Jeanne greeted her with delight but then began to be very demanding. The poor child was upset by the change in routine.

Liam arrived home, looking drained. Jeanne climbed on his lap as soon as he sat down but was happy to sleepily cuddle into him without making demands for attention.

"How did today go?" Mary asked.

"It went all right. My new pupils are a nice group. The principal called me to his office at breaktime. He had heard the gossip, of course. He wanted to find out exactly what my situation is and assure me that he understood my difficulty but that I could not be absent from school. He reminded me that there are no spare teachers in a primary school and the children would be without a teacher if I missed any days. I explained that the family was helping me and that we had a paid babysitter but he still looked worried. Some members of the staff were giving me funny looks when I came back to the staffroom."

"Oh, don't let those things worry you. They just love a good gossip. It will be a ten-day wonder but then they'll forget all about it and life will return to normal."

"Will it? I hope so. Anyway, you'd better get home. We've taken up enough of your time. You needn't come here again in the morning. I'll make sure that everything is ready for Lily."

"I'll be off home so. I'm a bit worried about Mam. She's not really back to herself yet. I'll see you tomorrow."

"Thanks, Mary. I don't know what I would have done without you."

The house was very quiet when Mary got home – usually the radio was playing. James was sitting at the fire, reading the paper.

"Where's Mam?"

"She's upstairs having a lie-down. She said she would get up when you got home. Don't worry, she's fine, just a bit tired."

Ellen heard the voices and came down.

"How did it go? Is Jeanne all right?"

"Yes, of course, Mam. Lily was great. She even tidied the flat and washed out a few of Jeanne's clothes."

"Oh, thank God. I wish I could have helped."

"You've helped a lot already. Sit down now and I'll get some tea for us. Then I'll tell you all about my new class."

By the end of the first week, they had all fallen into a regular routine and it became easier. Mary only went to the flat after school and stayed for an hour or two. Jeanne settled down with Lily and seemed quite happy.

On Sunday Liam and Jeanne came to see Ellen and stayed for dinner. They had just finished eating when there was a knock on the door.

Mary answered it.

The young woman on the doorstep didn't look familiar.

"Hello. I'm Claire, Kay's friend." She held out her hand.

For a minute, Mary didn't make the connection. "Oh, you mean Kathleen! I'm Mary. Come in."

She ushered Claire inside and introduced her to the rest of the family.

"Jeanne has gone upstairs to check on her dolls – they were having a nap while we ate," she told Claire.

Ellen grasped her hand. "Oh Claire, I remember you from the play. Have you heard from her? We had a letter, but she didn't tell us very much. How is she?"

"I'm sorry, I should have called sooner. I just didn't

know what to say. I haven't heard from Kay since I left her in New York, but I'm sure she's getting along fine. She has friends there."

"Yes, she mentioned friends but no one in particular."

During this exchange, Liam was silent. He moved forward now and spoke to Claire.

"I'm Liam, her husband. Do you have you an address for her?"

Claire looked uncomfortable. She had presumed that Liam was one of Kay's brothers. "No, I'm sorry. We were staying in a boarding house with all the cast but she left it at the same time as the rest of us. Maybe if you sent a letter to the manager of the theatre, he might have a forwarding address. I can give you his name and the address of the theatre."

"That would be helpful. I'll get a pen and paper."

They were all still standing awkwardly around the kitchen.

"Sit down, Claire," said Ellen, "and I'll make you a cup of tea."

"No, no – thank you, Mrs Devereux but I really have to go. I just wanted to say hello and deliver these presents from Kay to you." She handed a large paper shopping bag with '*Macy's*' on it to Mary.

Mary looked in at the gaily wrapped presents. "We'll open them later with Jeanne. Thank you."

Claire wrote the address of the theatre on the page which Liam had given her.

"If I hear anything else that is useful, I'll let you know. I'm really sorry about what happened. I tried to persuade her to come home but she wouldn't listen to me."

She went quickly to the door, afraid that she was going

to dissolve into tears. Mary followed her into the street, out of earshot of her parents.

"Claire, is there anything else you can tell me about Kathleen? We are worried sick about her. Jeanne still asks for her and gets upset. It is very difficult for Liam to manage on his own. Do you think there is any chance that she might come back?"

"She didn't say very much to me. I had no idea that she was planning to stay until that morning when we were leaving. I knew that she loved New York and was always talking about the great opportunities for actors. She even talked about Hollywood and going there some day. I thought it was all wishful thinking. I never thought that she would leave her little girl, whatever about her husband. She didn't say much about him, but she talked a lot about Jeanne."

"Who are the friends that you mentioned?"

"Well, there was one in particular, Marco Mercadante. I didn't want to mention him in front of her husband and your parents. He was the manager of the theatre where we were performing. He was also an actor and a director and a very nice guy. I knew they became close and he showed her around New York a bit but it didn't seem like a romance. I'm sure Kay will get in touch when she is ready. I know she was devastated when she told me her decision. Now, I have to go."

The room was very quiet when Mary went back inside. Liam was still looking at the piece of paper with the address that Claire had given him.

Then Jeanne came down and spotted the Macy's bag immediately. She began to pull out the parcels. Mary handed her one with her name written on it. Jeanne tore the paper off. It was the doll. She was entranced by it. It

262

could open and close its eyes when she moved it. She held it up to show Mary.

"Look, my new dolly!"

"She's lovely. She's a present from Mammy."

The little girl looked puzzled and then her face crumpled. "Where's Mammy Kathleen? I want Mammy Kathleen!" She began to wail.

Liam took her in his arms. "It's all right, sweetheart. Daddy is here. Show me your new dolly."

"*I don't want a dolly! I want Mammy Kathleen!*" The wailing got louder.

Ellen took the child from Liam. "Come here, Jeanne. Do you want to sing with me? What song would you like to sing?"

Jeanne continued to sob quietly but joined in on the chorus when Ellen sang "Baa, baa, black sheep".

She cuddled in to her grandmother and the sobs gradually subsided. In a few minutes she was asleep.

"I'll take her, Mam, and put her up to bed," said Mary. "She can stay here tonight and I will take her to Liam's tomorrow."

"Thank you, Mary," said Liam. "I'll write a letter tonight to Kathleen at this address and try to persuade her to come home. Hopefully, it will get to her. We'd better put that doll away somewhere – it's upset Jeanne. I'll say goodnight then." He raised a hand in farewell to Ellen and James. "See you tomorrow, Mary."

Ellen saw the warm smile they exchanged and worried.

CHAPTER 33

After the first week of term, everything became easier for Mary and Liam. They found more time to prepare and mark schoolwork and they spent less time together.

Ellen had spoken to Mary about the time she spent in Liam's flat.

"I know that you love Jeanne and you want to help Liam, but I'm worried that you're getting too close to him. He relies on you too much. He's a married man and no good can come of it. Just be careful. People are always ready to gossip."

Mary knew that her mother meant well and was only concerned for her happiness. It was true that she had become close to Liam but it was Jeanne who had brought them close. Watching Liam with his daughter had made Mary realise what a good man he was. However, she listened to her mother's advice and spent less time, particularly at weekends, with him. She arranged to meet friends from college and enjoyed a lively social life. She even had dates with a few young men from the group. It was a welcome relief from the stresses of teaching and the added stress of looking after Jeanne. Yet she missed her chats with Liam and the young men she went out with seemed young and shallow by comparison.

Christmas and the end of term were drawing near. They had a free day from school on the eighth of December and Mary went in to Henry Street for some early Christmas shopping with some of her friends. The city was buzzing because it was traditional for people from rural areas to come to Dublin for their Christmas shopping on that day. There were carol singers outside the GPO and the girls stopped to listen to them for a while. The Christmas lights had been turned on and sparkled in the crisp air. All the big stores had beautiful window displays, some of them depicting Santa's grotto. The dealers were shouting out their Christmas wares on Moore Street and the fruit and flower stalls made brilliant splashes of colour on the crowded street. There was a smell of fish from the whiting and cod displayed on the fish stalls and, in the butcher's shops, plump bronze turkeys were hanging upside down with their heads still on. Bunches of red-berried holly and smaller ones of mistletoe were piled high among every kind of Christmas decoration. Arnott's had a wonderful display of lights and Mary knew that their Santa was renowned as one of the best Santa visits in town. She said as much to her friends, some of whom were not Dubliners.

"Visiting Santa in Arnott's was one of the highlights of Christmas for me when I was a child. I remember going into the store and you had to queue in a sort of cave or grotto to see Santa. The light in the grotto was eerie and the sound was muffled but all along the way were brightly lit, life-size tableaus, depicting the story of some fairy tale or other. The story changed every year and it was magic.

At the end, Santa waited in his snowy cave and each child got to sit on his knee while they told him what they wanted for Christmas. Then he gave them a present. One year, I remember, Santa gave my brother Joseph a gun. When Joseph saw what it was, he gave it back to Santa and said that he didn't want it! Mam was very embarrassed. Eventually, Santa gave him a painting set which he accepted."

They all laughed and some of them told their own stories about visiting Santa. Mary half listened but she was thinking about Jeanne. She planned to take her to see Santa as soon as the term finished. Perhaps Liam would come with them.

As they made their way along Mary Street, a dealer was shouting "*Get the last of your Cheeky Charlies!*" and brandishing a funny little monkey puppet. Jeanne would love it. She bought one and decided to call in to see her on the way home. Then it was time to go to Bewley's for tea and a sticky bun before they said their goodbyes and went their separate ways.

The bus was packed and the air was thick with the stale smell of damp coats and mothballs mixed with cigarette smoke coming from upstairs. She had to stand all the way, trying to hold on to her parcels and not to fall into someone's lap.

She had just alighted from the bus when she spotted Liam walking briskly ahead of her, with Jeanne in her pushchair. He didn't seem at all embarrassed to be seen pushing a child. He was the only man she knew who would do it. Even Harry, who was very good with his children, would carry a child but she had never seen him push a pram or pushchair.

She hurried to catch up and called him.

"Liam, wait!"

He stopped and waited for her, smiling.

"I bought a little something for Jeanne and decided to call in. Hello, sweetheart! Have you a kiss for Auntie Mary?" She stooped to let Jeanne kiss her.

"I see that you've been shopping. I'm sure the town was packed today."

"Yes, it was but the atmosphere was great and it was real Christmassy weather, crisp and cold but bright and sunny. There were carol-singers outside the GPO. and another group outside Arnott's. Carols really get you in the Christmassy mood, don't they?"

When they got to the flat, Jeanne held up her arms to Mary to be lifted.

"I'll take off her coat, Liam. You put on the kettle. I'd love a cup of tea. I had one in Bewley's with the girls but it was so hot and crowded on the bus that I'm parched. "

She took Jeanne into the flat and gave her the little monkey. Jeanne squealed with delight. She had a storybook in which a monkey was the hero.

"It's Mali the monkey! I'll show him my book about him." She went off to find her book.

Liam put two cups of tea on the table. "Sorry, I've no biscuits left."

"That's all right. I'm not hungry, just thirsty."

She knew it was hard for Liam to pay the rent, as well as pay Lily and buy the groceries. His own parents and Ellen and James were good to him, but it only took one visit to the doctor for Jeanne or one unforeseen bill to mean that there was no money at all left at the end of the week.

"Will you stay and have tea with us? We haven't had a chat in a long time. It's only beans on toast but you're welcome to stay."

"Yes, that would be lovely. Mam won't be expecting me anyway for a few hours."

Mary toasted bread on the long toasting fork at the fire while Liam heated up the beans. Jeanne was too interested in her monkey and the storybook to eat much.

"I can't believe how much Jeanne has grown in the last few months – and she's even starting to read. Of course, she'll be five at Christmas. When she goes to school next September it will make everything easier for you. Will you send her to our school?"

"I suppose so. It would certainly be easier although I'm not sure if it is a good idea to be a pupil in your father's school."

"I think Jeanne will be able for anything – she's very independent."

They continued to chat about Jeanne and the future for a while. Liam made another cup of tea and then Mary read to Jeanne from her book about the monkey. When the little girl began to look sleepy, Mary got up to leave.

"I hope you'll come to Mam's for Christmas, Liam. We would love to have you and Jeanne there for Christmas Day."

She didn't add that she was dreading Christmas without Joseph and Kathleen. Her parents would feel so lonely. Jeanne would be a distraction.

"I'd like that too and Jeanne loves Granny and Grandad Devereux. We can go to my parents' on St Stephen's Day."

It had become very dark and cold when she left the house so she decided to get the bus for the few stops rather than walk. Then she met Carmel, the young teacher from her school, also heading for the bus stop.

"Oh, hello, Carmel! What are you doing around here?"

"I was visiting my aunt. She lives in this street. Where are you coming from?"

"I was in town, doing a bit of shopping and I stopped off to give Jeanne, Liam's daughter, a little present that I bought her."

"Ah, the poor man! Isn't it very sad for him the way his wife left him? I suppose you're a great help to him with the child." Carmel put her head on one side and screwed up her face into what was meant to be an expression of sympathy as she said this.

Mary didn't say anything. The bus drew up and the two young women got on. The bus was full. Carmel pushed her way down the bus and Mary took the opportunity to go upstairs. She didn't like Carmel and the insinuations in her tone.

When she got home there was good news, a letter from Joseph. Her parents were both elated and saddened by the letter.

"Joseph got a job in a small publishing house in New York. He said he is an editor. What does that mean? Is it a good job? Would it pay well?"

Ellen was full of questions. Mary read the letter.

"He says that the pay is all right and that he loves the job. Apparently, when he approached them with his novel, they asked him if he would be interested in a job as an editor. That's good isn't it? He must have impressed them with his novel."

"What exactly does an editor do?" James asked.

"Well, when someone sends in a novel or short story the editor checks the spelling and the way it is written to make sure it is ready to be published. He might also make some suggestions about the structure and the plot. It's a good job. It mightn't pay well because it's a small publishing house but he will get good experience there."

"Yes, that's what he said. Max is working with his parents in their café. They are looking for an apartment for the two of them. His parents seem to be very good to them, from what Joseph says."

Ellen had taken back the letter and was holding it to her breast. "Thank God that he's all right. I'm very thankful for that."

James nodded. Mary could see how much they both missed their son. And, of course, they missed Kathleen too. There had been no letter from her since the first one. It was going to be a lonesome Christmas.

CHAPTER 34

Mary was busy with her class for the next few weeks, rehearsing them for the end-of-year carol concert in the parish church in which the whole school would participate. The children were excited because they would be performing with the bigger pupils and parents could attend. At last, they were word perfect and they had their last run through before joining the other classes for a final rehearsal in the school hall. The Principal, Mr Murray, and the parish priest and manager of the school Father Mongey, entered the hall and took their places in the front row.

The fourth-form teacher, who was also the choirmaster, stood in front of the assembled children, raised his hands and gave the signal for the choir to begin. Mary could see the rapt faces of her own class as they sang and felt tears coming to her eyes – they looked so young and so happy. Some of the other teachers looked tearful too. Father Mongey was his usual sour self as he moved his eyes along the rows of bright faces. She caught his eye and he gave her a stony stare. For some reason, she shivered. How could anyone look at those young, bright faces and not be moved by the scene? Máire, a little girl from her own class, was singing the first verse of "Away in a Manger" in a clear soprano. Then the rest of the choir joined in. This time, the tears spilled over and she had to wipe her eyes. The final carol was "Silent Night", sung in Irish and English. Then there was rapturous applause from the small audience of teachers. The choir master praised the choir and told them that they would be even better for the actual performance in the church which was on the following day. Then the classes dispersed to their separate classrooms.

Mary had brought a box of sweets to share among her class. They were giddy and excited as they chose sweets, unwrapped them and began to chew but she quietened them down by reading to them from *A Christmas Carol* by Charles Dickens. The children loved being read to and gave her their complete attention.

Suddenly, the door opened and Father Mongey entered the room, followed by Mr Murray. The children looked apprehensive and stopped chewing.

"*Good afternoon, Father! Good afternoon, Mr Murray!*" the children chorused with her.

"Shouldn't you be teaching them their catechism or reading about the Nativity rather than promoting this kind of sentimental nonsense?" The priest picked up her copy of the Dickens classic and threw it derisively down on the table, making the front row of children jump.

Mr Murray looked uncomfortable and embarrassed. "Miss Devereux, Father Mongey wants to have a word with you. Please go to my office with him. I'll look after your class."

The priest walked ahead of her down the corridor, his long black soutane swishing with each stride. He opened the door and went in to sit in Mr Murray's chair. He motioned for her to sit opposite him. The pale winter sun was shining through the window behind him, almost blinding her so that she had to squint to see him. He leaned back, pressed the fingers of both hands into a steeple and tilted his head so that he was looking down his nose at her.

"Miss Devereux, some very unwelcome information about you has come to my notice. It seems that you have been visiting a married man regularly in his house. You have also been seen leaving his house late at night and early in the morning. That is not the behaviour that we expect of our teachers."

For a few minutes Mary was speechless with shock. Then she found her voice.

"Father Mongey, I don't know who has been telling you these stories, but there is a simple explanation. Yes, I have been going regularly to my brother-in-law's house but only to help him look after his daughter, my niece. I go there every day after school for an hour until my brother-in-law comes home. She is looked after during the day by a local woman who has to leave by two o'clock to collect my brother's child from school. On occasion, I have gone there in the early morning, especially early in the term when we were just getting into a routine with Jeanne, my niece."

"And what about the late nights when you were seen leaving his house?"

"That must have been when we took Jeanne for an outing and I went back to his house to help put her to bed. I was never there later than eight or nine o'clock."

"That is late for an unmarried woman to be alone in the house of a married man, a man, moreover, whose wife seems to have left him. Miss Devereux, you must understand my position. You, a teacher of very young children, have been giving scandal by your actions. When parents get to hear about it, they will be scandalised. What kind of example are you giving to young people? A teacher's behaviour must always be beyond reproach." He paused to lean forward. "I am afraid I have no option but to inform you that there will be no teaching position for you here after Christmas. You may finish up the term and you will of course be paid a month's notice. I will not, I am afraid, be able to give you a reference since this is an issue of morality. Thank you, Miss Devereux, you may return to your class."

Mary didn't move. She couldn't. Her carefully constructed world that she had worked so hard to build had been shattered and was falling in pieces around her. Images chased each other across her mind: the bright faces of her class singing that morning, Jeanne holding up her arms to be lifted, her parents proud faces at her graduation, laughing with her friends as they went Christmas shopping, Liam smiling at her as they paddled in Bray with Jeanne held safely between them.

The priest stood up and left the room, leaving the door open.

The bell rang for the end of the day for the younger children, the beginning of lunchtime for the older ones. The sound of children erupting from classrooms, the pounding of feet down the corridors and the hubbub of talk was followed by silence. The other teachers would be in the staffroom, a few would be on duty in the playground. She couldn't face seeing anyone.

The door opened and Mr Murray came into the room

and closed the door. He sat down and looked into Mary's face.

"Would you like a drink of water?"

She nodded. He went outside and returned with a glass.

"Here, drink this. You've had a terrible shock. I'm sorry about the way it happened. He arrived this morning, I thought it was for the rehearsal, but he told me that he wanted to see you after it and the reason why. He insisted on seeing you immediately. He's the manager of the school and has the Church behind him so there was little I could do."

"Mr Murray, what he is saying is not true. I don't know where he got his information but it is not true. I have been helping Liam with his daughter but neither of us would do the things he is implying. But he believes the gossips and I have lost my job. He told me I couldn't come back after Christmas. He also said that he wouldn't give me a reference. How will I ever get a job again without a reference?"

She began to cry bitterly, mopping her eyes with her sleeve. She accepted the handkerchief that he offered.

"My parents will be so upset and they've had enough upset over the last few months. How am I going to tell them?"

The thought of her parents brought on another paroxysm of crying. A bell went.

"There's the end of lunchtime," said Mr Murray. "They will all be back in the classrooms in a few minutes. Then you can leave without seeing anyone. Will you be all right?"

She nodded.

"Don't come in for the last day if you don't feel up to it. I'll look after your class. I'm sorry."

Then he was gone.

She listened until she could only hear normal classroom

noises, then she made her way to the staffroom and collected her coat and bag. Outside, it was raining and windy and very cold. She stopped to think. She didn't want to go home to her parents in this state. As it happened, she didn't have to go to Liam's as Lily would stay with Jeanne until Liam got home – Harry's Maeve had been at home with a bad cold in recent days and didn't need to be collected from school by Lily. She thought of Julia. Julia was kind and understanding. Yes, she would go there.

She didn't get a bus because she didn't want to meet anyone who knew her. She was cold and wet and drained by the time she arrived at Julia's house. Maeve was at home because she had a bad cold and when Julia saw Mary's face she sent her daughter upstairs to her room to play.

"Oh Mary, you poor love, what happened to you?"

Mary began to cry.

"What is it, Mary? Let's get you warm and then you can tell me."

She drew Mary into the parlour where the fire was lit.

"Sit down there and I will get you some soup. You look frozen."

Mary took off her coat and hat and sat as close to the warmth of the fire as possible. Julia returned with a large bowl of soup and a sandwich.

"My mother used to say that everything looks better after a good bowl of soup. Now eat that and then you can tell me what happened."

Mary ate in silence. Then, as she thawed out, she recounted the events of the morning.

Julia listened, her eyes wide with disbelief and shock.

"I can't believe the way you have been treated, Mary.

Listen, I hear the boys coming in from school. I'll just give them a hot drink and settle them in the kitchen to do their homework. Maeve can sit with them."

Harry arrived home early because the Dáil was in recess and was alarmed and upset to see the state Mary was in. He sat beside her and held her hand while she recounted the whole story to him. He wanted to confront Father Mongey that very evening. Julia calmed him down.

"No, Harry. I don't think that will help. Father Mongey has the power to dismiss Mary if he thinks he has grounds to do so. Any hint of scandal at all is enough to convince him. It will be very hard to make him believe that there is no truth in the rumours. How it looks is all he cares about."

"If I talk to the Minister for Education –"

"The church has the final say in their own schools. It might be worth approaching Father Mongey in a day or two, when you have calmed down. If Mary's own family vouch for her good character, he might listen."

"I think you're right, Julia. I'll wait a day or so and then approach him. In the meantime, Mary, what do you want to do? Do you want to go home? If so, I'll drive you. Or, you could stay the night here and I'll go and tell Mother."

"I plan to go in to school tomorrow for the carol concert. My pupils would be very disappointed if I didn't hear them singing. Harry, I'd be grateful if you would drive me to Liam's flat now. I don't want him to hear about this from anyone but me, so I'll tell him tonight rather than have him hear it from the gossips in the morning. After that, I'll get a taxi home."

"If you are sure that's what you want to do, Mary. Right, I'll get our coats and we'll be off."

CHAPTER 35

In the car Mary was absorbed in thoughts of how she was going to tell Liam about her dismissal.

"I can come back for you tonight if you want to stay with us," Harry said as he pulled up, interrupting her train of thought,

"No, thanks, I won't stay long, just long enough to tell Liam what happened and then I'll get a taxi home. Thanks, Harry. You and Julia have been very good to me. I'll see you in a few days when we finish school." Her voice trembled on the last word.

She got out and waved as the car pulled away.

Liam was surprised to see her. "Mary! I didn't expect to see you at this hour. Come in. Jeanne has just gone to sleep. "

"Liam, I have something to tell you."

She followed him in and they sat down.

Liam looked at her anxiously. "What is it, Mary? You look very upset. Is it one of your parents?"

"No, Liam. It's me – I've lost my job." She hadn't meant to put it as baldly as that. Then the tears came again.

"*What?* You lost your job? How? When?" He came over to sit beside her.

"Yesterday, after the concert rehearsal."

She sobbed out the whole story. Liam listened in stunned silence.

"Father Mongey? How could he think that? But he has it all wrong. This is so unfair. You were only helping me. You did nothing wrong. Someone has been telling him lies. The sooner I see him and tell him the truth, the better. I'll go and see him in the morning and tell him how you have helped me. Without you, I couldn't have managed. I'll make him see that."

"I don't think he'll believe you, Liam. He seemed to have his mind made up and didn't really listen to me."

"He will have to listen to me." He thought for a minute. "Will you come over here early in the morning, say about seven o'clock? I'll go to see Father Mongey before I go in to school. He usually says seven o'clock Mass so I can catch him after that."

Mary nodded. "Of course I will but I don't think it will do any good. I have to go home now, Liam. Mam will be wondering where I am. It's a terrible night so I'll get a taxi. I shouldn't be spending money on taxis but I got drenched once already today on my way to Julia's. I couldn't face going home so I went there instead. With a bit of luck my parents will be gone to bed when I get home."

"I'll walk down to the hotel on the North Circular Road – there's usually a taxi there or I can phone from there for one. You poor girl, you've had a terrible day and it's all my fault. I shouldn't have relied on you so much. I hope I can make it right tomorrow."

Mary gave him a hug. "It's not your fault."

She didn't think the priest was the type to change his mind. She had seen the look on his face when he dismissed her. But maybe Liam would be more persuasive than she had been.

All the lights in the house were off when the taxi dropped her outside her door. Her mother called down from the bedroom when she heard the front door opening.

"*Is that you, Mary? There's some stew on the range if you want something to eat!*"

"No, thanks, Mam. I had something earlier. God bless and sleep well."

She thanked God that her parents hadn't seen her in that state. Now, she would try to sleep so that she would look normal in the morning.

She did sleep because she was so exhausted but when she woke she looked pale, with dark circles under eyes that were still a bit swollen. She didn't usually wear much make-up but she searched in Kathleen's drawers in the chest and found some foundation and rouge. Inexpertly, she applied some of each and the result was an improvement.

Downstairs, her mother was preparing breakfast.

"Oh, there you are, love. Aren't you a bit early?"

"I have a lot to do today with the concert and end of term, so I want an early start." She ate her porridge quickly, swallowed a cup of tea and left.

Liam was ready to leave when she arrived. Jeanne was still asleep.

"Wish me luck. Bye." He set off, looking very determined.

As soon as Lily arrived, Mary left the flat. There was no sign of Liam when she got to school. When the bell went, he still hadn't arrived and she had to go to her class. At breaktime, all the school walked to the parish church for the carol concert. She couldn't see Liam. The church was festive with red poinsettias on the altar and an almost life-size crib waiting for the Baby Jesus who would be installed on Christmas Eve. Each class filed past the crib to admire it which gave her a chance to look around for Liam. There was still no sign of him.

Then the concert began. The children were wonderful and she enjoyed listening to them but her thoughts were distracted. Father Mongey was in the front row of the church and he had completely ignored her when she filed past him with her class. At the end of the concert he thanked the children and the parents who had come, wished them all a happy and peaceful Christmas and gave the children the rest of the day off.

She walked back to the school with her class to collect their bags and they all left with choruses of "Happy Christmas, Miss!"

She was standing outside the school gates when all the children had gone, wondering whether to wait or walk towards the flat when she saw Liam coming towards her. She ran to him.

"What happened, Liam?"

"Let's walk and I'll tell you as we walk."

They set out, Mary's heart sinking as she noted how downcast he looked.

He took a deep breath. "I caught Father Mongey in the sacristy after Mass. He was surprised to see me. I told him that I knew about his interview with you yesterday and that I felt that he had been misinformed. I told him that you and your family had been very good and helpful when

I had to look after Jeanne on my own. I said that your parents were aware of the fact that you came to my flat to look after Jeanne sometimes. I swore that everything was above board and innocent and that you are a very good person. I reminded him that your brother is a TD and will vouch for you. He listened without saying anything. When I finished, he said that whether you were a good person or not was beside the point. You had to be seen to be a good person and your behaviour said otherwise. He could not allow a teacher who was giving scandal to remain in one of his schools. He then said goodbye and left the sacristy. I ran after him and said an injustice was being done and that I would take the matter to the Department of Education and the Irish National Teachers' Organisation. That made him really angry. 'How dare you threaten me!' he said. 'I am the manager of this school and I have a duty to ensure that all the teachers are seen to be good-living people. You are as guilty as Miss Devereux. If either of you go to either the Department or the INTO, I will have no choice but to dismiss you too."

"Oh Liam, you shouldn't have threatened him! You can't afford to lose your job too."

"It's a matter of principle. You've been dismissed because of people spreading gossip about you, gossip that is completely untrue. If we don't do something about it, you will never get another teaching position in Ireland. We have to move quickly. The Department and the INTO will finish for Christmas in two days. I've made an appointment with both of them for tomorrow. Could you look after Jeanne for me? I gave Lily the two weeks of the school holidays off and I know that she is travelling to England to her daughter for Christmas."

"Yes, of course I will. What time do you want me to come?"

"About two o'clock. I should be home by four."

The following day, she left the house after her dinner on the pretext of doing some last-minute shopping. Jeanne was delighted to see her and they spent the afternoon reading storybooks and doing jigsaws.

Liam arrived home about five o'clock, later than expected. She couldn't tell from his face what the outcome of the meetings had been.

"How did it go?" she asked.

"Not well, I'm afraid. I'll tell you later."

After she got Jeanne to bed she went down and took a seat on an armchair opposite the couch where he sat.

"I'm sorry, Mary. I'm afraid that I got no satisfaction from those meetings. The man in the Department said that they would contact Father Mongey immediately but added that the manager of the school could dismiss a teacher if he felt he had a legitimate reason. It would take them months to investigate and, in the meantime, the teacher in question would be suspended. That would apply to both you and me in this case. The INTO were not any help either. They are known not to be sympathetic to cases brought by women."

"I know that. They allowed the government to introduce the Marriage Bar which prevented married women from applying for teaching positions and forcing any woman in a teaching job to resign on marriage."

"As well as that, there are no women on their executive. Two men listened to my story and said that, since Father Mongey was the manager of the school, he had the power to dismiss people. I was so disappointed with the outcome of these two meetings that I decided to call in on Mr Murray who I knew would be in his office in the school today because the builders are in doing some renovations. He's a strict man but a decent one and I thought that he was the best person to ask for advice. I told him the whole story. He knew about your dismissal of course, but he didn't know that the same thing had happened to me. He looked very shocked. I am sure he was thinking that he would be two teachers short in January but he didn't say anything about that. He simply said that going to the Department of Education and the INTO wasn't a good idea. It would simply polarise positions. He also said that those two organisations would not stand up against the Church."

Mary had been listening patiently but now she broke in.

"D'you mean that there is no hope of either of us retaining our jobs?"

"No, no hope. I am afraid that is the gist of what he said. He agreed it was unfair but said that there was nothing he could do about it."

"But, Liam, what are we going to do? Jobs are scarce enough but the job we have studied hard to be qualified for is no longer open to us. How will you look after Jeanne?"

"I don't know. I'll have to think about it. I'm just so tired that I can't think at the moment."

He looked so exhausted and defeated that Mary's heart went out to him. She went over, sat beside him on the couch, put her arms around him and soothed him like she would a child.

"Don't worry, we'll think of something in the morning."

He lifted his face to hers and suddenly they were kissing, gently at first but then hungrily. He stopped and drew back to give her a chance to move away but she didn't – she moved closer.

"Liam, I love you. I always have."

"I love you too, Mary, more and more every day. Can you forgive me for how I treated you?"

"Yes, of course I can. What are we going to do?"

"I don't know. I'm just glad that we love each other."

They kissed again and began to caress each other.

Liam pulled away. "Are you sure that this is what you want?"

Mary nodded, held his hand and pulled him towards the stairs.

The sun streaming in the window woke Mary. It was a beautiful morning. For a few minutes she felt happy. Then she remembered. She turned around to find that Liam was already awake, leaning on one elbow and smiling at her.

"Good morning, Mary, my love."

"Good morning, Liam. It's a lovely morning."

"Yes, it is. And it was a beautiful evening."

Mary smiled shyly. "Yes, it was. I love you, Liam and I want to be with you always. Now, we'd better get up before Jeanne wakes."

"Before we get up, I want to tell you some of the thoughts that went through my mind when I woke up this morning. When I talked with Mr Murray, he suggested that I might go to England and find a teaching job. He said that Irish teachers are very well regarded there and he has contacts with some head teachers who were students with him in Dublin. He offered to contact them on my behalf. Maybe you could get a job there too."

"Go to England? But Liam we would be leaving our

families and everyone we know behind. We couldn't get married. We would be living in sin. We couldn't take the sacraments. Our parents would be so upset. Jeanne wouldn't see her grandparents. Do you really think that is the only solution?

"Yes, I do. You said yourself that there are very few jobs around. So many people of our age have to leave their own country and go to England or America. It'll be an upheaval, I know that, but it is the only way we will be able to work as teachers again."

"You're right."

"Mr Murray also said that he will give me a reference. As long as I don't look for work in a Catholic school, there will be no problem about references. When I get a job, I could leave Jeanne with you and your family until I am settled and then I could bring you both over to join me. What do you think?"

"I just want us to be able to live together – you and me and Jeanne. I don't want to leave Ireland and my family, but if I must I will."

"We wouldn't be able to have a relationship if we stayed here. We've already experienced the havoc an innocent relationship between us has caused. I might have grounds for an annulment but it costs a fortune and takes years. Would you be willing to come with me and live with me and Jeanne in England?"

"Yes. I want to marry you but, if I can't, then I will live with you as your wife. My parents will be very upset and they'll find it difficult to accept us living together without being married, but I hope that they'll eventually see that it is the only thing that we can do. I just wish that Joseph hadn't left as well so recently. We won't tell them until after Christmas. Let them at least enjoy that."

"I'll go back to see Mr Murray today. He gave me his address. The sooner he lets his contacts know that I am looking for a job, the better. I'll take Jeanne with me. She will enjoy the walk."

After breakfast, Mary said goodbye and walked to her parents' house. She was wondering what they would say about her absence last night. Her mother looked up from ironing when she came in.

"Mary, love, I was worried about you last night. What happened?"

"Oh, the weather was terrible so I stayed with Harry and Julia. Sorry if I worried you." She hoped that Harry and Julia would go along with her story.

"That's all right. You must be glad to be on holiday now. Have you any plans for the next few days?"

"I'll probably meet the crowd from college one day. Otherwise, I'm free so I'll be able to help with the preparations for Christmas."

"I'm looking forward to Christmas although it won't be the same with Joseph and Kathleen away from home. I love the preparations and seeing the excitement of the children on Christmas Day. Maeve was very funny last year. She insisted she saw Santa putting the presents at the end of her bed! Will you help me put up the decorations tomorrow?"

"Of course I will, Mammy! We'll make it a lovely Christmas, as it always is."

CHAPTER 36

On Christmas Eve, there was a buzz of preparations in the house. Liam and Jeanne arrived early to help. James and Liam put up the paper chains and decorations. James had been to Moore Street the day before where he'd bought mandarin oranges, dates and other seasonal fruits which Mary arranged in a bowl. He also bought holly, ivy and mistletoe.

With the aid of Jeanne, who selected choice pieces, Mary arranged the holly and ivy over pictures and mirrors. She also hung the mistletoe in the time-honoured way from the central light. To do that, she had to stand on a chair. While she was looking up, attaching the mistletoe to the light, she swayed a little and Liam rushed to steady her. His arms were around her waist and their heads were together, directly under the mistletoe. Ellen saw the way they smiled at each other before he helped Mary down.

They managed to get an overexcited Jeanne to bed early and the adults settled down to listen to the radio which was broadcasting a Christmas concert. Harry called in later to say hello and chatted with James for a while. He and his family would be arriving for Christmas dinner the next day.

On the overmantel were cards from family and friends, including Kathleen and Joseph. They had both enclosed letters and Kathleen had also included a forwarding address, much to her parents' relief. Harry read both letters while he was there. Joseph's letter made him laugh with its descriptions of the eccentric people who worked in the publishing house. The final few paragraphs were moving and he turned away from the others to read them.

As you can see, I am enjoying my time in New York and my job. It doesn't pay very well but I am making good contacts with other publishers. I have revised my first novel and am writing the second one which is a sequel. A couple of major publishers are interested in them so I may get rich!

Max and I are living in a very small apartment in Greenwich Village. It's a very friendly neighbourhood with lots of small cafés and bars, many of which have live music in the evenings, mostly jazz. A bit different to Willie Ryan's! Many of our neighbours are actors, writers and musicians. I can walk to work in ten minutes. It is very cold here at the moment but it is a dry crisp cold with no dampness. It does rain here at times but not as regularly as it does in Dublin. Sometimes, I miss the rain.

Max's mother is going to cook a special dinner for me on Christmas Day so that, she says, I will feel at home. I'm sure it will be lovely but it won't be home and I will miss you both, Mother and Father, and all the rest of the family, especially the children. I will be thinking of all of you and wishing that I was there with you.

Have a lovely Christmas.
Your loving son,
Joseph

Harry had to blink rapidly and swallow a few times before he could turn around to face the family. He missed his brother. He too had got a card and letter from Joseph and it had reduced him to tears when he read it.

Ellen had been watching him as he read, going over the contents in her own mind, which she knew by heart, having read it over and over.

When he finished reading, she said brightly, "Well, he is happy and has good friends around him, that's the most important thing."

Harry showed no emotion as he read Kathleen's typically short letter. She had written only to her parents.

Dear Mam and Dad,

I hope you and all the family have a happy Christmas. I will be thinking of the family gathered in your house on Christmas Day and I will miss every one of you. Jeanne is always in my thoughts and I know you are all looking after her very well. I hope the presents I sent her arrive in time for her birthday.

I will be spending Christmas Day with the family of Marco Mercadante, one of the friends I told you about. They are Italian so the whole family will gather just like we do. That is our only day off because we are both appearing in the Christmas show at Radio City Music Hall. For the first time I have got the opportunity to sing as well as act and

I am really looking forward to it. I will send you some pictures of the show next time I write.

I have a small flat in Brooklyn now as you can see from my address. I share it with another girl from the theatre. I hope you will write to me and tell me all about Jeanne and perhaps send me a picture of her.

I miss Jeanne and both of you very much.
Your loving daughter,
Kay

"Well, she seems to be settled in New York for the present," Harry said. "There is more in the letter about her role in the Christmas show at Radio City than there is about how she misses her daughter." He glanced at Liam. "There seem to be lots of friends around her, anyway."

He didn't mention her specific reference to her good friend, Marco Mercadante.

Ellen defended Kathleen as she had always done. "Kathleen was never any good at expressing emotion unless she was playing a part. I'm sure she misses Jeanne and Liam and all of us very much. Christmas is a sad time if you are away from family."

"Well, I'd better be off," said Harry. "It will be difficult to settle the children tonight so I will go home and help Julia. See you all in the morning."

After he left, the four adults sat companionably around the fire and had a Christmas drink. They chatted for a while and then Ellen rose.

"I'm going to bed now. I want to go to early Mass tomorrow so that I'll be home in time to cook dinner before Harry and his family arrive."

"I'll come with you in the morning, Mammy," said Mary, "and then I will look after dinner. You should take it easy."

"I will, Mary, but I love doing the Christmas dinner. Goodnight, Liam. God bless, Mary. I'll call you so, when I get up."

James bid them goodnight and followed his wife. As soon as they were gone, Liam moved close to Mary to enjoy the only few moments of privacy that they had had all day.

"When are you going to tell them, Mary? Maybe you should tell them about losing your job before you say anything about us going to England."

"No. I'll tell them everything at once. There is no point in prolonging the agony for them. I just have to find the right time. Let's get tomorrow over first. Maybe when you and Jeanne go to your mother's on St Stephen's Day would be the best time."

"I'd like to be there to support you."

"But then Jeanne would be there too and she would be upset. She understands more than you think. No, it will be better if I do this on my own."

Next morning, Ellen called Mary and they set out for early Mass. It was a frosty morning and icy underfoot, so Ellen linked Mary as they walked. She smiled to herself at the feeling of closeness to her daughter which this gave her. They greeted people along the way and chatted to each other about the Christmas dinner and what they planned to do. The church was packed, mostly with women who, like themselves, were anxious to get back in time to put the turkey in the oven. At the ringing of the bell after the consecration, Ellen got up to go to Communion. She waited for Mary to get up too. She didn't. After a minute, Ellen went to the altar alone. When she returned, Mary had her face sunk in her hands and seemed to be deep in prayer.

After the Mass, people were anxious to shake hands with friends and neighbours and wish each other a Happy Christmas. They managed to extricate themselves and set off homeward. The sun was shining wanly but was just warm enough to ensure that the frost had gone.

Ellen had no reason now to link Mary but she did so anyway.

"Mary, love, is everything all right? You don't seem yourself these days."

"I just have a few things on my mind, that's all. Come on, we'd better hurry up – we have a lot to do."

She started to talk about the toys they had got for Jeanne and how happy she would be when she saw what Santa had left. They had bought a little pushchair for her dolls and a doll's blanket to tuck them in. Jeanne had outgrown her own pushchair and refused to get into it even on long walks. Liam usually ended up carrying her home but she wouldn't give in. She had also asked Santa for some books and jigsaws.

Ellen listened and talked about her own present for Jeanne but she was studying Mary as she talked. Mary usually looked bright and healthy but today she was pale and tired-looking. Maybe the teaching was too much for her. She was very sensitive and the boisterous six-year-olds that she taught were probably very exhausting. She wondered about the reason that Mary didn't go to Communion. Maybe she hadn't had time to go to Confession before Christmas.

Yes, that was probably it – Mary was so scrupulous.

They arrived home and Mary started bustling around immediately, taking all the most difficult jobs for herself.

"My, this turkey is huge! I hope we can fit it into the oven." She was filling the turkey with the stuffing Ellen had made the previous day.

"It's smaller than the one we had last year, so it will definitely fit," said Ellen. "Joseph and Kathleen were here then too so I got a sixteen-pound turkey. This is only twelve pounds." She tried not to think about the previous year. Little did she think then that two of her children would emigrate before the next Christmas.

With the turkey in the oven, they got to work on the vegetables.

When Liam and Jeanne arrived downstairs, the little girl was in a state of high excitement, showing off the doll's pushchair which she had found at the end of her bed. She was wearing a dress that Kathleen had sent but they hadn't told her where it came from. Any mention of Kathleen now seemed to confuse and upset her.

Mary set about making porridge for Jeanne.

When the time came to go the Mass Jeanne was reluctant to leave her new toy but went off with Liam and James happily enough in the end when they reminded her that she would see the crib at the church.

That gave Ellen another opportunity to talk to Mary. By now, she was convinced that there was something wrong.

When they had all the food prepared and cooking, they sat down at the kitchen table, face to face, for a well-deserved cup of tea.

"Mary, love, I know there is something wrong," Ellen

said. "Please talk to me. Maybe I can help. Is it something to do with your job?"

Mary was startled and shocked at the mention of her job. "What makes you say that?"

"I don't know. You just seem so preoccupied and upset. Please let me help."

Mary began to cry. "I've lost my job, Mammy."

"Oh, love, I knew there was something wrong! What happened?"

Mary was crying so much that she couldn't speak. The door opened and Jeanne rushed in, looking for her new toy. Liam followed her in. He saw the state Mary was in and went to comfort her. Mary pushed him away and ran up the stairs. James came in just as she left the room. He looked at Ellen and moved towards the stairs.

"Leave Mary alone for a while, James," said Ellen. "She's a bit upset. Will you put extra chairs around the table for Harry, Julia and the children?" She was trying to keep the atmosphere as calm as possible.

She noticed that Liam was still looking up the stairs.

Harry and Julia arrived eventually with three excited children. They had brought some of their presents from Santa and wanted to show them off. Jeanne wanted to show off her new toy and for a few minutes there was mayhem as toy cars, dolls and cowboy outfits fought for space on the floor.

Julia sensed the tension in the air and realised what must have happened.

"Children, let's go into the other room and you can play there. Granny is trying to set the table."

Julia gathered up some of the toys and shooed the

children out of the room. She came back out when they were all playing happily.

"Will I go up and see how Mary is, Mother Devereux?"

Ellen nodded.

Mary was lying on her bed with her head buried in the pillow. When she realised Julia had come into the room, she sat up.

"I told Mam that I lost my job. She asked me directly about it and it just came out. I didn't mean to tell her like that. I wanted her to enjoy Christmas Day before I told her. But I didn't tell her why I lost my job," she sobbed. "I don't know how I am going to tell her the whole story."

Julia put her arms around her. Mary continued to sob.

"Do you think you will feel able to come downstairs later? The children are asking for you."

"I'll come down in a while. I don't want to ruin the day for everyone."

Julia sat with her for a while, soothing her as she would one of her children. When Mary was calmer, Julia stood up. "I'll go down and help your mother. You come down when you feel ready."

Ellen was setting the table, her face tight and drawn. Harry was talking to his father, trying to distract him. Liam was looking at the floor.

"Mary will be down in a little while. I see everything is almost ready for dinner. Is there anything I can do, Mother Devereux?"

"Thanks, Julia. Just put the plates to warm by the range."

They were already sitting around the table when Mary came down. The children immediately clamoured for her attention. She admired their presents from Santa and their new clothes and sat between Jeanne and Maeve. Ellen and

Julia began to serve dinner and James poured a drink for everyone. Liam was sitting directly across the table from Mary and he smiled at her in relief that she had come downstairs. The tension in the room eased.

Mary looked at her mother and said, "I'm all right, Mam."

Ellen smiled back and leaned over to pat her daughter's hand. The meal progressed just as it did every Christmas Day. By the time they started pulling Christmas crackers, everyone had relaxed and could laugh at the silly mottos and toys that were inside them.

After dinner the adults sat and talked about the letters from Joseph and Kathleen. Then the children announced that they would put on a concert. The master of ceremonies was Michael. First to perform was Pádraig who played a slow air rather shakily on his tin whistle. Next was Maeve who sang "Silent Night". The star of the night was Jeanne who sang "O Holy Night" in a clear soprano. Mary had taught it to her earlier in the year. Jeanne looked so like her mother Kathleen when she sang that they were all tearful by the last note.

Julia saw the way the mood was going and introduced a pack of cards and suggested that they play Snap. All the children wanted to play and they insisted that Mary join them. The men moved over to sit beside the fire and Julia started to clear the table for the card game. They played Snap very loudly for about an hour but then the children began to get tired and fractious and Harry said that it was time to go home. He gathered up all the toys and put them in the car while Julia and Mary got them into their coats.

When he came back inside, he turned to Liam.

"Would you like a lift home with us, Liam? Jeanne has

an awful lot of presents to take home."

"That would be great, Harry. I was wondering how I would manage them."

"Mother, you three are coming to us for tea tomorrow, aren't you? I'll call for you about four o'clock."

"Yes, Harry, we'd love to come."

"How about you, Liam?"

"I'm taking Jeanne to see my parents tomorrow. They wanted to see her on her birthday."

"Yes, of course, I'd forgotten! Julia told me that you're coming to us next Sunday to celebrate the birthday. The children will be looking forward to it."

Mary put Jeanne's coat on and helped collect all her presents. Harry took most of them and put them in the car. Liam collected the rest.

"I'll see you the day after tomorrow, Mary," he said. "We'll take a walk and call in. Thanks for the lovely day, Mrs Devereux. Thanks, Mr Devereux."

A sudden quiet descended on the house when everyone left. Mary began to tidy up and put things away.

Ellen sat down. "Mary, will you tell us what happened about your job? James doesn't know why you were so upset. "

"Mam, I'm too exhausted and upset to talk about it now. I lost my job and I have no hope of getting it back. I'll talk to you both about it in the morning. Now I just want to go to bed."

"All right, love. We'll talk in the morning. Sleep well."

James was full of questions when Mary went to bed but Ellen had little to tell him.

"You know as much as I do. I don't know what happened or why she lost her job. She will tell us more tomorrow. In the meantime, we'd better get some sleep. It's been a long day."

Mary spent a very disturbed night and dreamed about being on a ship on a very rough sea. Huge waves were crashing over the ship and Jeanne was almost swept away. She couldn't find Liam. She could see her parents adrift in a lifeboat. She woke up in a sweat in the middle of the night with the bedclothes tangled around her. She didn't want to go back to sleep in case the nightmare started again.

CHAPTER 37

Mary didn't want to get up the next morning. She lay in bed, listening to the familiar morning sounds of her mother cleaning out the range, setting the fire and making breakfast. She didn't call out to Mary that breakfast was ready as she usually did. Eventually, Mary felt that she could put it off no longer. She dressed and went downstairs.

Her mother greeted her with a hug and placed a bowl of porridge in front of her.

"There love, that will do you good."

Her father was already eating his porridge and he smiled at Mary and passed the milk. He started to chat to her about something he had heard on the radio that morning. Mary half listened but was mentally rehearsing what she would tell her parents about the plans that she and Liam had. When they had all finished breakfast, her parents remained sitting opposite her at the table. She knew she would have to begin.

"Mam, Dad, I told you yesterday that I had lost my job. I didn't tell you why I lost it. Someone has been spreading lies about me and suggesting that I have been doing things that make me unfit to be a teacher. Father

Mongey came to the school and interviewed me. He said that I had been seen coming and going from the house of a married man and that I was scandalising people. He said that I had to leave immediately and he wouldn't give me a reference. Without a reference, I will never get a job as a teacher again. That's why I was so upset."

James was shocked. "A married man? Did he mean Liam? But you were only helping him with Jeanne. Did you tell him that?"

"Of course I did but he wouldn't listen. Liam went to see him to explain. Father Mongey wouldn't listen to him either. Then Liam went to the Department of Education and the teachers' union – you know, the Irish National Teachers Organisation – because, he said, an injustice had been done to me. That really enraged Father Mongey and he fired Liam as well. Liam went to the Principal, Mr Murray, to see if he could do anything for us but he said that he couldn't, that Father Mongey was the manager and had the final say."

Ellen had been listening to all this in silence, only her pallor revealing the effect the news was having on her.

"I was afraid of this," she said. "Some people can be very nasty and love spreading gossip. It's bad enough that you lost your job but for Liam to lose his too is dreadful. How is he going to pay for his flat and look after Jeanne? Oh my God, if Kathleen hadn't gone to America, none of this would have happened."

"But it has happened, Mam, and we have to decide what to do about it. I have something else to tell you too that I think you may find difficult to accept." She paused. "The shock of all this has made Liam and me realise that we love each other, that we have loved each other since we met and we want to be together with Jeanne as a family."

Mary paused to let this sink in. There was a long silence during which Ellen and James looked at each other. Then Ellen took Mary's hand.

"I've realised for quite a while that you and Liam have feelings for each other, you know. But he's already married. He can't marry again, at least not in the Church. If you live with Liam, you will be cast out of the Church. You and Liam won't be able to take the sacraments. People will gossip and life will be impossible for both of you. You certainly won't get a teaching job again. And have you thought about the effect this will have on Jeanne? As she gets older, her classmates will know about it and call her names. I'm sorry, love, but I don't know what you can do to get out of this mess."

"Your mother is right, Mary. I know Liam is a good man but I can't see how you can live with him, not in Catholic Ireland anyway."

Understanding was dawning on Ellen. "You're thinking of going to England, aren't you? That's the solution."

Mary couldn't believe that Ellen had seen the solution so clearly and indeed, had called it a solution, not a problem.

"You're right, Mam. Liam and I have discussed it and it seems like the only solution. Mr Murray, the Principal, has friends, people he went to college with, who are heads of schools there, schools that are not Catholic. He was going to contact them and see if there are any opportunities coming up in the new term. He will give Liam a reference."

"That sounds like you might be leaving very soon."

Ellen felt that she needed time to come to terms with this bombshell but it didn't look like she would get it.

She went around the table to Mary, sat beside her and put her arm around her.

"You deserve to be happy, Mary. You're always thinking of other people. It's time we thought about you. We will always love and support you, won't we, James? We will miss you but England is not so far away." Her voice broke on the last words.

James' eyes were full of tears. "We will always be proud of you," he said.

"Thanks to both of you, for being so good to me always. I think I'll go and have a lie-down for an hour or so. I didn't sleep very well last night. Harry's children are a lively lot and I need to build up my energy for them."

She kissed them both and went upstairs.

Ellen wanted to go to bed herself and cry in private but she couldn't because, if she once started, she would not be able to stop. There would be plenty of time for crying. Anyway, they were going to Harry's for tea. She wondered whether Harry knew about Mary and Liam's plans. He loved his sister but it would be a great embarrassment to him as a TD if anyone found out that his sister was living in sin. Any embarrassment for herself and James didn't concern her. She had found out who her real friends were when James was fighting in France. She had been denigrated by some people as a "Separation" wife because of her British army allowance while her husband was absent. Her children had been made little of at school by some pupils and even some teachers. But her real friends, like Violet and Grace, had been very supportive and she was sure that they would be again in this situation. What really worried her was the fact that Mary would now find herself outside the Catholic church, refused the sacraments and destined for hell. It would also affect Jeanne. She didn't know how Mary would deal with that. For herself, she would pray that God would be merciful.

She sat and stared into the fire and thought about what Mary had told them. A third child of theirs would be leaving Ireland and, with her, a beloved grandchild. Many of her friends and neighbours had suffered a similar fate. Children gone to the far corners of the earth, seldom and possibly never to be seen again. At least England was close and regular trips home to Ireland would be possible. In the meantime, she could see herself waiting, like all those other parents, for the regular letters home and the annual visit.

One man had caused this havoc by listening to vindictive gossip: Father Mongey. There was no point in trying to do anything about it. The Church was all-powerful in Ireland. Ellen had always found great support and consolation in her strong faith but she found it impossible to accept that the God she believed in would sentence Mary to hellfire. Her head was bursting with conflicting thoughts. She dismissed them. Mary was her daughter and she would support her, whatever she decided.

James was putting some turf on the fire.

"I'll bank up the fire later so that we can riddle it into life when we come home. I think I'll take a walk now for a while and clear my head. Are you all right, Ellen?"

Ellen smiled up at him. James always took a walk when he had something difficult to think about.

"I'm grand. We had a late breakfast so I don't think we'll bother with lunch. You know what a lovely spread Julia puts on. I'll just sit here and have a look at the papers. I haven't read any for the last week because I was so busy."

When the house was quiet, she found herself dozing in front of the fire. It must have been a few hours later when she heard Mary coming down the stairs. She was wearing her new red jumper and was wearing a bit of make-up. The silver bracelet that Liam had given her, a long time ago now, it seemed, was on her wrist. Her face was pale but there was a new maturity and sense of purpose about her.

"You look lovely, Mary. I'll go and change and then we'll be ready when James comes back."

James and Harry arrived at almost the same time and they were all ushered into the car.

"It's lovely, isn't it? So comfortable," Ellen enthused.

"It's a very steady car – very safe for the family," James said.

Harry was smiling at the praise his parents continued to give to the car for the whole journey.

When they arrived, the house was looking festive and Julia had the table set beautifully. The children were excited to see them.

"Granny, do you want to see the new cradle I got for my doll?" Maeve immediately wanted Ellen's attention and sat on her lap. "I got some storybooks too."

Michael was showing James his new toy soldiers and Pádraig monopolised Mary with his Meccano set.

"I think he is going to be an engineer. He's always building things," Harry remarked. "Do you remember, Julia, the time he took some of the screws out of his cot and it collapsed on the floor with him in it!"

"Yes, and I remember the fright we got!" She smiled up

at her husband. Harry put his arm around her waist.

"Isn't Julia looking wonderful, Mother?"

"Yes, she is. That colour really suits you, Julia."

"It's younger-looking that you are getting, Julia," James said.

The two parents were happy to see the obvious love between their eldest son and his wife. Harry and Julia had always been the calm water in the turbulence of family life and everyone had gravitated towards them when they needed help. Then they seemed to experience turbulence themselves for a few years but now they were as happy and devoted as ever. Ellen sent up a prayer that her other children would find a similar kind of happiness.

Julia was calling them all to the table. As usual, she had prepared a delicious meal. Mary was quieter than usual, but the children were so animated that it was not noticed.

When the children went upstairs to play, she told Harry and Julia about the plans she and Liam had. They were surprised but not shocked that she and Liam planned to live together in England as husband and wife.

Harry looked thoughtful. "It's probably the best thing to do. It would be very difficult for you here in Ireland, even if you did manage to get jobs. You'll be able to make a good life in England. Has Liam thought about an annulment? He surely has grounds for one."

Julia broke in. "An annulment is very expensive, Harry, and takes a very long time. I heard about someone who tried to get one but was put off by the cost. Annulments seem to be for rich people."

"I don't really care about that," said Mary. "I just want Liam and Jeanne and me to be together. People would see it as sinful but I don't. Liam is a good man. He did nothing wrong. Neither did I. Why should we be punished for it?"

Mary had been dreading telling her family the whole story. She had expected Harry to take a more conventional attitude and was warmed by his and Julia's support. She would write to Joseph in due course and explain to him but she was sure that he would understand. She was lucky. Many families would have thrown her out or at best disapproved completely, but she could rely on love and understanding from her parents and two brothers.

By the time that Harry had dropped them off at their front door, Mary was feeling more relaxed than she had for days.

Mary slept that night and woke up feeling that she would be able for whatever the coming days would bring.

Liam and Jeanne arrived in the afternoon. There was a supressed excitement about him as he greeted them all. James chatted to him for a while and then departed for his usual afternoon walk. Ellen discreetly said that she was going to visit Violet and took Jeanne with her. She knew they wanted to talk.

Liam was excited. He sat down beside her, and the words tumbled out.

"Mary, I called in to Mr Murray's house on my way here and he had good news. A friend of his has a contact who is Head Teacher in a small private school in a place called Altrincham, near Manchester. One of his staff had a heart attack on Christmas Eve and was taken off to hospital. He apparently won't be able to return to work until September at the earliest. Seán O'Sullivan, that's the Head, urgently needs someone to take over his class for the rest of the year. It's the same level that I am teaching so it would suit me. The best of it is that there is accommodation available as part of the deal. Obviously, I can't take over the house belonging to the teacher who became ill because his wife is still living there. But there is another cottage on the grounds, which is available. I told Mr Murray that I would think about it and let Mr O'Sullivan know within twenty-four hours. When I do, I'll say that you and Jeanne will be coming too. I have his phone number. What do you think?"

Mary could hardly take in all of the information.

"It sounds ideal. But it's all happening so quickly. Are you sure they won't ask any questions about our relationship?

"I don't think so. Mr O'Sullivan seems to be desperate for a replacement teacher. As Mr Murray doesn't know him, the arrangements will be made by phone between me and Mr O'Sullivan.

"How soon would you have to be there?"

"By the second of January. New term starts on the third of January and, because it's a boarding school, some children will arrive on the second."

"My God, that's very soon."

"I could go ahead on my own and leave Jeanne and you here for a while."

"No, we'll all go together. It would be very upsetting for Jeanne if you left. That means we'd better leave on the evening of the thirtieth of December, the day before New Year's Eve. It would be too emotional for the family if we left on New Year's Eve itself, don't you think?"

"I agree."

"That would give us just about enough time to get ready. We won't be able to take much with us. I don't know what we will do with Jeanne's toys. She won't want to leave them behind."

"I think that it's possible to get large boxes sent by container to England. I'll find out about that."

"Oh Liam, in spite of everything, I'm very excited. I'm also sad to be leaving my family and Ireland and everything that is familiar. But in England we'll be a proper family and you will have a good job."

She leaned forward to kiss Liam. He put his arms around her.

"I am sure you will be able to get one too, as soon as we are settled. Children of the teachers at the school are allowed to attend there as soon as they are four so Jeanne will be starting school soon."

They could hear Jeanne at the door, followed by Ellen turning the key.

"Sorry, Mary, Jeanne insisted on coming back to get her doll's pushchair. She wants to show it off to some children on the street."

"That's all right, Mam. Liam has some good news. He has been offered a job in a place called Altrincham, near Manchester. They can offer accommodation as well."

Ellen tried to look happy. "Oh, that's great news. You must be pleased, Liam."

Liam told them all he knew about the school and the town where it was situated. When James came home, he had to start again.

"It's what they call a Prep School. They take pupils from the age of four to twelve. Many of the parents are working abroad and want the children educated in England. The school is on its own grounds with lovely gardens all around. The cottages where the staff live are close to the school. I've been offered a two-bedroomed furnished cottage."

"That sounds very good, Liam. When do you have to start?"

"On the second of January – that means that we'll have to travel very soon – on the thirtieth of December."

There was a pause.

"So you won't be here for New Year's Eve?" Ellen said.

"No."

Ellen looked at her husband, her face tight.

There was a commotion at the door as Jeanne arrived back to the house with her doll and pushchair and two of her little friends. For the rest of the day there was no further mention of Mary and Liam's plans.

The next few days were busy ones. Mary knew that they couldn't carry much with them but the problem of selecting what to take and what to leave, especially with regard to Jeanne's possessions, was difficult. Ellen helped Mary as much as she could. One afternoon, she called Mary upstairs. She had taken out an old, carved box which she had brought from India. She kept her few precious items of jewellery and keepsakes in it. Mary had seen it a few times as a child. There was a lock of baby hair from each of the children in it as well as James' medals from the war. Ellen handed Mary a ring. It was broad and made of a yellow gold.

"Oh, it's beautiful!"

"It's for you, Mary. You can wear it as a wedding ring.

It was my mother's and I treasure it. I know that you will take good care of it."

Tears choked Mary as she put the ring on her fourth finger. "Mam, I don't know what to say. Thank you. I will treasure it. Look, it fits perfectly. "

They hugged each other. Ellen could feel the tears rising in her throat so she said in a matter-of-fact tone, "Now, we'd better get back to the packing. Liam will be here shortly with his own possessions from the flat. We'll have to find space for them."

Ellen had thought about how emotional the departure of the family would be and how best to plan it. She discussed it with James and they decided that they would invite family and friends for a meal before Liam and Mary had to leave for the ferry at seven o'clock. Having them there would make it easier to say goodbye.

Harry and Julia and the children arrived in good time followed by Violet and then Grace. The children made it easy to behave normally and a party atmosphere soon developed. James proposed a toast to Mary and Liam and wished them success and happiness in their new life. Liam said that he wanted to thank everyone for their support. Mary could not bring herself to speak.

At last Harry announced that it was time to leave. He helped Liam put their bags in his car. Julia brought Jeanne to the car and kept her amused while Mary said goodbye to her parents. She hugged them and then held a hand of each.

"I promise, Mam and Dad, that I will come home at every opportunity – Christmas, Easter and summer holidays. You will be sick of us."

The tears were rolling down her cheeks as she turned

to get into the car. Liam shook hands and got in beside her. He put his arms around her. Jeanne was waving at her cousins out the window. Julia gave a last wave and shepherded her children into the house.

Ellen and James managed to hold back the tears until the car went down the hill and turned left to Infirmary Road. Then James put his arms around his wife and she buried her face in his shoulder. Their friends, Violet and Grace, brought them both in out of the cold to sit beside the fire.

Violet said, "You won't feel it now until it's the Easter holidays. Jeanne will love coming home then."

"And Mary is a great writer. You'll get letters every week. They'll be great at keeping in touch."

Ellen looked bleakly into the fire. Yes, there were things to look forward to. They would look forward to the first letter and the first visit. That would keep them going.

A small hand crept around her neck. "Granny, can I sit on your knee? I want to make you better."

Ellen lifted Maeve up and settled her on her lap. The child was looking anxiously at her grandmother. "Granny, can I stay with you here tonight? Then you won't be lonely." She turned to her mother. "Mammy, can I stay with Granny tonight?"

"Of course you can, sweetheart, if Granny is not too tired."

"I'd love you to stay here tonight, Maeve, love. You can keep me and Grandad company and tell us some of your stories."

James had an arm around each of his grandsons. He made an effort to smile at Ellen.

"We are lucky to have such good grandchildren, aren't we, James?" she said.

He nodded and the two boys looked up at him. He swallowed but couldn't speak.

CHAPTER 38

As Harry drove down Infirmary Road, Mary had her face buried in Liam's shoulder. Beside her, Jeanne finished waving out the window and sat down, looking anxiously at Mary.

"Daddy, why is Auntie Mary crying? Is she very sad?"

"She's a bit sad because she won't see Granny and Grandad for a while. She will be all right when we get to the ship."

"When will we get to our new house, Daddy?"

"Well, tonight we'll sleep on the boat in a cabin with bunk beds. That will be good fun, won't it? Then in the morning we'll leave the ship and get a train to our new house. You'll have your own bedroom there, just for you and your toys."

Jeanne began to cry. "I don't want to go to the new house! I want to go to back to Granny's! If Mammy Kathleen comes home, she won't know where to find us."

Mary sat up and put her arms around Jeanne. "It's all right, sweetheart. If Mammy Kathleen comes, Granny will tell her where we are. And, don't worry, I will look after you now."

"Will you be my mammy, Auntie Mary?"

"Yes, I will, love."

"I'll call you Mammy Mary so."

Mary shot a look at Liam. This was like an answer to prayer – a solution to a serious problem that had been occupying their minds: how to tell Jeanne that she mustn't call Mary "Auntie Mary" any more.

"I'd love that, darling." She kissed the little girl and wiped away her tears with her handkerchief. "No more tears now. We'll go back to visit Granny and Grandad in a few weeks. You know that Daddy has a new job and that is why we're going to the new house. It's beside the school where he'll be teaching. You might be able to go to school there too. Would you like that?"

"Will I be able to read like Maeve and have a schoolbag?"

"Yes, of course. And you can choose your own schoolbag."

Harry had been watching the exchange in the mirror. He smiled at Jeanne.

"I think you'll be a very good reader, Jeanne, maybe better than Maeve," he said.

Jeanne relaxed and snuggled into Mary's arms. They were now driving down the quays, heading for Dublin port.

Harry slowed the car as they approached the docks.

"Look, Jeanne, that's the big ship that we'll be travelling on." Liam pointed out the window.

"Liam and I will manage the luggage if you just look after Jeanne, Mary," said Harry. "I can park quite near to where you go on board."

There weren't many people in the queue to show their tickets. Those that were waiting were subdued, a few of them tearful.

They look like emigrants too, Mary was thinking when Harry broke in on her thoughts.

"It's a quiet night. It's just as well. The crossing can be a bit rowdy at times. You should be able to get a good night's sleep before you arrive in Liverpool. What time is the train to Manchester, Liam?"

"The ship arrives in at eight o'clock and the train leaves at ten, so we will have more than an hour to get to the station. The Principal, or the Head as they call them there, Séan O'Sullivan, is going to meet us. He insisted because otherwise we would have had to take a taxi from Manchester to Altrincham and he thought it might be difficult to get one."

They were almost at the top of the queue. Harry left down the bags he was carrying beside Liam.

"Right, I'll say goodbye here. Give me a big kiss, Jeanne."

He turned and held Mary in his arms. "Take care of yourself, Mary."

He shook hands with Liam. "Look after the two of them, Liam. I might pop over to see you all soon, just to see how you've settled in. Have a safe journey."

Liam had the tickets ready. Mary took Jeanne by the hand and picked up one of the suitcases. They were moving forward and could see the ship.

Harry had moved back and was waving as they started to climb the gangplank. A seaman took Jeanne in his arms and carried her up and onto the ship. He looked at their tickets and directed them to their cabin.

The cabin had four bunks, two on each side and a hand basin. There was a little ladder to get to the top bunk. Jeanne immediately climbed up the ladder and sat on the edge of the bunk. Mary was wiping her eyes. Liam tried to think of a diversion.

"Do you want to go up on deck for a while, Mary?"

"No, it's too cold. Besides, I don't want to see Ireland fading into the distance. We'll wake up to a new life tomorrow and I'll be ready for that." She squared her shoulders as she spoke and put her handkerchief away.

"You're right. We may as well go to sleep then. We have a long day tomorrow. Mary, you and Jeanne take the bottom bunks. I'll sleep on top."

Jeanne protested. "Mammy Mary, I'm not sleepy. Can I play for a while?"

"All right, love. You can play for a little while on the top bunk. Get into your pyjamas first."

By the time they unpacked the things they needed and got into their nightwear. Jeanne was already looking very drowsy so they tucked her in with Mali, her monkey, and she was soon asleep. Mary would have liked the comfort of sleeping in Liam's arms but the bunks were too narrow. He held her in his arms for a few minutes before she lay down. She could feel the reverberations of the engine going through her body. She hoped that they would be able to sleep. Liam caressed and soothed her.

"We can make a good life in England, Mary. I'm looking forward to having our own place and being able to hold you in my arms every night."

He kissed her and then climbed up to his own bunk. Mary blinked back the tears and tried to focus on the following day. In a few minutes they both fell into an exhausted sleep.

Next morning, a change in the sound of the engine woke them. They could hear that other people were awake too and moving up and down the corridor outside. They dressed Jeanne and themselves, repacked their bags and made their way down the corridor and up the stairs onto the deck. It was a clear morning and they could see that the ship was slowly making its way up the Mersey and into Liverpool. They stayed on deck for the half hour that it took for the ship to dock before returning to the cabin to get their bags. Then they were ushered down the gangplank and into the customs hall.

All around them they were conscious of the Liverpool accents which made every statement sound like a question. Jeanne stayed close to Mary and held onto her skirt. Mary's hands, and Liam's, were occupied with suitcases, putting them up for inspection by the customs officials, opening them and then closing them when the inspection was over. At last they were out of the wide, echoing hall and asking directions to the train station.

Liam bought some tea and toast with jam for them at the railway café. He had to look carefully at the unfamiliar money when he proffered a five-pound note and got his change. They ate quickly and then it was time to board the train.

Mary felt that their surroundings were strange yet somehow familiar. She said as much to Liam as they settled themselves in the railway carriage.

"It's probably because you're so fond of going to the pictures. I was reminded of George Formby and Gracie Fields by some of those people in the café."

"Yes, you're right. Jessie Mathews also came into my mind. It's the accents, I suppose, and because we're so used to seeing English locations in films. The people seem very friendly, don't they?"

Liam was unwrapping a large lollipop for Jeanne

which he had bought at the café. "There, pet, that should keep you going until we reach Manchester. We should be there in about an hour."

Once they got out of the built-up area around Liverpool, Mary was surprised to see that they were travelling through an expanse of lovely countryside.

"I always had an image of England as being very industrialised but there seems to be lots of unspoilt country."

"Altrincham, where we're going, is in Cheshire and has lovely countryside around it which is mostly farmland, and it's not too far from Wales. I believe that Wales is famous for its beautiful strands. We might be able to go there for daytrips on the train."

Jeanne had been listening intently. "Strands? The seaside? Will it be like Dollymount or Bray? Can we go there, Mammy Mary?"

"I'm sure we will." Mary smiled at Jeanne's use of "Mammy Mary".

Liam was smiling at it too. He was glad to see that Mary was looking more relaxed. The grief of the previous few days seemed to be retreating further away.

Séan O'Sullivan was waiting for them at the station in Manchester. He was a big man with a mop of red hair and a strong, intelligent face. Mary had already noted him as the train drew into the station. He picked them out quickly and strode towards them.

"I'm Séan O'Sullivan. You are very welcome to Manchester. Let me take those bags, Mrs O'Broin." He shook Liam's hand, patted Jeanne on the head and took the bags from Mary with a smile. "My car is just over there. We haven't got very far to go."

He spoke with an Irish accent – Cork, Mary guessed. She was hugely relieved that he had assumed that she was Liam's wife.

He quickly loaded up the boot and ushered them into the car. As he drove, he told them that he was from West Cork and had been in England for twenty years. He pointed out some of the well-known buildings which were mostly of red brick and the amenities that the city had to offer. Then they were out of the city and heading for Altrincham.

Mary was pleasantly surprised to see that Altrincham looked more like a large, friendly village than a town. Most of the buildings were red-bricked, as in Manchester, but others were black and white, like the Town Hall which Séan pointed out. He also showed them the place where a market was held every week and the Catholic church, St Vincent de Paul's, where he and his family worshipped.

The school was situated on the edge of the town, an imposing old house with substantial gardens around it. Séan passed the school and a number of cottages which, he said, housed some of the staff.

They came to a stop outside a small red-bricked cottage which had a few plant pots each side of the front door. Snowdrops were peeping out of one of them.

He turned to look at Mary. "This is your house. I hope you will be happy here. My wife, Vera, is probably inside. She said that she would come over to light the fire and welcome you."

As he spoke, a pleasant-looking woman of about forty opened the door and came out. She had a little girl about the same age as Jeanne by the hand. She came over to the car as Mary and Jeanne got out.

"You must be Mary and this lovely little girl must be Jeanne. My name is Vera and this is Rose, our daughter. Welcome to Altricham and to St Crispin's. You must be tired from all the travelling. Let's go inside."

Her accent was English.

She led the way inside. Mary noticed how low the lintel of the door and the ceiling were. Liam almost banged his head as he came in. Seán had to stoop.

A log fire was blazing in the grate and the table was set.

"I thought you would be hungry after your journey so I made a shepherd's pie," said Vera. "It will be ready soon. I know it's a bit early for lunch but I thought you might be hungry after all the travel." She opened the gas cooker, checking on various dishes in the oven. Yes, everything is ready."

"Oh, it smells delicious," Mary said. "You are very good to go to so much trouble."

"Oh, It's no trouble. We'll eat here with you and have a chat and then we'll leave you in peace to settle in. Come on, girls, join us for lunch."

Jeanne and her new friend were chatting animatedly. They reluctantly joined the adults at the table.

Seán and Liam were discussing the school and the expected arrival of the pupils on the second of January.

"Tomorrow is a holiday so you can relax and recover from your trip," Seán said. "Then the next day come up to the school about ten o'clock. I'll show you around and explain your duties to you. You'll meet some of the other staff too. The first of the pupils are due to arrive about twelve o'clock. We'll all have lunch with them and help them unpack and get them settled into their dormitories. Later we will show them around the school and grounds.

Then we will all have tea and some social time together."
He turned to Mary. "Why don't you join us, you and
Jeanne? You can meet the pupils and get to know the
school. Liam was just telling me that you are a qualified
teacher. I hope that you will be doing some teaching for us
too. We are a bit short-staffed at the moment."

"That would be lovely. Thank you." Mary glanced at
Liam, delighted at this.

"Rose will show Jeanne around," Vera said. "She's in
the lowest class. Maybe Jeanne will be joining her. There
are no other girls in that class so they will be company for
each other."

Mary had already noticed how well the two little girls
were getting on. She looked gratefully at Vera.

"Yes, Jeanne is looking forward to starting school. If
we had remained in Ireland, she would have started next
September." She looked wistful as she said this.

"She'll love it here," said Vera with a smile.

After the meal, Vera began to carry plates over to the sink.
"I'll just tidy up and then we'll leave you to settle in."

"Oh please, Vera, leave the tidying to me. It was very
good of you to have a meal ready for us. It made us feel very
welcome. You and Seán must have so many things to do in
preparation for the new term so leave the dishes to us."

"If you're sure?"

"I am."

"Now, you're welcome to come over this evening and
have a drink with us to celebrate the New Year," Seán
said. "But don't feel obliged. I'm sure you all must be very
tired after the trip."

Mary glanced questioningly at Liam.

"Thank you, Seán," he said, "but you're right – we are pretty exhausted and I don't think Jeanne will last too long more without needing to be tucked up in bed."

"Well, in that case you must join us for lunch tomorrow – let's say one o'clock?"

"That would be lovely," said Mary.

The two little girls were reluctant to part but soon they were all saying goodbye. Mary closed the front door and sat down by the fire.

"Séan and Vera are lovely people and Rose will be a good friend for Jeanne. I feel much better about our future here having met them."

Liam joined her. "So do I. I'm looking forward to meeting my new pupils. Now, there is something that I have to do. Stand up, Mary."

Puzzled, Mary did as she was bid, and Liam suddenly lifted her up in his arms. He managed to open the front door and carried her outside. Then he turned and carried her back in again and put her down.

"I wanted to carry you over the threshold of our new home." He kissed Mary who responded by kissing him back.

"*Carry me over too, Daddy!*" Jeanne wanted to join in the fun.

When he had carried her out and back in, he pretended to be exhausted and collapsed onto the couch. Mary and Jeanne sat down either side of him.

They all hugged and sat for a while until Mary said, "Let's have a look at the rest of the house."

CHAPTER 39

On the first day of term, they walked up to the school together, already feeling at ease in their new surroundings. They had spent a very pleasant New Year's Day at Seán's house the day before. Vera had served a lavish meal and they had truly been made welcome. A restful evening followed in their lovely new house and they woke refreshed and ready to face all the challenges the new year would bring.

A small group surrounded Seán and Vera, obviously the other teachers. They were introduced and then Seán showed Liam and Mary around the school while Vera stayed with the two girls. The building was larger than Mary had expected, and housed as well as the classrooms a library, a refectory, kitchens, a sitting room or common room as they called it, dormitories and bathrooms for the children. Liam's classroom was big and bright with a window looking out onto a lawn which ended in a line of beautiful old trees, bare at the moment but their branches graceful as dancers.

They returned to the refectory where tea and biscuits were laid out for the staff, a few of whom, she was glad to see, were about the same age herself. They had a chance to chat to them before the first of the pupils began to arrive. Some were as young as five, while the oldest was about twelve. They all looked sad and tearful as parents and guardians said their goodbyes and left. Then, a transformation happened. They began to find their friends and were soon chatting animatedly about their doings during the holidays.

The four new pupils looked lost and lonely and two of them were crying. They were about the same age as Jeanne and Mary's heart went out to them. Vera quickly gathered the newcomers around her and introduced them to each other. Mary joined her and soon they had the group chatting and looking a bit happier. Then they took them to their dormitory and helped them to unpack. Tears started again as they took out photographs, mementoes and treasured toys. Once more, Vera managed to cheer them up before they returned to the refectory to join the others for lunch.

After lunch, Séan asked to have a word with her and led her out onto the corridor.

"Mary," he said, turning and facing her, "I told you that we are very short-staffed. I want to ask if you would be interested in working part-time alongside Vera with the youngest class? We will have to take up references et cetera but I would really like you to begin tomorrow if at all possible?"

Mary thought quickly. "Yes, that's the level I was teaching before and Jeanne will be in that class. I'd love to help Vera."

Inside, she was trembling. She had her teaching diploma with her. It was in her maiden name but that would not be a problem. Getting a reference would be more of a problem but there might be a way around it.

Séan was delighted. "Excellent. Now, let's go and join the others."

Back in their house that evening, Jeanne was still exhilarated by the fact that she was now a "big girl" who went to school. She was delighted with her readymade group of new friends and excited about seeing them again the next day.

Mary made a quick dinner and, soon after, Jeanne was ready for bed.

Before Mary had finished reading her a bedtime story, she was asleep.

Exhausted, Mary and Liam wasted no time in getting into bed themselves.

They quietly talked about the day and Mary shared her delight and worries about the offer that Séan had made her.

"Once Séan realises what a good teacher you are, he will be delighted to keep you on. We'll have time to think about getting a reference. Don't worry, it will all work out."

"I hope so."

They held each other close and Liam asked, "Are you happy, Mary?"

"I don't know, Liam. But I think I will be."

The following week passed very quickly with all the new experiences and responsibilities. Mary found that she had Monday and Wednesday afternoons free while Vera was free on Tuesday and Thursday afternoons. Liam also had Wednesday afternoon free while his class had PE so he was able to accompany Mary into Altrincham to do some shopping.

There was a small grocery shop quite near the school, run by the Patel family who were Pakistani. The husband and wife were very friendly and helpful. They brought regular deliveries to the school on a Friday so that they were happy to also bring groceries for the individual staff members. Mary and Liam took some essentials home with them but left the heavier items like potatoes to be delivered. On the way home they exchanged notes about the school and what was expected of them.

"It's just the length of the day that makes it so tiring," Mary said. "I'm enjoying it, but I just feel so tired all the time."

"I feel the same. But I think it's all the travel and having to leave our families that is affecting us as well as the work. We'll feel better in a few weeks. It's great though, having our own house and not having to travel to work in the rain."

"Yes. I love the house. And Jeanne is very happy. That's a blessing."

Liam was right. They did begin to feel better by the third week. The rest of their possessions arrived from Ireland and they set about making the small house feel like home. Jeanne greeted her toys like old friends and brought her new friend Rose to see them. The two girls played happily for a while.

Then Rose said to Jeanne, "Mummy said that your mummy would take me home at five o'clock."

Jeanne turned to Mary. "Mummy, can Rose stay for tea?"

It took a minute for Mary to realise that Jeanne was calling her "Mummy". She was amused at being called by this more English version of "Mammy" but also touched by it. "Of course, sweetheart. I'll just pop down and tell Vera."

From then on she became "Mummy" to Jeanne. Liam was delighted. This was even better than "Mammy Mary". Jeanne never mentioned Kathleen now and seemed very happy in her new life.

Mary showed her Teaching Diploma to Séan and he seemed satisfied. He reminded her about getting a reference. She discussed it with Liam and they felt that if she wrote to Mr Murray and said that she was applying for a few different jobs and asked him to send her a reference to her, he would do it. He would know that women applying for teaching jobs usually found it more difficult than men and ended up applying for a number of jobs before they got one. A few weeks later, the reference arrived in her mother's house and Ellen posted it on, to Mary's profound relief.

Once Mary knew the routine of the school and got to know her charges, she felt happier. But she still felt an overwhelming tiredness at the end of the day. She had been so busy that she hadn't thought about her time of the month. Now she realised that she was a few weeks overdue. At first she panicked and wondered how people would view a pregnancy. Then she began to think rationally about it. As far as the Head or anyone at the school knew, she was Liam's wife. After a quick calculation, she reckoned that the baby was due in early September. They must have conceived the very first time they made love, after she lost her job. Summer holidays began in mid-July so she would be able to continue to teach for the rest of the school year. She would welcome a new baby, a sister or brother for Jeanne, and she thought Liam would too. Easter would be early this year so she would be able to go home to Dublin without her pregnancy being too obvious to the gossips. After the way her family had supported her and Liam, she had no doubt that they would be supportive in this too.

When Liam came home that evening, she had a festive meal waiting. She told Jeanne that they were celebrating their first few weeks in England. She was delighted and insisted on getting into her best clothes. Mary changed into her red Christmas jumper and put some rouge on her pale cheeks. Liam was surprised but joined in the celebrations. Jeanne kept them entertained throughout the meal with stories about her friends and their doings in class. It wasn't until she went to bed that Mary had an opportunity to tell Liam her news.

He looked at her with shock, disbelief and joy registering on his face in quick succession. Then he jumped up and embraced her.

"I don't know why I'm surprised! I am absolutely delighted, Mary! Our own baby and a sister or brother for Jeanne!"

"I won't tell Jeanne about it for a few months. She'll be delighted but she'll want to talk about it all the time and tell everybody. I'm not going to tell anyone at all for a few months, not until it shows. I'd like to tell my parents the news myself, in person. Do you think we should still go home at Easter?"

"Of course. Your parents and family will be thrilled

when they hear about the baby. I don't know about my family, though."

"Oh, they'll come around. When I first realised that I was going to have a baby, I was worried about what people might think. But here, everyone sees us as a married couple. At home, our family, or mine at least, have supported us as a couple and I am sure they will continue to support us. Maybe your own family will surprise you."

The weeks flew by until Easter. Mary experienced some morning sickness but by the end of the third month she was feeling very well. Liam booked their tickets back to Dublin and soon it was the day of their departure. Séan offered to drive them to the station in Manchester and brought Rose with him. The two girls sat in the back with Mary while Liam sat in front and discussed school matters with Séan.

"I have two grannies and two grandads in Dublin and an auntie and uncle and cousins. We'll probably have a party in Granny Devereux's when we get home," Jeanne boasted to Rose.

"I have a granny and grandad in Cork and we'll see them in the summer. But I wish I could go to Dublin with you now."

They arrived at the station and Séan unloaded the bags. There were fewer of them this time so Liam managed them alone. The train was already huffing and puffing, emitting clouds of steam, ready for departure. The girls waved madly as the train pulled away and then the family settled down to enjoy the journey.

At Liverpool, again a seaman carried Jeanne up the gangplank and they went below deck to a familiar-looking cabin.

Jeanne was all chat about who would meet them in Dublin. "I hope Uncle Harry brings Maeve with him. I want to show her how I can read."

"I can't wait to see Mam and Dad," Mary said wistfully. She was thinking about the evening they had parted.

This time, they braved the cold and went up on deck as the ship was making its way down the Mersey and into the Irish Sea. There were many more people on board this time.

As they were going back to their cabin, they passed the lounge where a singsong had started. The familiar Irish ballads made them feel at home.

Next morning, they were up on deck in time to see the Kish lighthouse as they passed it. The morning was cold and they shivered on the deck, but they wanted to see the first glimpse of Ireland. Jeanne cheered and jumped up and down when the misty green outline came into view.

An hour later, they were coming out of the customs shed into pale sunshine. They immediately saw the tall figure of Harry and, beside him, Julia's unmistakeable red hair and the smaller figure of Maeve, jumping up and down with excitement. Mary and Jeanne ran and embraced them, followed more slowly by Liam who was burdened with the bags. There was a joyful reunion with hugs all around.

When they stopped outside the house on Aberdeen Street, Mary couldn't wait and jumped out to knock on the door. It opened immediately to reveal Ellen.

Mary and her mother embraced.

"I was just coming out to see if there was any sign of you. Oh Mary, you look wonderful. And Jeanne, you've grown so big! How are you, Liam? You look very well. Come on, let's go inside. James is just building up the fire. You must be cold after your journey."

Ellen still had her an arm around Mary and was holding Jeanne's hand as they went in.

Mary saw her father and ran to him. She was crying so much that she couldn't speak.

"Mary, my pet, I am so glad to see you." James was crying as well. "Come here, Jeanne, and give Grandad a kiss."

Ever practical, Julia said, "Harry, you and Liam take the bags upstairs. Then we can all sit down and have something to eat."

The two little girls went into the parlour, each of them carrying a book.

As soon as the two men came downstairs, Mary wiped her eyes and blew her nose. She stood beside Liam and looked around at everyone.

"I have something wonderful to tell you all. Liam and I are going to have a baby. It is due in early September."

There were cries of delight all around and then more hugging and kissing.

"I'm very happy for you, Mary," Julia said, smiling.

"We'll have to have a glass of porter to celebrate that," James said and began to assemble glasses and bottles for the men.

"I think we women will have a cup of tea," Ellen said as she bustled around, urging everyone to sit down.

The talk turned to the new life that Mary and Liam were enjoying. Although Mary had written to her parents and brother with all the news about their new home and jobs, they still wanted to hear it again.

"We had planned to come home again in the summer but I don't think I'll be able to travel. I hope, Mam and Dad, that you two will come to England before the birth and stay on for a while. We could have the christening then."

"The last time I travelled was when I was coming home from the war. That was a long time ago." James turned to Ellen. "What do you think, Ellen?"

"The last time I travelled, we were coming home from India with the children. That was an even longer time ago. I think it is about time we made a journey. We'd love to see your new home, Mary. And being there for the christening would be wonderful."

"I was hoping you would say that, Mam. We can give you our room and we'll move in with Jeanne. You'll like Altrincham."

The two weeks they had in Dublin passed by very quickly. They saw relatives and friends, shopped in the city centre and visited the Zoo with Jeanne and Harry's children. Mary spent as much time as possible with her parents, accompanying James on some of his walks and sitting chatting to her mother in the kitchen while they cooked or baked. Liam's family were reasonably supportive about the baby although Mary suspected that it was only because they were living too far away to be an embarrassment. Jeanne had a wonderful time with her cousins and friends and was very tearful when the morning came that they were leaving.

Mary managed to smile when they were saying goodbye, clinging on to the prospect of the planned visit of her parents. She reflected that, although she was upset at parting from her family, she was looking forward to returning to her teaching and the little house that had become home. Jeanne began to chat about seeing Rose and her other friends as soon as they were on the ship. Liam took out a novel that he was planning to read with his pupils the following term.

CHAPTER 40

Mary told Jeanne about her expected brother or sister once they were settled back in their house. The little girl was delighted and asked endless questions. Vera kissed and hugged her but looked wistful at the news.

"You are very lucky and blessed to be having another baby. Séan and I wanted more children but it just never happened. We are lucky to have Rose because she was very delicate when she was born. You would never think that now! Jeanne must be delighted."

"Yes, she is, and she wants to talk about it all the time. She wants to choose the name for the baby. I told her that she and Daddy and I will choose it together. She called her latest doll Candy so we will have to be careful!"

Séan was very happy for them and also pleased that she would be able to finish out the term. Letters from her mother and Harry became more frequent, enquiring after her health and planning their trip to Altrincham. Her parents had booked their passage and hoped to be there for the birth. Harry and Julia planned to come for the christening and would stay in an old inn in Altrincham, within walking distance of the school. Joseph wrote to congratulate them.

Some weeks later, a letter arrived from Kathleen. Liam looked at the unmistakeable flowery script on the envelope and opened it nervously.

New York
10th April 1938

Dear Liam,

Mam has been keeping me informed about Jeanne. I was surprised to hear that you and Jeanne had moved to England and even more surprised to hear that Mary went with you. You are both very brave to bring down the wrath of the Church on you like that, not to speak of the gossip.

I don't want to give up all rights to Jeanne but I think it is the best thing for her. I love her more than anyone or anything in the world, but I am not the kind of person that makes a good mother. Mary is that kind of person and I know that she loves Jeanne and will always do her best for her. Mary is my sister and I love her although she might not believe it. We are just very different people. I am glad that you have found happiness with Mary. I should never have stolen you from her, I know that now.

I have not been very happy since I decided to stay in New York. I miss Jeanne and my parents very much. However, I am beginning to find some contentment in my life. I have a very good friend here, Marco Mercadante, who I met in the theatre when I first arrived. He has supported me when I was at my lowest. He wants us to be together but I am not sure if I can make someone happy. I have my own flat, shared with another girl and I have been getting good opportunities in the theatre.

I wish you and Mary happiness in the future. Please don't let Jeanne forget all about me. I know that Joseph is in New York. Mam sent me his address so I will contact him.

I should have written to you before this. I tried a few times but just couldn't do it.

I hope that, in time, you and Mary will forgive me. Kathleen

When Liam had digested the letter, he read it aloud to Mary

"Well, what do you think of her that?" he asked.

"Well, she sounds more mature than I remember. I'm sorry that she has been unhappy, but she brought it all on herself. I can't understand how she could abandon Jeanne in that way. But at least she wants the best for her."

"Do you think we should tell Jeanne a little more about where her mother is?"

"When she is a little older. It wouldn't be fair to talk to her about that now. Besides, she'd tell everyone, and our relationship would be under scrutiny."

"That's true. And she's happy with things as they are. She's settled so well – and she's really looking forward to the new baby." Liam put his arm around Mary. "And so am I! Motherhood really suits you, love. You look wonderful."

The following months seemed to pass very quickly until it was nearing the end of the school term. Mary made regular visits for check-ups to the small local hospital. By June, Mary was beginning to feel uncomfortable and needed to rest more. Séan suggested that she take every afternoon off. The children were doing more outdoor activities and preparing for the school sports and Mary's duties for those were taken over by a young newly trained teacher called Edward. Some afternoons she simply rested, on other days she took a chair and watched the children at their activities.

On the last day of term in mid-July, she attended assembly with the whole school, said goodbye to her class and waved off excited children as they climbed into cars and taxis with their parents. The school and grounds seemed very quiet when they had all gone.

"We'll have a few weeks now to recover and a chance to prepare for the baby. I'm sure that there must be lots of things which we need to buy." Liam was looking tired after the last few hectic weeks, but he was full of anticipation for the birth of their baby.

"Yes, I think we'll take a trip into Manchester to get what we need. As Vera gave me those baby clothes and the pram she had for Rose, we won't have a lot to buy. I want to get a present for the baby from Jeanne and one from the baby to Jeanne, probably yet another doll, a baby doll this time. Vera was saying that it will help her to accept the new baby. She has been an only child for so long that she will find it strange to have a brother or sister."

"Oh, I'm sure she'll be delighted. Then, of course, your parents will be arriving."

"I can't wait to see them. They'll be so happy to see where we're living. Séan has kindly offered to meet them in Manchester." She paused. "Liam, there's something else we have to do. I want to see the priest in St Vincent's about the christening. I know we've spoken to him a few times when we attended Mass there but he doesn't really know us. I hope he won't be difficult about the christening when he learns that we're not married. He will need all the details for the baptismal certificate."

"He seems like a decent man. We can ask to speak to him after Mass next Sunday."

The following Sunday, they waited after Mass until the young priest, Father O'Connor, had bid goodbye to the rest of the congregation and then they asked to talk to him. He invited them to the nearby presbytery to have a cup of tea with him. He chatted to Jeanne as they walked over to the house.

Once they were all seated in the parlour, his housekeeper brought in tea and biscuits.

"Maggie, I think Jeanne might like to see my dog," he said.

The kindly woman took Jeanne's hand and took her off to the kitchen.

"Jeanne will enjoy playing with the dog while we have a chat. What did you want to speak to me about?"

Mary looked at Liam and began. "We are expecting a baby in early September. We wanted to ask you about arranging the christening." She paused.

Liam took over. "There is a slight complication. We are not married."

The priest showed no surprise. "That's not a problem. We would not deny baptism to a child because of that." He turned to Mary. "Of course, on the baptismal certificate it will show your maiden name, Mary. I presume you have two people who are Catholics to be godparents?"

Mary nodded. "Yes. Some of my family will be here for the christening."

"Then that's all we have to worry about. Once the baby is born, Liam, come and arrange the date of the baptism with me. It is usually a week or so after the birth in Ireland but here it can be a little later. Jeanne is a lovely child. Is she your daughter too, Mary?"

"She's Liam's."

Then the whole story came out.

The priest listened and then said to Liam, "It seems that you two were the innocent parties in all of this. Would you think of seeking an annulment?"

"We have thought of it but it's too expensive and takes too long."

Jeanne came running in at that point, followed by a small black terrier.

"This is Oscar, Mummy and Daddy. Isn't he lovely? He likes playing with his ball. Can we get a dog?"

"Not for a while, sweetheart. We're getting the new baby first."

When they were leaving, Father O'Connor said, "I hope that you will invite me to the christening party. I love meeting Irish people. I miss home."

"Yes, of course we will. Thanks, Father."

Liam and Mary smiled at each other with relief when they emerged from the house.

"Now, all we have to do is decide on godparents," Liam said.

"I have thought about it already. I'd love to ask Vera to be godmother. She has been very good to me. And I'd like Harry to be godfather. He has been so supportive. He's my own godfather, you know."

"Is he? I didn't know that. That's all settled then. Let's have an ice cream to celebrate."

CHAPTER 41

James and Ellen arrived in Altrincham on the twenty-sixth of August. Liam and Jeanne went with Séan to meet them in Manchester. When the car drew up outside, Mary was waiting at the door.

"Oh, Mam and Dad, I am so glad to see you both! Come on in, I am dying to show you our house."

She embraced her parents awkwardly.

"Mary, love, you look so well." Ellen held Mary's hand as they led the way into the cottage. "Oh, it's lovely. So quaint and pretty! You must be very happy here."

James was looking out at the garden. "It's lovely to be able to look out at some greenery. And it is so quiet here, not like living in the city."

After a quick goodbye, Séan promised to see them during the week. Jeanne assembled some of her dolls to show her grandparents who were now sitting side by side on the sofa.

Liam appeared from the kitchen with a tray of tea and scones and Mary poured the tea.

"The scones are homemade by Vera. I'm afraid I am not up to baking at the moment. We'll show you around the house later. Vera loaned us another bed so we have that in Jeanne's room and you have our room. I hope you'll be comfortable. I can't believe you are here. I have been looking forward to it so much." She started to cry. "Sorry, I'm very emotional at the moment. Everything makes me cry. Liam picked some flowers and put them in a vase for me this morning and that made me cry."

Ellen leaned over and clasped her daughter's hand. "We're delighted that we will be here for the birth. By the look of you, it will be soon."

For the following week, Mary rested but went for short walks around the grounds of the school with one or both of her parents. Ellen investigated the kitchen and took over the cooking. James played with Jeanne and listened to her reading from her favourite books. He was amused at her Cheshire accent.

Then, one morning, Liam brought Mary breakfast in bed. She looked at it but did not want to eat it. "Liam, I think the baby is coming. We'd better get to the hospital."

He helped her out of bed. "I'll run down to get Séan while you're dressing. I won't be a minute. Your mother is up so I'll send her in to you."

James and Ellen were sitting at the kitchen table. He told them what was happening.

"Jeanne is out in the garden. I'll take her for a walk for a while," James said as he rose from the table.

Ellen immediately went to Mary and found her sitting on the side of the bed, bent over in pain.

"I'm all right, Mam. I just got a sudden pain. Will you help me to dress? And will you get my suitcase out of the wardrobe? It's already packed."

They could hear Séan's car drawing up outside.

"Mam, will you come with me to the hospital and stay with me?"

"Of course I will, love."

They were all silent on the short drive to the hospital. Liam was pale and kept looking back at Mary from the front seat. She smiled wanly to reassure him.

At the door of the hospital, Mary linked her mother.

"I'll be fine now, Liam. Mam is going to stay with me until the baby comes. You go home with Séan. This is no place for men."

Liam kissed her and reluctantly got back into the car.

When Liam got home, Jeanne was reading to James. He looked up hopefully.

"Any news? No? I suppose it's a bit too soon. Men feel so useless at a time like this."

They all settled down to do a big jigsaw but Jeanne got annoyed with them because they weren't concentrating. Liam prepared sandwiches for lunch but only Jeanne was hungry.

At last, at three o'clock, Séan was at the door. He was smiling.

"Congratulations, Liam, you have a son! Ellen just phoned from the hospital. Mary is fine and the baby weighed eight pounds. You can visit her after six o'clock."

Liam collapsed onto the sofa. "Oh, thank God! I know Mary is strong but I couldn't help worrying."

Jeanne was looking from one man to the other.

"Where's Mummy? Did the baby come? Is it a boy? When will he come home? What will we call him? Can we call him Oscar like Father O'Connor's dog? Please! Can we go to see him?"

"Come here, sweetheart. Mummy is in the hospital for a few days. She is tired after having the baby. Yes, it's a little boy. He will come home with Mummy in a few days and then we will decide what to call him."

That evening, Liam and James walked to the hospital after dropping off Jeanne at Vera's house. She couldn't wait to tell her friend Rose the good news.

When the two men arrived at the hospital, James said, "You go in on your own for a while. This is a special moment for you both. I'll follow in about half an hour. I'll have a walk around and get to know the area."

Mary was sitting up, holding the baby in her arms. She looked radiant. Ellen was smiling, sitting in a chair beside the bed.

Mary offered the baby to Liam. "Here's your son, Liam."

Liam took the baby who was making little contented noises. He had blonde to sandy hair and a pert nose, just like Mary's.

"I've just fed him so he is sleepy now. Isn't he beautiful? He looks very like you but also a bit like my father. I'd like to call him James after my father and Liam after you – Jimmy, for short. He looks like a Jimmy, doesn't he?"

Liam could hardly speak. He nodded and leaned over to kiss Mary. He smiled at Ellen. "Thanks for being with Mary."

"Oh, Mary did all the work. She was wonderful. I just held her hand. James will be very proud that the baby will be called after him. Did he come with you?"

"Yes, but he wanted to give us some time together so he took a walk."

"Well, I'll do the same. I could do with a bit of fresh air." She took her coat, kissed Mary and left.

"Was Jeanne excited when she heard the news?" Mary asked.

"Very. She wanted to name the baby there and then. She wants to call him Oscar, after Father O'Connor's dog!"

"Oh, no!" Mary laughed.

"She's with Vera and Rose at the moment."

"They want me to stay here for a week or so. I'm looking forward to getting home."

Exactly a week later, Mary and the baby came home. By then, Ellen had taken over management of the house. She and James had moved into Jeanne's room and left the bigger room for Mary, Liam and the baby.

Vera, Rose and Séan came to see the baby, bringing flowers and a lovely little suit for Jimmy.

Vera offered to help with the catering for the christening which Liam had already arranged for the following Sunday.

"We'll keep it simple," Ellen promised.

Harry and Julia arrived on the Saturday before the christening. Harry was delighted to be asked to be godfather.

"I remember your christening well, Mary. I was only a child myself, only about twelve, but I took my role very seriously."

The next day, Sunday, Mary insisted on going to the church for the christening.

"Are you sure you are feeling well enough to go?" Ellen was anxious. "In my day the mother never went to the christening. Mothers stayed in bed for about three weeks after the birth."

"I feel perfectly well, Mam. Thanks to you and Liam, I've been doing nothing but having breakfast in bed and resting on the sofa. Séan is going to drive me to the church. I don't want to miss this important day."

The whole family except Mary, Vera, Ellen and Liam walked to the church. The others set off in good time and arrived at the same time as the priest. They were to attend Mass before the christening. The whole group sat close together for the Mass.

Afterwards, Father O'Connor called them up to the altar rails. He explained the duties of godparents before starting the ceremony. Jimmy remained quiet in Vera's arms until the cold water was poured on his head. Then he cried loudly until the end of the ceremony.

When they returned to the house, Vera and Ellen set about making sure that everyone had something to eat. James and Harry looked after the drinks. Another group of friends, young teachers that Mary and Liam had become friendly with, then arrived. Jimmy was passed around and admired until it was time for him to be fed. Mary retired to the bedroom with the baby and Liam. The baby made contented little sounds as he fed. Liam looked at his wife and son.

"I could never have imagined this time last year that our lives could have turned out like this. I am the happiest man in the world with a beautiful wife and a wonderful daughter and son. We have a lovely house, we have good jobs and we are surrounded by family and friends."

"I know. I thought my heart would break when it seemed as though I had lost you. Then, when we had to leave Ireland, I was heartbroken at leaving my home. Now, I hope we will return to live in Ireland someday but, until then, I'm very happy to be here with you and our children."

Liam went over to put his arm around her shoulders and stayed like that until Jimmy started to fall asleep.

Mary changed him quickly and put him down in his crib. She freshened up, brushed her hair until it shone and powdered her shiny nose.

"Now, let's go and join the party!"

As soon as they opened the door, people turned towards them and raised their glasses.

James looked around at their family and friends.

"I want to propose a toast to little Jimmy, his sister Jeanne, and Mary and Liam. God bless them all!"

"*God bless them!*" was the resounding response.

The End

Also available from Poolbeg.com

A SOLDIER'S WIFE

MARION REYNOLDS

Ellen, romantic and naïve, falls in love with James, an Irishman serving in the British Army. He is posted to India and this, for her, is a dream come true. After seven years of heartache and joy, and a lifestyle which is leisurely and luxurious, they return to Ireland and James is demobbed.

They settle with their three young children in Dublin, a city rife with political and civil unrest, and beset with terrible poverty. When World War I is declared, James re-enlists. Ellen is left to bring up her children alone, in a city which views the wives of British soldiers with suspicion.

If James survives and returns, it will be to a different Ireland, one which has lived through the 1916 Rising and its aftermath, where anti-British sentiment grows stronger every day.

Ellen longs for James but worries. Will there be a place for them in this new Ireland?

"An intimate portrait of a young mother as she attempts to navigate the political and social complexities of early 20th century Dublin. Full of social and historical detail – but always warmly human" Catherine Dunne, author

978-178199-781-9

Printed in Great Britain
by Amazon